EIDOLON
A NOVEL

Grace Draven

Grace Draven
Grace.Draven1@gmail.com
www.gracedraven.com

Book Layout ©2013 BookDesignTemplates.com
Cover Illustration © 2015 by Isis Sousa
Cover Layout Design by Isis Sousa

Eidolon/ Grace Draven. – 1st ed.
ISBN – 13: 978-1-5332-6365-0
ISBN – 10: 1-5332-6365-5

Dedicated to my father, D. W. Walker

I love you, Dad.

To my editors Lora Gasway and Mel Sanders: once again you saved me from myself.

To my intrepid beta reader Jeffe Kennedy: the wine is on me, lovely.

Thank you all.

PROLOGUE

When Kirgipa accepted the coveted position of second nursemaid to the youngest of the Kai heir apparent's brood, she never imagined the role entailed consecutive days of sleep deprivation and exile to the farthest corner of the palace. The baby in her arms nuzzled her shoulder, grunting like a badger. Her small fingers twitched against Kirgipa's sleeve, thin black nails scoring marks in the fabric. Kirgipa tapped her gently on the back in steady rhythm as she paced back and forth across the room under the watchful eye of a royal guard.

The chamber housed a pallet for Kirgipa, a more luxurious bed for the baby, a chair, and a basket of supplies for feeding and changing an infant. Beyond that, it was a room spare of comfort, tucked far away from the nursery and anyone else who wanted to sleep, undisturbed by a colicky, fractious child's cries.

Kirgipa ignored the ache in her arms from holding her charge for hours and eyed the simple pallet with longing. It wasn't much protection from the hard, cold floor but after days of almost no sleep, it looked as inviting as an eiderdown mattress.

"Have you worn holes in your shoes yet?" The guard, a man she now knew as Necos, offered a sympathetic smile. As the guard assigned to day watch for Prince Harkuf's youngest child and only daughter, he kept Kirgipa company in the stretch of time when the rest of the palace slept. Mostly silent, he sometimes surprised her with inquiries into her health or brief suggestions for how to soothe the baby. Kirgipa often sneaked glances at him during the long hours, admiring the sheen of his black hair and the way muscle rippled under taut gray skin. He possessed elegant hands, his black claws neatly filed.

"Not yet, but close," she replied softly and began her hundredth, maybe thousandth circumnavigation of the chamber. "If I counted the steps I trod across this floor, I suspect I could have walked to Saggara and back."

Times such as these, when her eyes were scratchy as dried thistle and her lids heavy as stones, she wished she had accompanied the royal family's young prince Brishen and his entourage to the garrison of Saggara months earlier. Instead, she'd chosen to stay behind in Haradis. Her short tenure as second maid to the prince's human wife had aided her in capturing her current position, but this was much harder work. The human *hercegesé*, so different from the Kai in appearance, had been a fright to look upon but was of pleasant disposition and held to a more merciful sleep schedule.

Kirgipa idly wondered how the new princess Ildiko had adapted to her home among the Kai. Whether brave or reckless, any woman who stood up to the formidable Kai queen Secmis possessed the backbone necessary to cope and succeed in any situation.

The Kai feared Secmis—a fear beyond that of lesser nobles for a ruthless monarch. Maybe since Brishen's bride had not been Kai and unfamiliar with the queen's reputation, she hadn't understood the need for caution. Whatever had moved the *hercegesé* to take such risks, Kirgipa wished she had witnessed firsthand the initial confrontation between the two women.

She ran a soothing hand down the baby's back as the little one squirmed into a more comfortable position. The guard, Necos, tracked her path with his gaze as she passed in front of him once again. "This is dull duty for a soldier," she said.

He shrugged. "It is still duty, and I am bound to it." His eyes shimmered in the room's shuttered gloom. "There are worse assignments than keeping watch over the newest royal child and her pretty nurse."

His compliment surprised her, and her face heated. She lowered her head, hoping the action hid the telltale blush she suspected swathed her cheeks. Necos was a well-favored man, a decade or so older than she were she to guess his age.

His position as a royal family guard denoted both fierce loyalty to his king and experience in battle. During the many days Kirgipa and her charge spent under his protective watch, she had learned he was kind but not inclined to flirtation. A compliment from Necos carried weight and meaning. Her blush burned under her skin.

She was saved from forming a witty reply by a noise rising from the palace's lower levels. The floor beneath her feet vibrated with the sound. It fell away into an absolute silence that made the fine hairs on her arms rise. She met Necos's eyes. "What was that?"

He shook his head, the easy half-smile replaced by a grimness that made her shiver almost as much as that wrong-feeling sound. Even the baby, slumbering restlessly in her arms, stilled.

The noise rose again, sly whispers like the soft chattering of aristocrats exchanging salacious gossip or the quick patter of tiny nails from vermin trapped in the walls. Her skin crawled at the second thought then nearly leapt off her bones at the sudden piercing scream that overrode the strange whispers. Another followed it, louder, tortured, as if whatever wailed convulsed in the throes of suffering beyond comprehension.

The baby startled awake with a squawk. Frozen in place by the horrific sound that swelled and tapered and swelled again outside the chamber's door, Kirgipa clutched the youngest royal and stared wide-eyed and silent at the guard.

Necos drew his sword. He threw the bolt, locking them in. Any hint of softness in his expression had vanished, and he made a sharp cutting motion with his free hand, indicating she back to the farthest corner of the room away from the door. The screaming became a chorus, resonating through the floors and the walls, punctuated by the whispers. Kirgipa's knees turned to water, and she huddled against the wall to hold herself up. Necos pressed his face to the wood, one eye squinted closed as he peered through the peep hole in the door with the other.

"Necos, open the door! Open the door!"

Kirgipa recognized the voice—Dendarah, the night guard who shared watch duty with Necos. He leapt to do her bidding, throwing back the bolt and swinging the door wide. The infant princess was now wide awake and indulging in a full, screeching tantrum. Kirgipa could hardly hear Dendarah over the cacophony.

The guard barreled into the room and skidded to a stop, pale and haggard. Her silvery hair hung in tangled locks that had escaped her braid. "Close the door and bolt it!"

Necos did as she commanded. "What's happening?"

Dendarah ignored his question, her gaze lighting on Kirgipa in her corner with the baby. "We have to get them out of here and to the river." Her hands curled into fists, and a great shudder wracked her frame. "Someone has released *galla* into the palace."

Kirgipa whined low in her throat and hugged the baby. *Galla.* Demons. Their name meant destruction in the old tongue. Necos could wield ten swords, and it wouldn't matter. Clean steel didn't kill *galla.*

Necos froze, turning as pale as Dendarah before resheathing his sword. "How much time do we have?" He spoke as he turned to Kirgipa's pallet and ripped the linens from the mattress. He tossed a blanket to Kirgipa. "Make a sling," he ordered.

"They've overwhelmed the entire south and east wings and the first three floors of this one." She joined Necos in stripping bedding and cutting it into long strips they knotted together into a makeshift rope.

The baby halted her crying when Kirgipa plopped her on the floor at her feet to fold and knot the blanket into a sling. "The others? The royal family? The nursery?" Her questions were rhetorical, but she asked them anyway, hoping against hope that someone had survived to escape. Sorrow warred with horror inside her. All that screaming. Men, women, children. Consumed by the *galla.*

Dendarah's gaze mirrored Kirgipa's turmoil. She gestured to the small child, whimpering and hiccupping at Kirgipa's feet.

"Demons have overrun all the lower floors. For now, behold your new queen," she said flatly.

The screams continued, joined by the sounds of twisted revelry, of laughter bloated with malice as if something fed off the terror and the agony and found it delicious.

"Hurry," Dendarah said. She and Necos finished knotting the rope. He anchored the end to the iron shutter bar riveted below the window while Dendarah threw open the shutters to a punishing sunset that bloodied the western horizon.

Kirgipa shrugged on the makeshift sling and lifted her charge with shaking hands. Queen of the Kai. The baby settled into the sling, finally quiet and content, unaware of the abominations that boiled and frothed and consumed below them, unaware that tragedy crowned her in the role of monarch.

Necos tossed the length of rope out the window. It rippled down the outside wall, stopping short of the ground. "We'll have to drop a ways," he said. "Enough to rattle your teeth when you land, but if we're careful enough, we won't break anything."

"I've never climbed before." Kirgipa stared out the window, at the descent to the ground that seemed to go for leagues. "What if I drop the baby? What if I fall?" Her reason told her that plummeting to their deaths would be far cleaner than any death meted out by *galla*. Still, she didn't want to die at all, didn't want to harm the innocent who rested trustingly in the sling against her body.

Dendarah gave the rope a last yank, testing its strength and the knot Necos had made to fasten it to the bolt ring. "If you fall, one of us will catch you." She turned her attention to Necos. "How old are you?"

"Thirty and four," he said.

She nodded. "I'm forty and one. My magic is stronger. You go first and wait for the nurse. I'll follow her."

Necos nodded as if what Dendarah said made sense. Confused, Kirgipa watched as he wrapped a section of rope around his forearm and slung a leg over the windowsill. He paused. "Climb fast," he instructed both women and swung out of sight.

They leaned out the window and watched as he rappelled down the wall. Dendarah turned Kirgipa to face her and checked the knotting on the sling. "Your turn, little maid." Behind her, the sound of demonic revelry rose to a fevered pitch, drawing ever closer.

Kirgipa stared at her. "Why does it matter that your magic is stronger?"

Dendarah glanced out the window once more. "You know the tales. The *galla* feed on magic. I'm the more enticing meal. If they breach the door before we escape, they'll feed longer on me than they would on Necos. It will give you more time to get away." Kirgipa gasped, rendered speechless by the woman's practical courage. The guard ushered her closer to the window. "He's down. When he tells you to drop, let go of the rope. No hesitation." She helped Kirgipa across the sill, offering additional instructions for how to rappel down the wall and not injure the infant.

Her descent was harrowing, stomach-churning, and she was soaked with sweat by the time Necos called out "Let go!" She released the rope. Her stomach wedged itself into her ribs as she fell, slamming back into place when she landed solidly in Necos's arms.

He tipped her out of his hold and onto her feet and grabbed her hand. "Run!" he shouted and yanked her toward the herb gardens that surrounded the palace's western side.

Made fleet and nimble by terror, Kirgipa easily kept up, feet flying over the ground as if she'd grown wings from her heels. Her heart thundered in her chest, thundered in her ears, almost drowning out the sickening shrieks that raged behind her. Had they breached the door? Did Dendarah escape in time and raced to catch up?

She didn't dare look back at the palace, but she glimpsed movement from the corner of her eye—a blackness that writhed and clawed as it spread over the palace grounds toward the city of Haradis like a dark tide. Oh gods, the city. Her mother and sister were there. Everyone's mother and sister were there. Sons and daughters. Fathers and brothers.

"We have to warn them!" she shouted to Necos.

His iron grip on her hand made her fingers throbbed. "Someone will. Someone may already have. We must get to the river."

A stitch in her side burned, and her shoulders ached from the baby's weight as they raced the seething black tide purling toward Haradis. She almost fell once, slipping on a slick stretch of grass that reeked of decay and burned refuse. Necos clapped a hand over her mouth to muffle her scream.

The slippery patch had once been a Kai. The only way Kirgipa could tell was by the single yellow eye that floated in a viscous gray puddle peppered with bone splinters and the remains of a mouth that impossibly opened and closed over and over like a fresh-caught fish gasping out its last breath.

Necos's voice shook even as he steadied her and pulled her along once more. "Don't look. Keep running."

Dry sobs rattled in her throat as she clutched the baby and sprinted alongside the guard. *The river, the river, the river.* The two words echoed in her mind in sync with her heartbeat.

The great Absu, born as a stream in the far Dramorin Mountains, bisected the city as it rushed toward the sea several leagues south. Its waters, deep and perilous, had broken ships and drowned sailors. Now it was the salvation of the Kai. The old tales spoke of how *galla* couldn't cross over flowing water, bridged or not. Kirgipa prayed the tales were true.

They reached the city outskirts, plunging into streets filled with panicked Kai. Necos was right. Someone had warned the denizens of Haradis, creating a beast made of terrified people that heaved and labored toward the Absu's banks.

Necos shoved his way through the solid wall of bodies, clearing narrow wedges of space for Kirgipa to pass. The crowd didn't part before them. They were like the rest—ordinary folk desperate to save themselves from the boiling darkness erupting from the palace to spread across fertile fields and toward the city. The infant queen was nothing more than a baby clutched by her frightened mother and protected by her soldier father.

A cry, resonant with terror, rose above the mayhem. "THEY ARE COMING!"

All of Haradis screamed in reply, and the crowds transformed into a stampeding mob. Kirgipa shouted Necos's names as the surge wrenched her from his grasp. She held the baby close, fighting to stay on her feet as others fell around her and were trampled to death. The guard struggled against the wave of frenzied Kai to reach her but to no avail. He disappeared in the throng, swept away, as she was, toward the riverbank.

The infant queen squalled in Kirgipa's arms, her tiny features lavender from her bellows. Kirgipa rammed her elbow into the face of man who literally tried to climb her and others to walk atop the crowd. He toppled, fingers clawing her dress in an attempt to gain his balance. She stumbled, falling toward him. He grunted as she tried to kick herself free. Her skirt ripped through to the hem, snapping the tether that bound her to him. He let go of her, his plaintive calls for help silenced beneath the crush of running feet.

A powerful hand gripped the back of her shirt and shoved her forward. "Step lively, little maid. We're almost there," Dendarah said near her ear.

Were they not in the midst of a panicked herd of people with *galla* at their backs, Kirgipa would have turned and hugged the royal guardswoman. Instead, she doubled her efforts to reach the Absu, Dendarah beside her, doing as Necos had done-using brute strength to clear a path.

The Absu's icy waters swirling around her legs robbed the breath from her body. People crowded around them, packed tighter than salted fish in barrels and shivering in the frigid air. More Kai stood on the opposite banks, pulling their wet, shaking brethren onto the banks and the docks.

"Can you swim?" Dendarah asked in a voice pitched loud above the din. Kirgipa nodded. "Good. We have to cross the river. Stay as far away from others as you can. Those who can't swim will drown those who can in an effort to save themselves.

You have to hold the baby so I can protect you both and help you cross."

They navigated slowly across the river, pulled by the rushing current. Kirgipa recited every prayer of deliverance and protection she learned in childhood, her teeth chattering as her sodden skirts weighed her down in the cold water. The baby rested high on her shoulder, kept dry except for the sling's trailing ends. Dendarah swam beside her, rising out of the current twice like an avenging water nymph to shove away other swimmers who drew too close.

The protected side of Haradis swelled with people—those fleeing the *galla* and those who patrolled the banks to help the swimmers ashore. Dendarah was helping Kirgipa to her feet when a dripping wet Necos rushed up to them and wrapped his arms around both women and the baby. All three squawked in protest until he let them go.

"I thought you were *galla* meat, woman," he told Dendarah, a faint smile flitting across his lips.

She didn't smile back. "Almost." Her gaze turned to the opposite shore and the twitching, gibbering darkness that had swallowed all the fields and seethed into the first streets of Haradis. "And I may well be yet."

The screams and warped laughter that had followed Kirgipa and Necos as they fled the palace echoed in the avenues and alleyways. Some of the Kai had not run fast enough or had been unable to flee. Kirgipa closed her eyes, praying her mother and sister were among those who swam across and were somewhere in the throngs of people finding sanctuary on this side of the Absu.

More people clogged the river, struggling to reach the opposite shore. Kirgipa's mouth dropped open when she caught sight of a group of Kai doing the exact opposite. Clothed in their armor and mounted on horses, they plunged into the Absu, cleaving a path to the side vulnerable to the *galla*.

"What in the name of Emlek are they doing?" Necos said, his eyes wide. "They can't fight those things with swords."

Kirgipa glanced at Dendarah who watched the commotion for a moment before answering. "They aren't." She pointed to the group. "Look at them. All are old, long retired from service. They aren't there to fight; they're there to die."

Dendarah was right. The contingent of armed Kai consisted of men and women who might have been her own grandparents. They rode to the opposite shore, dismounted and set the horses loose. The leader, a Kai man with his black hair silvered by advanced age, faced his troops and the river. Hunched and elderly he might be, but his voice carried strong and true over the dying screams of the Kai and the howls of the *galla*.

"There is no better legacy to leave than this—to die in the effort to save our descendents. Join with me so that those who came after us will live to remember."

He then put his back to the river and spread his arms. Those who followed him lined up on either side, grasping forearms and linking to each other until they forged a living chain that stretched along a portion of the riverbank.

Kirgipa's heart ached at their bravery, and she hugged her small charge to her breast for solace. Beside her, Dendarah's voice rang hard and bitter. "Duty is a weighty burden." She met Kirgipa's eyes, her face drawn and aged. "My first purpose is to protect your charge. It is your purpose as well, and Necos's. But I would be lying if I said I don't wish with all my heart to be among those who stand unyielding before the enemy." She pointed to the river. "See there? The words of a brave leader are their own powerful magic."

People left the water's sanctuary, mostly elderly but some in their prime. They waded to land, unheeding of the frantic relatives who tried to hold them back. Others abandoned the safety of the opposite shore and swam the river after them. Grandfathers and grandmothers, soldiers long retired from the field and many whose professions bore nothing of war and glory. They joined their comrades, bound together in a line that now stretched far down the river's banks.

Kirgipa's heart lurched to a horrified stop at the sight that met her eyes. Her mother, Tarawin, wet from the river, joined the chain. Atalan, Kirgipa's sister, stood hip-deep in the water, begging her not to go. Kirgipa screamed and lunged toward the shore, forgetting the baby in her arms and the guards who watched over her. "No, Muta! Don't!"

She would have fallen into the water had Necos not hauled her back. Dendarah plucked the baby out of her arms, leaving Kirgipa's hands free. She swung at Necos, writhing in his arms to get free. "Let me go! That's my muta in the line! My sister in the river!"

Necos shook her so hard, her vision blackened at the edges. "Stop, Kirgipa!" He spun her to face the river, his grip on her shoulders like shackles, unbreakable, unyielding. He pointed to a spot in the chain. "My oldest brother is there," he said, indicating a man of middle years. He pointed to the man beside him. "Our uncle." He turned her to face him, and Kirgipa keened at the grief in his eyes. "They have made their choice, and it's a courageous one. Our memories will preserve their sacrifice as heroic. Honor that choice by staying alive and doing your duty."

She could only gasp and moan, sick with the knowledge that she and her sister were about to watch their mother die. "My sister," she said on a hiccup. "She's in the river."

Assured that Kirgipa wouldn't try to rescue her mother, Dendarah returned the infant to her. "Can she swim?" Kirgipa nodded. "Then she's in the safest place of all."

She had no opportunity to argue. The *galla* ravaging that side of the city reached the riverbank. The Kai locked arm and arm along the riverbank began to chant, and then they began to glow. Their magic, the strength of earlier generations, arced across their linked arms until it suffused their entire bodies, creating a luminous blue barrier that brightened the oncoming night and whipped the living darkness into a frenzy.

Not a barrier. Bait. Kirgipa shuddered, her gaze frozen on the shimmering column of cerulean light that was her mother. The Kai still in the river and those on the shore had gone silent. The river's dull roar filled the quiet, along with the chant of spells that awakened a Kai's magic and the ravenous screeches of *galla*.

Dendarah forced Kirgipa to face her. The guard's features were pinched. "Do not let this be your last memory of her. I will watch. I will remember." She glanced at Necos. "I'll do the same for you."

Necos shook his head, his gaze locked on the spot where his brother and uncle stood. "I carry the burden of this memory willingly."

Kirgipa clutched Dendarah's sleeve. "Promise you'll save my sister when it's done."

"I'll do my best."

She knew when the *galla* struck by the collective gasp inhaled by the Kai standing around her. She almost turned, stopped by Dendarah who pulled her into her embrace, the baby between them.

More screams, these loud and long and so piercing as to crack the moon above them. They were the cries of the dying and the cries of those who watched them die. Kirgipa shuddered in Dendarah's embrace and prayed that their suffering would speedily end, that her mother would perish instantly and not know agony.

In the end, she couldn't judge if the attack lasted moments or months. It seemed to last lifetimes. When Dendarah freed her long enough to face the river, the blue glow born from Kai magic and the men and women who formed it was gone. Only a wall of writhing shadow fenced the far shore, nebulous shapes made of crimson eyes, pointed claws and jagged fangs that dissolved into smoke and char only to reform again and again. The river itself was bloated with more people. Those who had sacrificed themselves to the *galla* had allowed everyone still trapped on the shore to reach the water in time.

The mass churned at the river's edge, its frustration at not being able to feast on the victims just beyond its reach, palpable. Howls and rapid clicks, as of teeth gnashing together, filled the air. Behind the black wall, the palace rose in the distance, a ravaged silhouette under the rising moon's light.

Dendarah spoke behind Kirgipa. "So falls the kingdom of Bast-Haradis."

CHAPTER ONE

Ildiko clenched her fists and cracked her knuckles within the folds of her gown as she viewed the kitchen's main worktable. Saggara's head cook had laid out a sampling of each dish to be served at the banquet she and Brishen would host the following day in celebration of *Kaherka*, the Kai feast of plenty.

"For you, *Hercegesé*." The cook handed her a plate and flashed Ildiko a sharp-toothed smile.

As hostess of this gathering and mistress of the household, it was her responsibility to taste and approve the dishes created by Saggara's kitchen staff. Ildiko didn't normally balk at this particular duty. She enjoyed many of the foods the Kai prepared and ate—all save one: she gripped the plate and tried not to stare too hard at the scarpatine pie that breathed and beckoned at the opposite end of the table, the sharp point of a venomous barb poking through a crust glistening with butter.

Cook was obviously watching her much closer than Ildiko guessed. She strode to the pie perched on a decorative tray and lifted it with a coaxing gesture. "Do you wish to try this first, Your Highness?"

"No!" Ildiko cleared her throat and lowered her voice. "No thank you, Cook. I'll start at this end." She hoped by the time she made it to where the pie waited to do battle, her stomach wouldn't try to flee her body via her throat at the idea of eating a steaming, freshly butchered piece of scarpatine.

17

She took her time, nibbling at the small portions cut or scooped and placed onto her plate. A few had once made her hesitate. The dishes she had grown up eating as a Gauri noblewoman didn't include such things as honey-roasted locusts or the *sipla* grubs smoked, then stewed in a spicy pepper sauce that threatened to burn her tongue to a pile of ash when she first tried them. The scarpatine pie grew ever closer, and Ildiko ate slower and slower. Beside her, Cook shifted impatiently from foot to foot.

Ildiko almost leapt across the table to hug the steward in gratitude when he appeared in the doorway. Mesumenes flinched at her grin before his features smoothed into a stoic expression. "*Hercegesé*, if I may, a moment of your time."

Cook's eyes narrowed as she stared at the steward, her tall frame stiff with annoyance at the interruption. "Shall I save this for your approval later, Your Highness?"

Satisfied with what she'd already tried and thrilled not to have to sample the pie, Ildiko handed Cook her unfinished plate. "No, of course not. I've enjoyed everything I've tried so far, and I'm sure our guests will too. I have every faith that all of these dishes will be enthusiastically devoured." Any of the guests were more than welcome to her share of the scarpatine.

Cook preened at her praise, directed a last sniff of disapproval at Mesumenes and ordered her small army of cooks and scullions back to work.

Ildiko accompanied the steward into the dark corridor outside the kitchens. He led her to a pool of yellow light spilling from a single torch mounted in an iron sconce bolted to the stonework. He handed her a bound stack of documents.

"You've the look of a man with a weighty question, steward." She glanced at the first page, noting the writing was in a mix of both Common and Gauri.

Mesumenes clasped his hands behind his back and settled his weight on his heels, a sure sign he was about to give Ildiko an earful. "The first cargo of trade goods from Gaur has arrived by barge. It's docked outside of Escariel township. The crew has unloaded Gauri goods and is waiting to load the shipment of amaranthine specified in the trade agreement."

Silence stretched between them until Ildiko coaxed him into further expounding with an "And?"

Frown lines cut paths in the space between his eyebrows. "A messenger from the township sent this manifest from the dock master. They can't take possession of the Gauri goods until they can verify accurate shipment."

Ildiko looked back at the papers in her hand, flipping through each one slowly this time. The more she read, the angrier she grew. She met Mesumenes's glowing gaze. "Is this supposed to be a joke? Who decided to send a manifest with weights and measures in Gauri Old Form?"

He shrugged. "No one can say, but neither the dock master nor I are familiar with the language, so we can't calculate the amounts to make sure that what's listed is what has been delivered."

The heat of an embarrassed blush crawled up her neck, burning her cheeks and ears. This was the first real trade exchange between the two countries enacted beyond sheaves of parchment signed and stamped since she and Brishen married, and someone in Gaur had decided to try their hand at a bit of deceit and trickery. Such an action cast her people in a poor light.

The agreement between Gaur and Bast-Haradis had been the trade of luxury items to the Kai: exotic teas and spices, semi-precious stones, high quality glass, cotton fabrics and gold-spun embroidery. All for the valuable amaranthine dye, processed and sold only by the Kai.

Indignant and ashamed, Ildiko crinkled part of the manifest in her tight grip. Mesumenes took a cautious step back when she spoke. "Tell the messenger to wait and have a horse saddled. I'll accompany him back to Escariel."

She didn't shout or snap, but the steward leapt to do her bidding. In no time, a mount was readied, along with a contingent of a half dozen soldiers who accompanied her on the half-hour ride to Escariel.

They arrived at the docks that hugged the Absu's deeper banks where a crowd of Kai mingled amongst cargo unloaded from boats. Bales of cloth and sacks filled with various goods occupied any available space alongside rows of baskets, amphorae and barrels. The river swelled with flat-bottom barges moored to bollards with lengths of rope. The barges nestled together, creating wharves of their own as the crews busily transferred shipments according to the shouted orders of a dockmaster or barge captain. It was an orderly chaos carried out under moonlight and beneath the flicker of torchlight.

The messenger who had brought the manifest to Saggara led them through the throng. Ildiko ignored the weight of Kai gazes as she passed. She had resided in Saggara for over a year and grown used to the curiosity she represented. The Kai living in villages closest to Saggara were more used to the sight of humans than the insular population in the capital. They stared not because she was a human among them but because she was a human married to one of their own.

They rode past barrels marked with magenta-colored hashmarks and stamped on the lids with the Saggara territorial seal. Amaranthine waiting be loaded and transported to Gaur. The cluster of clerks who sat behind makeshift desks constructed of planks of wood laid across empty barrels argued in a mixture of bast-Kai and Common with three humans. Ildiko listened as the exchange grew increasingly loud and hostile, with Kai refusing to release the barrels until they verified the manifest and the humans demanding to load cargo without more delay.

The argument ceased abruptly when she and her escort halted before them. The Kai scrambled to their feet and bowed together. The three humans stared at her for a moment, puzzled, until they too realized who paid them a visit. Like the Kai, they bowed.

"Your Highness," one group said in Gauri.

"*Hercegesé*," the other said in bast-Kai.

Ildiko dismounted, manifest in hand. She nodded to the clerks. "Where is your dock master?"

"I'll fetch him directly, *Hercegesé*." One of the clerks sped away and disappeared into the crowd.

Ildiko eyed the three humans, her gaze settling on an older man, grizzled by the elements and years spent sailing the waterways. "Which of you is the barge captain or second mate?"

Her guess was correct. The man stepped forward and bowed a second time. "Your Highness, I am Captain Glay of the *Sly Fox*." He jerked a thumb toward the barge behind him.

Ildiko raised an eyebrow. Considering their current problem, she thought the barge name appropriate. She waved the stack of papers she held at him. "We have an issue with the cargo manifest, Captain. It seems the port master in Gaur gave you one that, unless you're a Gauri priest or tutored by one, is impossible to read."

The captain's smiling features turned shuttered, and his shoulders tensed. "I wouldn't know, Your Highness," he said in carefully bland tones. "We loaded from the sailing ship *Seahorse*. Her captain assured me all cargo was accounted for. It all looks right to me, so we'll take the dye and backhaul it to Gaur if you please."

Ildiko flipped through the pages, chewing on her lower lip as she perused the lists of items with their quantities and weights—all of it in Gauri Old Form. "I don't please," she said. "The Kai clerks can't verify your manifest because they can't translate it." She thrust the manifest at him. "Can you?" She smothered a laugh when he took a step back as if she handed him a live viper. "I didn't think so. That's because someone thought it would be a good idea to list amounts in temple language. Why that someone would assume Gauri priests linger at Kai wharves to accept tithes and offerings is a puzzle, wouldn't you say?"

Captain Glay's gaze slid to one side. He shrugged as if such things happened all the time. "I suppose, Your Highness. However, I assure you, the delivery matches the manifest."

She did laugh then. He obviously thought she meddled in affairs unsuitable for a woman and should trust him because they shared a commonality—they were both human. She addressed him over her shoulder as she made her way to one of the desks where the Kai clerks tallied cargo. "I'm sure it does, but you'll have to humor me. You and the Kai may not be able to translate Old Form, but I can."

Thank the gods for the Gauri custom of having priests tutor the nobility. Ildiko had found the lessons excessively dull, and she was an average student at best, but average was all she needed right now to translate the manifest.

She pointed to one of the desks vacated by a clerk. "May I?"

A selection of stools for her sit on and quills with which to write were donated by all the clerks, their fangs gleaming ivory in the semi-darkness as they smirked in triumph at the barge captain.

He was far less accommodating. His hands clenched at his sides, and he spoke through clenched teeth. "Your Highness, this will take hours and put me behind schedule."

Ildiko clucked her tongue in false sympathy. "An unfortunate result of another's inappropriate humor. I suggest, that when you return, you speak with whoever drafts these manifests and strongly encourage them to use the language of trade instead of temple." She ignored his glare, opened the manifest to the first set of lists and dipped her quill into the nearby inkpot. "Let's get started shall we? I'm sure none of us want to still be here at dawn."

The dock master arrived before the captain could offer up any more argument. He bowed to Ildiko, not hiding his surprise at the sight of her perched behind the makeshift desk. "Saggara received my message. I expected Mesumenes with a reply, not the *hercegesé* herself." He sounded both pleased and confused. "How may I be of assistance, Your Highness?"

Ildiko waved her quill at him. "I'm only here to translate. I leave the coordination of all this cargo to you."

Had she been a Gauri priest herself, the translation would have gone much faster, but years had passed since she labored over lessons in temple text, and she muddled slowly through the list. The captain paced and muttered and sometimes left her for his barge only to return moments later, bestowing hot glares on her that she blithely ignored.

Dawn had not yet cracked the black horizon when she finished, but it was close, and her fingers curled cramped and ink-stained around the quill before she set it aside and exhaled a relieved breath. "Done," she said and smiled triumphantly at the dock master. He nodded and the barge captain pumped a celebratory fist in the air.

He gave her and the manifest a wary look. "We're free to go then?"

Ildiko shrugged. "You've still to work out a credit with the dock master for those goods damaged in shipping, but my work here is done." She stood, wincing at the low ache in her back from sitting on the hard stool for so long. "Good evening." She glanced at the thin edge of glowing light in the distance. "Or good morning as the case may be."

She accepted the dock master's profuse thanks for her help and promised a return visit should they experience a similar problem in future shipments. Her gaze settled on the captain who was busily snapping orders to his sleepy crew to ready the barge to sail. She hoped a lesson in delays might prevent him and others from trying another stunt like this one in the future.

The fortress was still a hive of activity as the household staff worked to prepare for the next evening's feast. Ildiko didn't stop to inquire how things progressed. As long-time steward of

Saggara, Mesumenes handled such events with an expert hand. She simply stayed out of his way and approved or requested changes when he or Cook asked specifically for her input. At the moment, she was doubly grateful for their efficiency. All she wanted was a bath to wash away the stink of the wharf. Her maid Sinhue waited for her in her bedchamber, her nose crinkling before she smoothed her features into a polite mask.

Ildiko laughed. "No need to hide it. I know I smell foul. I've the wharf's reek on me."

The two women worked together to strip off Ildiko's clothing, and soon she was naked except for a light blanket she wrapped around herself to ward off some of the room's chill. She huddled in a chair by the lit hearth for warmth while Sinhue left for the kitchens to order a hip bath and food.

Were Brishen here, she'd order a bigger bath for the two of them to share. Ildiko sighed, staring into the flames dancing merrily in the fireplace. He'd taken Anhuset and a patrol with him to his territory's western border. Word had reached Saggara of numerous raids on Kai homesteads, with the theft of cattle, sheep and horses and the death of one family. Reports had been mixed as to who the culprits were, with some proclaiming them as Kai while others swore they were Beladine raiders crossing into Kai lands from Serovek Pangion's territory.

She hoped it wasn't the second. Since Serovek's help in rescuing both Ildiko and Brishen, not to mention Anhuset, he and Brishen had gone from amicable neighbors to close friends. A fine thing except for the fact their respective kingdoms took an ever more belligerent stance toward each other. Ildiko prayed neither would declare war. She hated the idea that the two men might have to face each other as enemies on the battlefield.

Sinhue returned with a contingent of servants bearing the tub and jugs of water, along with covered platters of food. In no time, Ildiko sat submerged to her waist in hot water. Sinhue occupied herself with setting a nearby table until her mistress was ready to wash her hair.

While the tub wasn't designed to recline in, one side had a high back, similar to a chair, that allowed Ildiko to rest against it. Were it not for the delicious smell of the nearby platters teasing her nose and making her stomach gurgle, she'd sit for a long soak. Instead, she hurried through the bath and hair washing, eager to sit and eat.

She was in the midst of wrapping a warmed drying cloth around her torso when the door connecting her bed chamber to Brishen's opened behind her. Sinhue bowed in that direction, and Ildiko turned, spotting her husband in the doorway.

Still dressed in mud-splattered armor and leather and a cloak whose hem dripped more mud onto the floor, he stood on the threshold, his grin both sensual and sharp. "Hello, pretty hag," he said in tones that sent a pleasant shiver down her back that had nothing to do with the cold.

"Brishen!" Heedless of the fact she was still standing in the tub, Ildiko lunged for him, tripping over the tub's edge in her haste to reach him. Sinhue's quick reflexes saved her from an embarrassing sprawl.

The grinning servant passed her to Brishen who'd cleared the distance between the doorway and the tub in a quick stride. "I leave the *hercegesé* to your care, *Herceges*." She bowed a second time. "Ring if you need me."

Ildiko waited until the door closed behind Sinhue before speaking. "Well, there went my plan to greet your homecoming with dignity and grace," she said in a rueful voice.

Brishen's mouth quirked, and his right eye shone with a nacreous gleam. His left eye was gone, gouged out months earlier by raiders in a bout of torture. A black patch covered the empty eye socket but didn't hide the jagged scars that split the skin above his eyebrow and below the eye rim. "I like this plan much better." His long-clawed fingers traced a delicate line along the edge of her towel where it lay against her breastbone, one corner tucked into her cleavage. He held her hand in a light grip with his other hand. "Miss me, wife?"

"Eh, maybe a little," she teased. She leaned into him, savoring his touch. Despite the lethality of his claws and his ability to use them like knives, she harbored no fear for her safety. For all that he was a warrior born and bred, with the superior strength bequeathed to all those of his race, Brishen Khaskem had always been a gentle husband. Ildiko tried to embrace him and frowned when he stepped out of reach, still retaining his hold on her hand.

"I'm filthy, wife, and need a bath of my own." His nostrils flared, and his voice lowered to a more guttural timbre. "Lover of thorns, but you smell good enough to eat."

She arched an eyebrow and glanced at the platters on the table. "Considering our people's respective histories, not to mention that wolf smile when you say such a thing, I'm not sure if I should be flattered or scream for help."

Her comment recalled a conversation from a few months earlier. Anhuset, not he, had been the one to verify a bit of gruesome history shared by Kai and human. Ildiko was sure she'd gone pale as chalk when Brishen's cousin told her how the Kai once hunted humans for food.

She'd stared at Anhuset for a long moment, trying to determine if the other woman teased or spoke fact. "Then Serovek wasn't bluffing when he threatened to turn that Beladine raider over to the Kai as road rations if he didn't tell us where they held Brishen."

Anhuset had shaken her head. "He wasn't. Threats work best when they're grounded in truth."

Brishen's stomach growled. Ildiko tugged her hand free and took a step back. "I'm certain I taste like a boiled potato," she declared.

He scowled. "Then you're safe from me, my beauty." He strode toward the table with its enticing scents and lifted the covers off the various plates. His eye closed in ecstasy as he popped a tidbit into his mouth and chewed. Ildiko's knees wobbled, and a burgeoning heat began to pool in her belly and between her thighs. Who knew someone could look that seductive while eating?

He stole another bite before offering her an apologetic shrug. "I haven't eaten since yestereve. We tracked a band of cattle thieves to the western boundaries. We killed two and took the other ten prisoner."

She dreaded his answer to her question. "Kai or Beladine?"

"Kai."

Her shoulders sagged. She did her best to hide her relief. Killing his own countrymen was surely not an easy thing for him, but at least there was no increased chance of cross-border hostilities if Brishen had meted out Kai justice to Beladine thieves.

She peered more closely at him, touching on his face, shoulders and slender waist thickened by layers of armor, his legs encased in heavy woolen trousers and boots laced to the knees. He bore the splatters of mud but not blood, and there were no rips in his clothing.

After more than a year of marriage, he had grown far more adept at reading her expressions. Something in her face must have revealed her concern. "I am well, Ildiko. Just tired and starved."

She sighed. "I can't help it. I worry for you when you lead these patrols. I don't sleep until you return."

His features softened. "Then you don't dream of me when I'm gone," he complained before giving her a wink.

Ildiko turned to gather up the night rail Sinhue had laid out on her bed and casually let the drying cloth drop. She smiled but didn't turn at Brishen's gasp. "Now that you're here, I can sleep. Then I will dream of you."

His voice took on a noticeable rasp, thick with desire. "Put that thought away now, Ildiko. There'll be no sleep for either of us for many hours."

She shivered, both from the cold and anticipation before slipping on the garment. A disappointed exhalation made her glance over her shoulder at him. "Well then, *Herceges*, why are you just standing there pilfering my supper? Shed that muddy armor and make good on your threat."

Brishen chuckled. "Not a threat, a promise." A knock at the door separating their bedchambers turned his attention from her for a moment. "That would be Etep with my bath and food. Will you join me?" He grabbed both trays off the table set for her by Sinhue.

That he would even have to ask such a question made her shake her head. "I would have ordered those for you if I'd known you were here, husband." She followed him to the door, frowning when he sidestepped her attempt to touch him once more. Her fingers practically throbbed with the need to caress him—a need born from desire as well as concern that he was well and whole.

Brishen nudged the door open wider with his boot to reveal his personal servant Etep standing across the room setting another table with more food while the same group of servants who filled her tub emptied buckets of water into another bath. "I was barely through the entry hall's door when I begged for these things. I've several days of road dirt on me, and I stink of cattle."

Unlike the hip bath delivered to Ildiko's room, this one was a full tub that allowed the bather to stretch out. Steam, scented with the cool fragrance of juniper, rose off the water's surface in wispy tendrils.

Brishen's bedchamber was an icy crypt compared to hers, the fire in the hearth as yet unlit. A servant crouched at the opening, preparing kindling around the logs. Ildiko shivered and excused herself to retrieve a heavy robe and slippers from one of the clothing chests in her room. When she returned, the servants were gone except for Etep who set to work helping Brishen out of his armor.

She settled into one of the chairs next to the food-laden table, pulled her knees up to the seat, and tucked her cold feet under her robe.

Brishen regarded her with a narrowed eye as she sampled the various offerings set out for their supper. He shrugged out of the loosened brigandine cuirass and handed it to the waiting Etep.

"See you don't devour it all, Ildiko. I'm hungry enough to eat the plates."

"I'll try and control myself," she promised in a casual voice. She grinned at his low growl. "Bath or food first?" The scent of spicy pepper and savory sauce tickled her nose and made her mouth water.

"Bath." Brishen dismissed Etep when he was down to his long shirt and trousers. "I'm dirtier than I am hungry." He stripped off the shirt, flinging it to a far corner of the room. The trousers followed. Ildiko's sharp inhalation made him pause as he stepped into the bath's hot water. His eyebrows arched, and a faint smirk played at the corners of his mouth. "Why are you staring like that, wife?"

Ildiko snorted. What a silly question. The Kai were, by nature, a leaner, more muscular people than most humans, and Brishen was no exception to the rule. He possessed a horseman's solid thighs and the arms of a man who trained often for war. Smooth gray skin stretched taut over broad shoulders and a sculpted chest and stomach. Were he to turn, she'd be treated to an equally impressive view of a powerful back and firm buttocks.

Her gaze settled on his thighs and stayed. While a Kai male differed in some ways from his human counterpart, the two shared the same construct when it came to the endowments of manhood. They also shared the commonality of bragging about and comparing said endowments. Living in a military garrison among rough soldiers, Ildiko had inadvertently overheard more than a few masculine boasts.

Brishen, both confident and humble, didn't brag, but judging by the impressive erection that rose under her steady gaze, he certainly had cause to do so. "Now look what you've done," he complained.

She laughed. "You brought it on yourself. How can I possibly look away with you prancing about in all your glory?" She rose and tightened the belt on her robe. "Stop dawdling and get in. I'll play lady's maid and wash your back and hair."

He did as she instructed and breathed out a pleasured sigh when he sank into the water to his neck. "I think I'll like being a lady."

The fire in the newly lit hearth crackled merrily. Ildiko left Brishen to float lazily in the bath, an expression of pure bliss gracing his features as he rested his head on the tub's edge and draped his arms over the sides. She moved the stack of drying cloths closer to the hearth to warm and poured a dram of wine from a carafe into a goblet.

He looked asleep when she returned to the tub, goblet in hand. His right eye was closed, the left eye socket still concealed by the black eye patch he wore when he sank into the water. Neither vanity nor shame moved him to keep it on. He'd simply forgotten he wore it. He opened his good eye and caught her admiring him.

"You're either planning my seduction or my demise," he said in a voice slurred by fatigue. His long fingers wrapped around the goblet, and he raised it in toast to her thoughtfulness.

A small footstool by the hearth served as an excellent perch, and Ildiko placed it behind the tub where Brishen's head rested. "Neither," she replied. "I'm planning to wash your hair." She gave him time to drain the wine while she retrieved a shallow pail, pitchers of cold water and a cake of soap.

Brishen's appreciative "Mmmmm" as she slid her fingers gently through his tangled hair made her smile. Ildiko rolled up the sleeves of her robe, tucked the hem under her seat and set to wetting, soaping and rinsing his long locks. She tried to imagine him as an elder Kai man, with hair turned silvery white instead of its current sloe darkness. He'd still be as handsome and regal as he was now. She chuckled under her breath, amused at the idea that she once thought him hideous.

One yellow eye peered up at her. "What amuses you, wife?" The question fell away to a moan as she rubbed his scalp.

"I was just thinking you are far too handsome for your own good."

"It's the scars," he said. "They give me a certain air."

Ildiko lost her smile. Those scars. She'd have nightmares about them until she died. Not because they made him hideous but because they'd been inflicted with purpose and merciless brutality. Never in her life did she imagine she'd order the death of other men, but she'd done it to those who tortured her husband and wouldn't hesitate to do the same a second time.

She twisted his clean hair into a heavy rope, ignoring his accusation that she was trying to scalp him. His protests changed to wordless hums of approval when she soaped his back, her slippery hands gliding over the curve where neck met shoulder and the deep valley where his spine bisected the hard slopes of his back.

His protests started anew when she passed him the soap and a cloth. "You can finish the rest while I fill a plate for you and pour more wine."

"But you said you'd play lady's maid to me."

"Sinhue does not bathe me all over."

Brishen grunted. "Wasted opportunity that." He coated the cloth in soap and began scrubbing, his frown forbidding at her chortle.

It was her turn to frown when he stood up from the tub and reached for the drying cloth she held out to him. The movement made him pivot into profile, and Ildiko got her first glance of the ugly indigo bruise stamped on the back of his thigh.

She held back the cloth and drew closer, gaze on the bruise. "What is this?"

Wet and shivering, Brishen glanced down at himself, still semi-erect. The faint smirk reappeared. "Proof of my consuming passion for mollusk."

Ildiko scowled, her fingertips dancing lightly along the bruise's dark edge. "Not that. This."

He shrugged. "Gift from an annoyed cow. I'm a better fighter than a drover. Felt like someone hit me in the leg with a hammer." Taking advantage of her distraction, he snatched the drying cloth out of her hand.

"You should summon a healer." A part of her recognized she was being unduly concerned. Many a night Brishen had returned from the training field patterned in purple bruises from knee to neck. Still, she couldn't help her overprotective response.

As if recognizing the source of her fear, his voice gentled, and he twined her still damp braid through his fingers. "There's nothing one can do that I didn't already take care of on the road, Ildiko. It's a small thing and will heal soon enough."

"You still should have sought out a healer."

He wrapped the towel around his middle and took the second one she handed him to dry his limbs. "I was in too much of a hurry to return home. I had a wife waiting. And food." He flashed a fanged grin at her. "Not one and the same of course."

She swatted him lightly on the arm before scampering away on a screech when he returned the gesture with a hand to her buttock.

They caught up with each other's week as they ate. Brishen's foray sounded miserable, complete with rain, fighting and bad-tempered cattle. He was on his third plate of food when he mentioned the barge carrying trade goods to Escariel's docks. "We saw the barge as we traveled back to Saggara. I expected it to be much further down the Absu. Was it delayed?"

Ildiko leaned back in her chair, twirling the stem of her goblet slowly between thumb and fingers. "You could say that. Someone in Gaur decided it might be amusing to list the weights and measures of the cargo in Gauri Old Form." She described the visit from the messenger and her anger at seeing the manifest completed in temple script as well as the long hours at the dock completing translations.

Brishen's dismay made her own irritation over the entire affair flare once more. "You're an excellent helpmeet, Ildiko, but it's disappointing this happened. I'd hoped the actual trade exchanges wouldn't start out so contentious."

She caressed his forearm where it rested on the table's surface. "I as well, though I suspect we won't see much more of that in future shipments. This was someone testing the waters."

He shook his head. "You'd think they'd find better ways to waste their time and ours." He finished the rest of his wine and helped her stand. His undamaged eye was at drowsy half mast, and he'd tossed aside the patch earlier while bathing. Scar tissue welted the curvature of bone around the empty socket in a corona of pale, jagged lines.

Ildiko slid her thumb along the grouping below his collapsed eyelid. "I know you've said they don't hurt, but it's hard to imagine you no longer feel the pain."

Brishen captured her hand and brought her thumb to his lips for a brief kiss. "They would only hurt if you thought me hideous because of them."

"That will never happen," she vowed.

"Then they will never hurt."

She spread her fingers across his soft mouth. "Come to bed. I'll massage you, then take advantage of your body while you're too relaxed to protest."

His eyebrows shot up. "Threat or a promise?" he murmured under her hand.

Ildiko gave him a coy smile. "Does it matter?"

He grabbed her hand and tugged her toward the big bed where the sheets were turned down. "Not at all."

The towel dropped, abandoned by the bedside. Brishen sprawled face down and naked across the bed, feet hanging over the edge, arms hidden under a pillow he tucked under his cheek. He closed his eye and gave a deep sigh when Ildiko seated herself on his lower back, knees and thighs pressed against his narrow hips. A drawn out moan followed the sigh when she began kneading his shoulders and upper back with hands slippery with scented oil.

Tight muscle loosened under her ministration, his smooth skin made even more supple by the warm oil. Ildiko rubbed and kneaded him from shoulder to calf, shifting position so she could reach the various spots on his body and still avoid the painful looking bruise on the back of his leg.

His breathing slowed, and he settled deeper into the mattress. Ildiko assumed he'd fallen asleep until he spoke in a somnolent voice. "Are your hands tired?"

She heard the thread of hope in his voice that her answer would be a "No." She lifted her weight and balanced on her knees. "Not yet." She shed her robe, giving a small shiver as a cold draft coursed over her skin. The hearth was doing its job of warming the room, but the air remained frigid. Brishen, on the other hand, lay hot beneath her. She bent, pressing her breasts to his back, and nuzzled his ear. "Turn over," she whispered.

He rolled to his back under her, his hands settling on her hips. He was fully erect, the head of his cock tapping against the folds of her night rail as his pelvis shifted. A bluish flush highlighted his cheekbones and washed over his neck and clavicles. "How long will you deny me, wife?"

The light scrape of her forefingers over his dark nipples made him gasp and arch his back. "How am I denying you?" She knew the answer; they played this game each time he returned to her, but she wanted to hear him say it.

His right eye had paled from vibrant yellow to glowing alabaster, and he replied in staccato breaths, broken each time she stroked his nipples. "You haven't kissed me yet. Not once since my return."

Of the many things they both had to adapt to in this marriage, a simple kiss had been the one Ildiko was certain had carried the most thought and planning. The Kai typically kissed each other with closed mouths and affectionate nuzzling of the nose and cheeks. Even in the heat of passion, they didn't kiss with open mouths and tongues—a bloody business considering the sharpness of their teeth.

Ildiko had taught Brishen to kiss her in the way that was human but not so dangerous. A careful dance of lips and tongues, his stroking hers in the hot space of her mouth, her licking and sucking on his lower lip. Neither fully human nor fully Kai, the kiss was solely theirs, altered to please each other, and made of pure magic. Ildiko delighted in kissing her husband and quickly learned that Brishen craved it, demanding she bestow that particular display of affection on him at every opportunity.

She stretched across his torso, his cock long between their bellies. "You're impatient, love," she said and punished him for the failing by drawing his right nipple into her mouth to gently suck.

Brishen nearly heaved them both off the bed. Powerful legs wrapped around hers, heavy arms crossed her back, and he thrust against her, caught in the tangling folds of her night rail.

Undaunted, Ildiko abandoned his right side for his left, showering the same attention before nipping and licking a path up his chest to his neck and the hollow of his throat. Brishen arched his neck to grant her greater access, and his pulse beat hard and fast under her lips.

His fingers flexed on her backside, the pointed tips of his claws spearing the cloth of her night rail to press into her skin. Ildiko shivered in his arms, as much from desire as from an instinctive wariness. He could easily bloody her. A careless twitch, an involuntary jerk, and he could flay her open. He didn't and never would. Her trust in him was absolute, and the danger implied by the Kai physical traits of tooth and claw, strength and speed, only heightened her passion for him.

"I do not deny you," she whispered against his temple, damp with perspiration. He tasted of salt and the cool sharpness of juniper. She feathered light kisses along his hairline, traveling across his forehead to the clear space between his eyebrows before gliding lower, over the bony bridge of his nose to the fan of scars and the collapsed lid covering his empty eye socket. The breath of a touch on mutilated flesh before she moved to his ear. "I will never deny you," she whispered and nipped his earlobe. He shuddered in her arms. "Ask anything of me, and it's yours."

Brishen's only reply was the tightening of his arms around her and the steady cadence of bestial growls vibrating low in his throat. Ildiko's lips mapped a path to his mouth, pausing for one incandescent moment. The room had grown hot, heated by more than one fire. Shivers still raced across her skin but not from the cold. She had successfully reduced her husband to incoherency and wordless moans that begged her for mercy. He, in turn, had set her alight. Every nerve ending tingled, from the top of her head to the arches of her feet. The interior muscles of her sex throbbed, and her thighs were slick as her body readied itself in anticipation. Brishen shoved the night rail up to her waist. They exchanged a mutual groan when his shaft pressed into her bare belly, the head smearing a trickle of seed below her navel.

She kissed him then. Not a peck on the lips or the click of teeth in the more violent throes of passion, but a slow, decadent play of mouths and tongues. She opened to him, both mouth and thighs. He slid in, filling both places until she'd burst from the fullness of him inside her. He swallowed her throaty whimpers.

His hands slid from her waist to her hips, holding her in place as he ground against her pelvis. Ildiko sucked on his tongue, all her internal muscles matching the rhythm as she squeezed his shaft. Their position didn't allow for greater movement unless they ended their kiss, and Ildiko waited until the last wisp of air emptied out of her lungs. She pulled away to inhale and rested her forehead against Brishen's.

"I won't last," he said in a guttural voice. "It's too good."

It was too good, and she didn't care that any prolonged lovemaking was no longer a choice. She had brought them both to fever pitch. The grind of his pelvis against her pubic bone, the swell of his cock inside her, the scent of him inundating her nostrils—all served to drive her to madness.

She rocked atop him, back arching, fingers kneading his shoulders as jolts of heat and sensation shot down her spine to spiral in her abdomen. She cried out, nails digging into Brishen's flesh as her knees clamped down hard on either side of his hips. Caught in the throes of climax, she only vaguely heard his responding groans and the cant of her name uttered in broken breaths as he clutched her buttocks and found his own release.

Ildiko hung her head, panting hard, before stretching atop Brishen's length. His chest heaved against her breasts. He tightened his forearm across her backside to keep her anchored to him and rolled them both to their sides. Dark hair drifted over his cheek and eye, and she caught the silky strands in her fingers before draping them back behind his ear.

He nuzzled his face into her palm. "I've thought of nothing else except that kiss since we started for home."

"And what about that which came afterwards?"

She squeaked when he hugged her even closer. "I didn't dare," he said. "Too much of a distraction. I'd likely have walked my mount into a tree with such thoughts occupying my mind."

They both laughed at the image his words conjured. Brishen yanked the covers one way, then another until he and Ildiko lay beneath them instead of on top. He plucked at her night rail. "This has to go." The garment ended up in the corner with his dirty shirt and trousers.

As naked as he was now, she huddled into the cove of his body for warmth. He caressed her back and rubbed his chin on the crown of her head. Both motions soon slowed and finally stopped. Deep, even breaths drafted across her scalp.

Ildiko tilted her head enough to glimpse Brishen's features. Despite his assurances they wouldn't sleep for hours, he'd drifted off, the shadows of exhaustion indigo-dark under his eyes. She smiled, settling deeper into his embrace and the warmth of blankets and furs. He was home; he was safe. He was in her arms. There was no better moment in all the world than this. She closed her eyes and joined him in slumber.

CHAPTER TWO

"I reviewed the agreements regarding water rights assigned to Natep Holt and those assigned to Istari Holt as well as the map drawn up showing the stream's path through the two holts. There's an error in the cartography which puts almost a league of the contended stream in Istari territory instead of Natep's. Both holts are now up in arms. Your Highness, I'm afraid no matter how I rule on this matter, the end result will require a martial intervention from Saggara."

Brishen nodded without comment, wondering idly how history might remember him if he impaled himself on his own sword in a last ditch effort to escape the soul-killing boredom of his vicegerent's conversation. It might be less excruciating to hear if he hadn't already heard it three times before—in excruciating detail. That, and the water rights conflict between those two holts was a long-running one, existing when Brishen's own grandfather ruled Bast-Haradis from Saggara instead of the current capital. The map was always wrong and the stream's geography seemingly as fluid as the water coursing through it.

He gazed longingly at the open doors that led from the great hall to the loggia outside. The silhouettes of figures danced and leapt near the threshold, their forms outlined by the many bonfires lit for the festival of *Kaherka*. Kai from every village and holt in a two-day's ride had gathered at Saggara to celebrate, from humble farmers who had labored in the fields to bring in their harvests to

43

the vicegerents who labored at their desks and now whittled away at him with their bureaucracy. *Kaherka* promised two days of eating, drinking, and lovemaking—none of which Brishen was enjoying at the moment.

The crowd in the hall was sparse, populated mostly by the provincial ministers who answered directly to Brishen and considered this an opportune time to bend his ear, and servants who ran to and fro between the kitchens and the serving tables laden with food. Those who feasted filled their plates and returned to the celebrants filling the loggia and spilling into the redoubt's outer perimeter. Music and raucous laughter drifted inside, and Brishen bit back a groan as a second vicegerent pressed him for resolution on a litany of concerns he was certain he already addressed during the previous month's visit to that particular province.

At least he wasn't alone in his misery. Ildiko, dressed in a gown of deepest indigo that highlighted her pale skin and red hair, traversed the hall from one corner to the other, stopping at each cluster of Kai to greet visitors and talk for a moment. As the only human in the gathering, she stood out like a beacon on a hill, drawing every gaze as she passed.

His presence in the hall and the awareness of rank assured none would be anything but courteous and even friendly to her. She might be human but she was also a *hercegesé*, a duchess through marriage to him, and outranked every Kai occupying Saggara and its provinces except himself. Still, he knew their thoughts. He once had them as well.

Serovek Pangion, the Beladine margrave whose lands bordered Saggara, had assured Brishen that to human eyes, Ildiko was pretty. Beautiful even.   To the Kai, she was ugly, and he'd received numerous pitying glances and overheard an equal number of whispers about how regrettable it was that the handsome Kai *herceges* was given such an uncomely creature to wife.

His gaze followed her as he listened with half an ear to his minister's relentless drone. Lust surged in his blood. A day in her arms wasn't enough for him, especially after a week spent away from her, knee-deep in mud, cow manure and blood. Surely there was some way he could spirit her away from the hall, out the doors and into the wild crowd that frolicked and cavorted under the light of a waxing moon. He'd dance her past the bonfires and the revelers to a quiet spot where he could assuage his passion for her in the tight grip of her body while she serenaded him with soft moans.

Ildiko caught his stare over the shoulders of a duo of Kai who chatted with her. Her eyebrows quirked upward as he mouthed a desperate "*Help me.*" Her gaze flickered back to her guests; she laughed at something one of them said, responded with something he couldn't hear and inclined her head in farewell before strolling to where he stood, his well-meaning ministers' prisoner.

The vicegerents' complaints faded at her approach. Each gave a low bow and polite "Your Highness" in greeting. She returned the salutations before turning her attention to Brishen. "My lord, please forgive the interruption, but I seek your advice on a matter that's come to my attention." Brishen clamped his lips tight against the laughter threatening to escape. As she spoke, Ildiko's right eye slowly drifted toward her nose while her left stayed in place.

"It's a small matter," she continued as if unaware of the bizarre ocular motions or the stifled horror they elicited in her guests. "I promise to return you to your companions as soon as possible." Her right eye snapped back to center and leveled a stare on the female minister to his left. The woman shuddered and audibly swallowed.

Brishen choked back a gasp of his own when Ildiko partially closed her right eye but kept the left one open. The eye rolled in a slow circle and repeated the action as if chasing a speck of dust stuck in the white sclera. Judging by the shocked silence and stiff postures of the vicegerents on either side of him, they were as repulsed as he was.

Muttered assurances that she wasn't interrupting and to take all the time she needed prefaced a flight toward the open doors and the sanctuary of the loggia where human women with chameleonic eyes didn't lurk to seek them out for casual conversation.

Ildiko watched the vicegerents flee until they were lost in the darkness beyond the doors. She turned to a grinning Brishen, her eyes steady and no longer capering about in their sockets. "And now we are alone. Was that the help you sought, love?"

He pulled her into his arms, hands splayed across her back and hip. "That was the most grotesque and formidable performance I've ever witnessed."

She "harrumphed" and tapped a finger against one of the ivory clasps that closed his tunic. "I've been practicing. And it's only grotesque because you're Kai. Had I done that to another human, they would have either laughed or ordered me to stop acting childish."

"My savior," he murmured against her cheek. "You've frightened my vicegerents and rescued me from an evening of dull complaints. What payment can I offer you?" He leaned back and wiggled an eyebrow. "Gold? Jewels? My body?"

Ildiko traced the pattern of embroidery decorating his tunic sleeve. Her lashes, a darker red than her hair, shielded her strange human eyes for a moment. "Hmmm, that is far too difficult a choice, therefore I choose all of them." The lashes lifted, and Brishen didn't mistake the mischievous gleam in her black pupils. "For now though, you can repay me with dancing. Nearly all of Saggara is outside celebrating, except us. This is my first *Kaherka* festival, and I don't want to miss it."

She didn't need to say it twice. Brishen meshed his fingers with her and strode toward the doors, wearing a scowl he hoped deterred anyone from stopping him. Ildiko jogged behind him, laughing and admonishing him to slow down.

A crush of people filled the loggia from one corner to another, clustered in small groups to drink and toast a successful harvest. Others danced around great bonfires while even more lingered at the long trestle tables dragged from the hall and laden with food prepared by Saggara's kitchen staff and brought by festival goers who had traveled from homesteads in Saggara's territory.

Brishen swung Ildiko into a crowd of Kai standing at the ready before a group of musicians. The dancers faced each others in two lines with a space between them, men on one side facing women on the other. Several applauded and whistled when the *herceges* and his human *hercegesé* joined them.

The musicians tuned their instruments, playing teasing notes that revealed the song they prepared to play. Brishen grinned, delighted when Ildiko clapped and laughed. "I know this song," she called to him over the din of voices and celebration.

"But can you dance to it?" Ildiko was an adept dancer, as a woman raised in any royal court was expected to be, but she wasn't dancing with Gauri humans. This dance, a reel, was fast, and the Kai were faster.

She cocked a hip, her expression challenging. "Better than you, I'll wager, Your Highness. It's a favorite Gauri dance as well."

More whistles and catcalls from the line of dancers met her reply and Brishen bowed. "I accept the gauntlet thrown, my lady."

The musicians spun out the first notes and rhythms with string instruments and percussion. The two lines danced towards each other, the men spinning the women around as they met before parting once more and widening the gap between the lines.

Drums beat faster and the players' fingers flew across strings as the dancers flew over the ground, spinning and jumping in a swirl of flying skirts and tunics. Ildiko threw back her head and laughed as Brishen caught her up in his arms and whirled through the serpentine line as it coiled and stretched, compressed and expanded to the increasingly wild music. The dancers spun, calling out encouragement to each other and to the musicians to play faster, play harder.

Ildiko was a feather in his embrace, and he tossed her high in the air. She screamed, not with fear but exhilaration. He caught her easily, snatching a quick kiss before spinning her away from him to her original place in the line. They slid around each other, a wordless courtship that fired the blood in his veins from hot to boiling.

His wife's hair had come loose and flew about her head and shoulders each time he spun her around him. Even in the light silvered by the moon and warmed by the bonfires, he could see the pink glow washing her pale skin. He'd once compared her coloring to that of a boiled mollusk. The mollusks and their bounty of amaranthine dye were the wealth of Bast-Haradis and Ildiko of Gaur the greatest treasure of Brishen Khaskem.

The beat of the song slowed in increments, finally coming to a halt. Brishen admired the quick rise and fall of Ildiko's breasts as she struggled to catch her breath. She massaged a spot on her side. He guessed she rubbed at a stitch similar to the one pinching his ribs at the moment.

Her eyes narrowed as she followed the line of his gaze. "And what are you looking at, *Herceges?*"

He drew her closer and pushed a lock of red hair off her shoulder to expose her neck, shimmering with perspiration in the half-light. "The exceptional stitchery on your bodice, madam." He bent and licked at the spot no longer hidden by her hair. She tasted of salt and flowers. "You're nimble on your feet, wife," he whispered in her ear.

She chuckled and stroked his arms. "I have to be if I don't want to be trampled by you and the rest of your kin. Heavier than an ox you are. My toes would be crushed beyond hope if I didn't keep them out of the way."

Brishen hugged her, careful not to squeeze too hard. She was human and far more fragile than a Kai woman, at least physically. If her physical strength equaled that of her character, she could carry a loaded wagon on her back up a mountainside and never break a sweat.

"What if I told you, I'm a sliver of a breath away from hauling you behind that barricade." He indicated a low wall away from the crowds with a thrust of his chin. His voice thickened. "Hitching your skirts and taking you against the timbers." Her soft sigh tickled the underside of his jaw where she nuzzled him. His trousers stretched tight over his erection, and he held her even closer, no longer aware of the many people eddying around them.

"I would tell you to remember to cover my mouth so I don't embarrass us both by screeching your name from the pleasure of it." She winked.

"Holy gods," he muttered before ending their embrace to grasp her hand and pull her toward their chosen trysting place. Once more, she jogged to keep up, her breathing as harsh as his in anticipation.

They made it three steps before a voice rose above the crowds and the music and the crackling bonfires in a bellow that brought silence down on the loggia with the force of a thunderclap. "*Herceges!*" Anhuset strode toward him and Ildiko, the gathering of Kai parting before her like grain before a thresher's blade. Her eyes glowed almost as silvery as her hair, her features harsh and leached to the color of cold ashes. Another Kai followed close behind her.

A warning roil gathered strength in Brishen's gut. Had his father died? Djedor was already an old monarch when he married Secmis and sired children off her. Brishen hated his mother and barely tolerated his father. The apprehension swelling inside him rose from something other than a sorrow he didn't possess for a parent he hardly knew, an instinct that warned of news more dire.

Anhuset's expression mirrored that of the man who accompanied her.

Anhuset inclined her head briefly toward Ildiko. "*Hercegesé.*" She turned immediately back to Brishen. "A messenger from the capital. You need to hear this." She stepped aside and motioned for the man to come forward.

Ildiko released Brishen's arm to step behind him, an observer now. The man looked as if he'd ridden off a battlefield, horror stamped on his haggard face. Brishen eyed him, noting the shadows of sleep deprivation, the ragged and dirty state of his clothing. If he'd ridden from Haradis to Saggara, he'd done it without stopping by the look of him. "What message do you have from Haradis?"

The messenger blinked at him slowly, as if unsure Brishen was real or simply an illusion born from lack of sleep. "They are gone," he choked out in a raspy voice. "All of them. Every one gone. Destroyed by *galla.*"

Startled cries and gasps broke the suffocating stillness. Brishen slashed a hand through the air, and they quieted. "Bring wine," he ordered and waited while someone rushed forward with a full goblet. The messenger took it with shaking hands and downed the contents in three swallows. He gripped the empty goblet as if it were a talisman, and he shuddered.

Brishen's heartbeat accelerated. "Who's gone? And what is this of *galla*?"

As if restored not only by the wine but also Brishen's calm voice, the messenger inhaled and exhaled a steadying breath before continuing. "Three days ago, someone summoned a *galla* horde." This time Brishen didn't bother to silence the chorus of gasps punctuated by fearful cries. "It started in the castle. Consumed everyone inside. The horde destroyed everything in the capital east of the Absu. Some in the city escaped into the river and swam to the other side. The rest were devoured, trampled or drowned."

A flare of heat pressed against Brishen's lower back—Ildiko's hand, touching him. He stared at the messenger, listening to his words as if the man spoke from the opposite end of a tunnel, and they carried back to him at the other end on an icy wind. "Are you certain of this?"

The other man nodded. "I saw it all myself. Ran to the river with the others. I rode my horse into the ground and stole another to get here. The *galla* are spreading from the capital like contagion. Survivors are keeping close to the Absu or fighting over boats. They're coming here to Saggara."

The roar of the frigid tunnel wind sounded in Brishen's ears. *Galla.* Survivors. Both streaming toward Saggara. "My family?" he asked softly, even though he already knew the answer.

Shoulders slumped, the messenger shook his bowed head slowly. "The royal house of Khaskem is gone. All perished. Except you. The king is dead." Mournful wails from the Kai surrounding them met his declaration. He fell to his knees before Brishen and bent to touch his forehead to the ground. "Long live the king."

The crowd's whispers rose to a dull roar. Brishen's stomach plummeted to his feet. He scowled and bent down to haul the man to up from the ground. "Off your knees," he snapped. "There is no king at Saggara until we know more."

His heartbeat echoed the earlier pounding of the drums from the dancing. The hot desire for his wife that had coursed through his body moments earlier was snuffed, replaced by detached purpose. He turned to Ildiko, noting her stricken expression and eyes made glossy with unshed human tears. "Find every vicegerent, mayor and clan chief in the crowd," he instructed in a calm voice. "Send them to the hall." She nodded without speaking and briefly caressed his forearm before disappearing into the sea of Kai.

Brishen motioned a grim Anhuset closer. "Summon Mertok. I want you two and a dozen of your best scouts in the hall with the ministers."

She leaned toward him, speaking in a low voice. "How did *galla* breach the barriers between worlds and enter ours?"

He met his cousin's firefly stare but didn't reply. The question wasn't how but rather who breached the walls for them. They both knew the answer. If the messenger was right and *galla* first appeared in the royal palace, then his mother, Queen Secmis, and her power-mad machinations had something to do with it.

He gestured to the haggard Kai who waited for his next command. "Come with me. There's more wine and food inside my hall and a promise of rest as well, but first I need your help."

Once inside, he sent Mesumenes to retrieve a set of maps from the library. Space was cleared on a trestle table and the maps rolled out flat. The messenger picked listlessly at the food served to him before abandoning his plate to join Brishen who studied the terrain illustrated on parchment.

One map depicted the known world, from frozen Helenrisia in the far north to the Serpent's Teeth in the south and all the lands between, including the kingdoms of Bast-Haradis, Gaur and Belawat. The second map focused solely on Bast-Haradis, and it was this one Brishen scoured first. He tapped a finger on the square that marked the capital of Haradis. "Show me which path the survivors are taking to reach Saggara."

"What about the *galla*?" The other man choked on the name.

"Such demons are drawn to blood and magic. Where the Kai travel, the *galla* will follow unless distracted by a greater food source or trapped by water."

The messenger paled. "Then they're bringing them here."

Brishen stared at him before speaking, that cold numbness inside him spreading throughout his body. "Possibly. We must figure out how to contain them before such a thing happens." He didn't point out the fact that containing *galla* was the least of their challenges, the most difficult, how to send them back to the chaos from whence they came.

The hall filled with more people as Ildiko ushered in the various village and clan leaders. Anhuset, Mertok and a company of other officers and scouts swelled the gathering until a sizeable group congregated around Brishen. They were no longer revelers enjoying a night of celebration but a somber troop faced with a possible catastrophe unlike any witnessed by Kai generations much earlier than theirs.

Ildiko and Mesumenes traveled back and forth between the hall and the kitchens and the hall and the loggia, directing the small army of servants to serve food and drink. The servants whispered among themselves, wide-eyed and frightened as they watched and listened to the arguments rising and falling around the two maps.

The exhausted messenger took the brunt of it, peppered with multiple questions, exclamations of disbelief and even an accusation of falsehood by one clan chief. That had almost erupted into a brawl. Brishen threatened to imprison the chieftain and tie the messenger to his chair if they didn't calm themselves.

No one spoke when the man described what he witnessed at the river, his voice broken. "We saw...we saw a line of elders, led by the old general Hasarath, make of themselves a wall near the riverbank so that others might reach the water in time. Their sacrifice saved hundreds, maybe more." His breath hitched, and he bowed his head. "No one should die like that."

Brishen knew the image conjured by those words would remain emblazoned on his mind's eyes until he died. He spent the next several hours planning and strategizing with his most trusted ministers and his garrison officers. Fear and the black of edge of panic saturated the air, heavy enough he could taste its bitterness on his tongue. When the meeting finally ended and the group disbanded to race to their respective homes or scout the territories Brishen had marked for reconnoitering, the sun was high in the sky and the exhausted Haradis messenger slumped over the table, asleep.

Brishen scraped a hand over his face and blinked a dry, itchy eye. Even the memory of his left eye itched. He swallowed, wondering when his tongue had grown a wool blanket, and gratefully accepted a cup of cold water from his heavy-eyed steward. Except for Mesumenes and the slumbering messenger, he was alone in the hall. "Did the *hercegesé* find her bed?" Ildiko had long since disappeared from the hall, and Brishen was desperate to hold her, find some steady point to grasp in a world suddenly spinning out of his control.

The steward nodded toward the hall's doors, now closed to the brutal daylight. "She's outside, my liege, seeing off the last of the ministers. As you know, she can withstand the light better than we can."

Brishen was tempted to follow her, but the events of the past few hours had drained him, the enormity of their circumstances threatening to overwhelm him. "When she returns, tell her to come to me."

He left the hall for the sanctuary of his chamber. A low fire danced merrily in the hearth, the windows shuttered closed tight against the daylight. Brishen dropped into the nearest chair and closed his eye.

A more cold-blooded side of his character reasoned it was probably fortunate that he wasn't close to any member of his family except Anhuset, and she was here at Saggara with him, thank the gods. Otherwise, the shock and grief over their deaths would cripple him.

Still, he sorrowed for his brother's children, for their mother, the quiet, biddable Tiye and for every Kai in the palace and in all of Haradis who never imagined the horror their own queen would visit upon them.

He'd grown up with stories of the *galla*. Even humans knew of them and called them by the same name. Savage, ravenous, they thirsted for blood and fed on magic. Some held they were created by the gods at the same time as the elder races. Most, however, believed them born of the Gullperi who sought to somehow purify themselves and transcend their worldly limitations by wrenching out the darkness in their own souls.

That ancient schism had wrought the *galla*, entities of such brutality and voracious appetite that the most powerful leaders of the elder races united and cast them out of the world. Unable to destroy them, they had sealed the *galla* in a realm outside of time and place, a prison without lock or key. The elders' punishment of those who had brought the *galla* into the world had been swift and merciless: a lesson to all that such an act repeated would be dealt with in the harshest way.

History, however, was long and memories short. Whatever lesson those long-ago elders tried to teach was either forgotten over time or disregarded. Centuries of record and mortem light memory told of instances where one or two of the *galla* had broken free of the prison realm, usually because of a sorcerer with more power and ambition than sense. Brishen firmly believed Secmis was the culprit mage in this instance.

He growled. Leave it to his murderous bitch of a mother to miscalculate the *galla*'s savagery and bring down an apocalypse on an entire kingdom. Maybe even a world if the horde wasn't stopped in time.

Brishen covered his face with a trembling hand. In a way, he understood the motivations of those misguided ancients who sought to cleanse themselves of their own malevolence. He was the child of a woman who had stained the world with her presence. Her blood ran in his veins. If he could somehow physically rip his maternal legacy out of himself, he wouldn't hesitate. His skin crawled with self-loathing.

The door connecting his bedchamber to Ildiko's opened on a faint creak before closing. He didn't look up. He recognized the scent of flowers and the light footfalls that drew near.

Ildiko remained silent except for the rustle of her skirts. Brishen dropped his hand from his face at the feel of her head pressed to his knee. She sat at his feet, her cheek against his leg as she stared into the fire. She hugged his calf to her breasts while her hands stroked and massaged him through his boot.

Brishen combed his fingers gently through her hair, his claws sliding easily through the silky locks. The giant knot inside his chest didn't unravel, but it did loosen. Her presence soothed him.

"Your ministers and chieftains have left Saggara for home as have many of our visitors from the nearby villages. Word of the *galla* horde is spreading like brush fires already."

He managed a small smile, admiring the way the firelight shimmered in her red hair. Ildiko would give him all the succor he wanted, but she was a practical sort and didn't shy away from the harsh reality of a bad situation. This one was dreadful.

"And unsubstantiated rumor fanning the flames," he replied. "Expect a wave of fearful visitors returning to Saggara with many questions over the next few days, wife."

"What will you tell them?" She hugged his leg even harder to her.

Brishen shrugged. "Very little. At least until the scouts I sent out report back with more news. I've instructed the holt and village leaders to set their own watches and coordinate a system of signal fires to warn each other in case any spot *galla* breaching their borders. Except for a single messenger's account, we know nothing at the moment." He spiraled a curl of her hair around one claw. "In all honesty, I hope he's delusional and spewing a nonsensical tale. I'd rather be made a fool than made a..." he stopped. *King.* He hid a flinch. Gods.

Ildiko stared up at him. Fatigue pinched and paled her face. "And if he's of sound mind?"

He bent, lifting her from the cold floor to settle in his lap. She looped her arms around his neck, fingers sliding under his hair to stroke his nape. He kissed her once, twice, before speaking. "He is. My gut tells me he is. Whatever news the scouts bring back to us, I'm afraid it won't contradict what he's told us."

Her eyes glossed over once more with tears. "Your family...surely someone survived."

The numbness wormed its way deeper into him, seeping into his soul. "You heard what he said, Ildiko. The *galla* spread from the palace first. No one survived such an attack."

"I'm sorry, Brishen. So very sorry." She kissed his face, soft pecks on his forehead and eyelid, his eyepatch and nose, cheeks and lips.

He caressed her hip. "There was no love lost between us, but I wouldn't wish a death like that—cruel and unclean—on anyone." Except his mother, and even death by *galla* attack was too merciful for such a viper. Rage cast ripples across the still surface of the numb pool inside him. He almost wished he'd been there to witness her demise. It might have been worth suffering the same fate just to watch her die. "I may be all that remains of the House Khaskem."

A vertical line stitched the space between Ildiko's eyebrows. "There is Anhuset."

Yes, thank the gods for Anhuset. He treasured his fierce cousin. "There is, but she isn't recognized as an official member of my house." Ildiko's eyes widened at the revelation. "She's *gameza*, a bastard sired by a stable hand on my father's sister. Khaskem by blood but not by validation." What little color remained in his wife's face drained away at his words. "Ildiko?"

She blinked, then shook her head, the brief smile flitting across her mouth tight and insincere. "Sorry. It's been a very long night."

He couldn't agree more. The day promised to be even longer. "Bed?" he asked.

Ildiko shook her head. "Not yet. Do you think Sec—"

Brishen pressed a finger to her lips to stall her question. He knew what she was about to ask. Anhuset had expressed a similar suspicion earlier. She'd made sure to murmur it low enough that only the two of them could hear, and such conjectures were best left unspoken at the moment. Those who suffered and those who feared would find someone to blame. The Queen was likely dead of her own twisted machinations, but her younger son and his immediate family were not. He refused to shoulder the blame of Secmis's evil.

Ildiko's gaze flickered, first in confusion, then in understanding. She took up the conversation when Brishen removed his finger as if she meant to speak something other than his mother's name in the first place. "Securing borders now is a good idea? What if the population panics?"

He smirked, admiring her effortless transition from dangerous conjecture to innocuous question. "Having *galla* show up unexpectedly on your doorstep would cause more than panic. Ignorance and oblivion are only illusions of safety."

"If word of a freed *galla* horde reaches Gaur or Belawat, there may be war."

Such a scenario had occurred to him and every Kai who gathered around the maps earlier in the great hall. "There's no possible way for us to hide the presence of a *galla* horde. We just have to hope the Gauri and Beladine leaders have enough sense to recognize we're all the least of each other's problems. I can't hope for an alliance between all three kingdoms, but if they manage to keep their swords sheathed and their armies from each other's throats—and ours—until we can resolve this disaster, I'll consider it a triumph."

"Wise words," she said. "Mark of a good man. Mark of a good ruler. Her expression turned even more solemn. You will make a magnificent king, Brishen."

Something in the way she uttered the last sent an icy splinter down his spine and urged him to gather her even closer. "You will make an equally glorious queen, Ildiko," he whispered into her hair.

She hugged him in return before pulling away. Her gaze was oddly bleak. "I'm ready to find our bed now. If what the messenger says is true and accurate, I suspect we won't see much rest after this." She slid out of his lap and stood, offering her hand.

He clasped her cold fingers and joined her, intuition warning him of some unnamed threat beyond the *galla* and everything their invasion entailed. Ildiko's appearance had never truly frightened him until now.

He resisted when she tugged him toward the bed. "Do you love me, Ildiko?" He forced the words from a throat closed tight.

She halted and gripped his hand harder, the crescents of her fingernails digging into his palm. "With everything I am, Brishen," she said in a soft, fervent voice. "And for as long as I live. You must never doubt it."

He believed her, yet her words churned his stomach and hummed discordant in his spirit. She uttered them, not as if they were a declaration of devotion but one of farewell.

CHAPTER THREE

The *galla* never rested and never quieted, but they learned from those they devoured and those they hunted. A writhing black wall of shrieking, gibbering shadow, the horde tracked the refugees who survived the attack on the capital as they followed the Absu's opposite shore toward Saggara.

Kirgipa did her best to ignore the horror across the water. The *galla* mimicked the dying screams of those they consumed—people, animals, anything born of magic or flesh and blood. The shocked and grieving Kai around her had gone silent after the first hours of their escape. She suspected that, like her, none wanted to hear the last cries of a dying relative or friend echoed back to them by the foul things that continuously screeched their frustration at the impenetrable barrier of water between them and their prey.

She risked a single glance and wished she hadn't. A section of the shadow wall twisted in on itself and reformed into Kai faces—twisted and terrified, frozen in mid-scream. She stumbled, clutching the infant queen to her breast.

"Eyes on your path, little maid." Dendarah clutched her elbow to steady her. "Nothing good comes from watching them, especially when you know they're watching you." She pivoted in front of Kirgipa. "Give me the child. You've carried her since early this morning with little rest in between." Her yellow gaze flickered over the procession of Kai who flowed around them as they trudged steadily toward Prince Brishen's garrison. "It's safe enough to put my sword arm to other uses at the moment."

Kirgipa happily shouldered off her sling and handed the sleeping baby to Dendarah. In this small thing, fortune had favored them. The normally restless child was quiet, as if sensing the threat on the other side of the river and the need not to draw attention. The palace guard slipped on the sling and tucked her burden gently against her brigandine. She handed Kirgipa the three skin flasks of goat's milk and single pack of *tilqetil*. "Considering the king's ransom we paid for those, you're still carrying precious cargo. Whatever you do, don't drop or spill."

Dendarah didn't exaggerate. She and Necos together had given up a sword, two daggers, and every piece of jewelry they wore to a Kai weaver on the safe side of the Absu in exchange for the milk and four thick cakes made of whipped animal fat, berries and dried fish. Kirgipa had never liked *tilqetil*, but she was grateful the baby did, and a little bit went far in making and keeping her full.

"Don't worry," she assured the guard. "I know the value of your weaponry and your jewels. I only wish I had contributed." She wore nothing of value on her with which to barter, and the weaver had shaken her head in disdain when she offered her plain shawl.

"You're her nursemaid. Your loyalty to her is your greatest treasure. Steel and baubles can be replaced. We don't barter loyalty or honor. Those can't be replaced." Dendarah's severe expression softened infinitesimally. "I know you worry for your sister, that you've been tempted to leave this child and search for her."

Kirgipa's throat constricted. They had traveled along the Absu for four days now. The majority of the capital's population had been devoured in the *galla* attack, but there were still many Kai who had made it to the river's safety and those who dwelt on its other side. Dendarah had kept her promise to Kirgipa and searched each day for Atalan, always returning alone. Today, however, Necos had volunteered to scour the crowds.

After a sparse breakfast of bits of *tilqetil* and water cupped from the Absu, he'd left them that morning, first to hunt in the forest for any game not yet flushed out by other Kai, then to seek Atalan. Kirgipa prayed he would find her. She had lost her brother in a Beladine raid during his service to Prince Brishen, then her mother in the suicidal defense of the fleeing Kai from the *galla*. She and Atalan were all that remained of her family. She considered herself loyal and honorable, but she was also terrified and missed her sister. "Please, Necos," she whispered under her breath. "Find Atalan."

As if she summoned him, he suddenly appeared beside her, returned not with Atalan, but with a split lip and bloodied knuckles. Kirgipa's stomach plummeted. Oh gods, her sister. Something happened to her sister!

She clutched Necos's arm. "Atalan! She's hurt!" He shook his head and pulled her to the outskirts of the crowd away from listening ears. The weight of a hundred stares settled between her shoulder blades.

Dendarah followed. "What happened to you?"

His gaze ran the length of Kirgipa's form, searching for something. "What?" she snapped and looked down at herself, confused by his action.

Satisfied by a discovery she couldn't see, he turned his attention to Dendarah, and his eyes narrowed. "She isn't wearing anything to give her away, but you need to strip your insignia and anything else you're wearing marking you as palace staff or guard."

Dendarah obeyed instantly, ripping the patch off her sleeve identifying as her one of the elite royal guards and handed it to Necos. He tucked the patch inside his brigantine and dropped to one knee in front of her before clasping the hem of the tunic she wore under her armor. Fabric tumbled into his hands as he cut away the hem of its amaranthine border.

Kirgipa gaped at both guards. "Why are you doing this?"

Necos stood and held up one of his injured hands. "I was attacked while looking for your sister. It seems more than a few folk want to punish me for the *galla.*" He hid the amaranthine border with the patch. His own tunic hem was torn and ragged, lacking the magenta-colored strip, and his sleeve bore a rip where his insignia had been stitched.

She licked suddenly parched lips. "Why do such a thing? It makes no sense."

"It does in its way." Dendarah's gaze slid past Kirgipa's shoulder to the boiling darkness defiling the opposite shore. "These are frightened people looking for someone to blame for their suffering and the loss of their loved ones and homes. The *galla* emerged from the palace first. Many saw it happen. The event has been recounted to those who didn't."

"They want revenge." Necos further destroyed his tunic by tearing off another strip, plain brown cloth this time, and using it to bandage his hand.

Dendarah shook her head. "They want justice, and the guilty are dead and beyond their reach. Except for her." She patted the baby's bottom. "And us."

Kirgipa bristled. "We didn't do anything! My muta died for those people! And this is a harmless baby."

Necos motioned with his hands for her to lower her voice. "It doesn't matter," he said softly. "That malice across the river sprang from the castle. Don't think anyone with time to wonder didn't suspect this disaster is the queen's doing. You are her granddaughter's nurse; we're palace guards. We're guilty by association."

Dendarah's severe features hardened. "We need to leave now. Follow the river but stay well ahead of the others. We're in as much danger from our own kin now as we are from the horde."

A rushing in Kirgipa's ears made the guard's words sound as if they came from a tunnel. They were leaving, parting from the protection of the Kai, leaving her sister behind. She slowly backed away. "No," she said," torn between her sense of loyalty to the royal line, ingrained in her since childhood, and love for her sibling.

Necos blocked her and turned her gently to face him. His handsome face, marred by the split lip, was its own comfort. His hands were warm and heavy on her shoulders. "Unless she's crowing to all and sundry that her sister is a royal nursemaid, then she's safer with the crowd than she is with us." His claws tickled her skin. "We are all traveling to the same place, Kirgipa. The three of us just need to get there faster, with that baby alive and well to greet her uncle."

She sagged under the weight of his hands and closed her eyes. "This is so hard." Her lids sprang open once more at the light brush of his lips across her forehead.

"Indeed it is, little maid," he said, using Dendarah's address for her. "Indeed it is."

She nodded once. "I still hold you both to the promise that you'll find Atalan and unite us."

Dendarah inclined her head. "And we will fulfill that promise." She turned to Necos. "The Absu meanders away from Saggara toward Belawat territory, but we can trek back. I'd rather take my chances with a longer walk and human raiders than being stuck in the open as *galla* food and no river in reach for safety.

"What will we do for food?" Kirgipa tapped the pack of *tilqetil* she held. "This won't last long, and most needs to be for her." She pointed to the infant resting peacefully in her sling.

"We'll fish from the river and raid farms if we have to." He sighed at Kirgipa's silent disapproval. "If we don't, the masses behind us will. The forests are already emptying of anything to hunt or forage. We're turning into locusts." He drove home his defense with "And we can at least warn some of them of the *galla*'s approach if we move fast enough."

Dendarah tightened the sling's knot at her shoulder. "Then we leave now. Walk all night and into the day. Sleep in short intervals and again walk at night. We won't be as fast as if we rode, but hundreds moving together are slower than three. We can put a fair distance in a short period of time between us and any Kai wanting vengeance."

"Horses have become rarer than gold and ten times more precious now. Stealing one will take some doing." Necos clasped

Kirgipa's hand, twining his fingers with hers. She drew strength from that reassuring grip. "Ready?"

She turned a last gaze at the Kai behind her. Somewhere in that gathering, her sister had found shelter and safety, temporary though it was. Kirgipa would pray for a lot of things; uniting with Atalan soon, a horse for Necos, delivery of the infant Kai queen to her uncle's protection at distant Saggara, and a way to send the *galla* back to whatever horrible place they thrived in and called home.

She briefly squeezed Necos's hand and nodded to the waiting Dendarah. "Lead on."

CHAPTER FOUR

Three days had passed since the messenger from Haradis arrived with the stomach-dropping news about Haradis, a full week since the fall of the city itself. Ildiko's breath fogged in front of her as she stood besides Mesumenes in one of Saggara's many storerooms. She wrapped her woolen shawl more tightly around her and stared up at the sacks of grain piled one atop the other until they covered most of the floor and reached nearly to the ceiling. This year's harvest had been a good one, a fortunate thing since half of Haradis was set to arrive in Saggara any day now, hungry, frightened, and homeless, with both winter and the *galla* hard on their heels.

"Are the other storerooms this full?" Were they in different circumstances, she'd rejoice at the bounty before her. A room of plenty were it not for the fact they'd soon have a city's worth of mouths to feed.

Mesumenes checked the roll of parchment he carried with him, running a claw lightly across tallies of numbers. "Most of them. One or two are about half this, but we've asked those fleeing their farms to bring what harvest they've stored, so we'll get a little more."

Ildiko skirted the perimeter of the chamber, waving away the clouds of grain dust floating in the air, burnished and sparkling in the torch light. "We'll have to start rationing immediately. I'll

71

need every grain sack weighed, and its contents calculated so we can estimate how many people each sack will feed."

Mesumenes's nacreous eyes rounded and flared. His horrified expression mirrored her own thoughts. Ildiko waited for the inevitable protest, pleased and surprised when none were forthcoming. The steward wrestled his stunned expression into a more stoic one, nodded, and scribbled additional notes on the parchment he held.

"I'll help with the counting," she said.

The quill paused. "That isn't necessary, Your Highness. This is a clerk's work."

"Such a counting is a monumental task and requires the work of an army of clerks and weeks to complete it. We don't have weeks. Every hand not busy with some daily task needs to be put to this one, including mine." The flick of a rodent tail caught Ildiko's eye before disappearing behind the shelter of the sacks. "I also want every available rat-catcher searching the storerooms and barns. We don't have the luxury of sharing food with rats."

Mesumenes cleared his throat before speaking. "The *herceges* may protest at you climbing up on grain stacks to count, Your Highness."

Were her husband of different character, Ildiko would be inclined to agree. Brishen, however, possessed a nature almost as practical as her own. "I doubt it. When he's not on patrol hunting *galla* or appeasing the parade of nobles arriving at Saggara, he'll probably help with the count as well." She didn't say it aloud, but she had no plans of allowing their noble guests to lounge about while everyone else worked themselves to exhaustion. Now wasn't the time for mollycoddling simply due to birth and rank.

The *galla* didn't differentiate between the nobleman and the peasant. Neither did famine. And now, neither would she.

She and Mesumenes planned their strategy for setting up a work force and dividing the storerooms between them, pausing only when one of the doors squeaked opened. Anhuset stood at the entrance, dressed in training garb: loose shirt and trousers with padding tied at the elbows and knees. She wore a padded breastplate and held similar gear in her arms, along with a bundle of sticks in various lengths.

"Are you ready, Your Highness?"

Ildiko sputtered. "You must be jesting. We don't have time for training, Anhuset."

Since Brishen's recovery from his capture almost a year earlier, Ildiko had trained with Anhuset, learning the basic skills taught to a young Kai barely off of lead strings. They met three times a week, every week. Ildiko held no delusions about her martial prowess, or lack thereof, especially should she ever face a Kai adversary, but anything was better than nothing. A damsel in complete distress was a burden to her protectors; one familiar with self defense, not as much.

Anhuset remained unswayed at Ildiko's protest. "There is always time for training, *Hercegesé.*"

"Now?"

"Especially now."

Ildiko accepted her fate and returned a sheaf of parchment to Mesumenes. "I'll join you again soon," she promised. She passed Anhuset who fell into step beside her as they crossed the open loggia toward the manor house itself. People, livestock, and wagons crowded the open space. Unlike at the firelit festival of

Kaherka earlier, the Kai wore grim expressions, their revelry forgotten with the news of the *galla* and the possible fall of Haradis. She was almost thankful for the mountain of preparation and work to be done. Fear found fertile ground in idle minds and idle hands.

She scowled at Anhuset. "I have another dozen storerooms and four barns to inspect with Mesumenes, not to mention finding additional quarters for a vicegerent, two mayors and their families. You're riding patrol and coordinating messenger and scout runs. Teaching me how to successfully hit one of you with a stick is an indulgence neither of us has time for."

Anhuset refused to relent. "While I'm here at Saggara, we train. No excuses."

"They're perfectly good reasons, not excuses." Ildiko sighed. "Fine. A half hour, not a moment more."

The other woman's lips quirked into the faintest smile, and the two trekked into the house and a small spare room devoid of furniture on the third floor. Ildiko changed into the trousers and shirt Anhuset handed her and donned the padding.

She stared down at herself, then at Anhuset, and frowned. No matter how many times she dressed in this outfit, she'd never grow used to the sight of it. She looked like a turtle, bulky, clumsy and slow, unlike her teacher who wore hers as naturally as a second skin and moved in it with all the lithe grace of a cat.

Anhuset untied the bundle of sticks she'd propped against the wall, handing two to Ildiko: a tall one nearly Ildiko's height called a *silabat* and shorter one, half the *silabat*'s length called a *sediketh*. "Which do you want to work with first?"

When they had first embarked on their training sessions, Brishen had volunteered to teach Ildiko the martial art of *gatke* or stick fighting, both women had balked.

"You'll be too soft on her," Anhuset declared.

Ildiko had echoed Anhuset. "The first time you even tap me, you'll end the lesson."

Brishen hadn't given in right away and countered with his own protest. "If Anhuset teaches you, you might not come out alive after the first lesson. I don't want to have to kill my favorite cousin for killing my wife."

It had taken a few indignant sputterings from Anhuset and several assurances from Ildiko that she'd survive before he agreed to relinquish his role as mentor to Anhuset. It had been several months since then, and while Ildiko always emerged from the encounters sporting a bruise or four, she hadn't died yet.

She hefted the shorter *sediketh* in her hand and set aside the *silabat*. She had better luck with the shorter stick. Its size made it easier to handle, and as Anhuset reminded her every chance she got, easier to conceal on her person.

"Your strength is the element of surprise," the Kai woman said before one of their first lessons. "No Kai, or human for that matter, will expect you to be armed or able to defend yourself. Learning the art of *gatke* will allow you to protect yourself long enough to flee or escape. You can hide the *sediketh*, and the *silabat* will give you both reach and distance. And you can turn just about anything into a stick." An ignoble fighting method, but an effective one.

The two women faced off, Ildiko dropping into the wide stance and half crouch Anhuset had taught her. They circled each other,

Anhuset loose-limbed and casual as Ildiko stalked her around the room.

She lunged and swung, her strike easily parried. They clashed several more times, Ildiko striking, and Anhuset either parrying with her own stick or blocking with her forearms. While Anhuset landed several stinging blows to Ildiko's arms, legs and backside, Ildiko didn't manage a single strike against her opponent. By the end of the half hour, she was breathless, sore and wet with sweat, even in the frigid room. She surrendered her stick to Anhuset, who looked none the worse for their encounter, and bent over, hands flat on her thighs as she fought to catch her breath.

The Kai woman stared down her nose at Ildiko, forehead creased in disapproving lines. "You're distracted."

"You think?" Ildiko said between gasps.

"We need to practice longer. A half hour isn't nearly enough time."

Ildiko limped to where her clothes rested in a neat pile and untied the padding at her elbows, wincing with every bend. "More than enough to earn my daily quota of bruises."

She peeled off her sweat-soaked training garb and dressed reluctantly in the frock she'd donned earlier. She was sticky with a coating of grain dust and desperate for a bath. That would have to wait as would her meetings with Mesumenes. She needed information from Anhuset first.

"How much do you know of your mother's history and that of King Djedor?"

The other woman lifted one shoulder and bound the fighting sticks together. "More than I wanted and none I can recall." She did raise her head then, giving Ildiko a close-lipped smirk. "I'm *gameza*, Highness. Bastards aren't taught about the pride of a long bloodline, when they are the shame and taint of that line."

Ildiko flinched. A bastard's lot was a hard and unfair one, no matter what culture they were born into. "I'm sorry, Anhuset."

Anhuset shrugged. "No need to be. I lose no sleep over it. Brishen is the one who can answer your question. He could recite Djedor's bloodline before he could read." She piled the sticks and Ildiko's training clothes in her arms and strode to the door. "You're still using that liniment I sent you?"

"Yes, but it smells foul."

She received no sympathy for her complaint. Anhuset opened the door, peered outside, then motioned for her to exit. "Just hold your nose and tell the *herceges* to do the same. If you don't use it, you'll be too stiff and sore tomorrow to get out of bed."

They parted company at the stairs, and Ildiko fled to her chamber where she shed her clothes for the third time and sponged down with a cake of soap and a basin of cold water Sinhue had filled for her earlier. By the time she finished, her teeth clattered hard enough to make her jaw ache, and her hands were so clumsy with the cold, she had only a quarter of the lacings tied before Sinhue returned to finish the rest for her.

Clean and warm in her heavy frock and shawl, she met Mesumenes at the bottom of the stairwell leading to the great hall. "Mesumenes, does Saggara's library keep records of the royal family's history?"

"It does, Your Highness."

They made their way to the expansive library, a glorious room with tall windows that looked onto the wild orange grove, and was filled with floor-to-ceiling shelves stuffed with both scrolls and precious bound books. A wealth of knowledge and information, unmatched by any library Ildiko had ever seen in Gaur. Even the Gauri royal library didn't compare, and Ildiko often wondered why such a treasure had remained at Saggara instead of moving to Haradis when the royal court did. It was a fortunate thing it hadn't, or all of it would be lost to them now.

Mesumenes stalked the shelves for several minutes, climbing ladders at times to retrieve a dusty scroll or two. By the time he gathered what he deemed sufficient, there was an impressive pile of parchment covering one of the tables that dotted the room.

Ildiko unfurled the first scroll, using river stones left on the table to hold down the corners. "I'll need your help translating. My knowledge of written Kai is adequate at best, and I'm guessing some of this is written in an older form."

She and the steward spent the next hour reviewing the scrolls he brought her. She took notes while he translated and did her best to hide the growing tremor in her hands as she scribbled the information he gave her. When they were done, and the scrolls rolled and tied, Ildiko thanked him. "The scrolls can stay here for now. I might want to look at them again. There's no need to stay with me. We've more storerooms to inspect and guests to sort. I'll join you soon."

Mesumenes bowed and left her in the quiet library. Candles flickered in the darkness, and she caught her reflection in the windows—solemn, pale, human.

Ildiko turned back to her notes and the rolled scrolls. They revealed nothing surprising, only verification of the thing she suspected and dreaded the moment Brishen explained that Anhuset was illegitimate and barred from line of succession to the throne. She rested her head in her hands and sighed.

If his father and his brother and children were dead, then Brishen was indeed the last Khaskem with the right to rule. If not him, then the throne would pass to another family. She flipped a page of notes to scan another one. If the Kai were like the humans, and in her observation during her brief sojourn in Haradis, they were in many ways, the major noble families tended to congregate at the royal court, in part to curry favor, gain influence and scheme against each other. It was also likely Djedor preferred it that way. His spies could keep a watchful eye on them and report back any information considered either beneficial or threatening.

That concentration of nobility in a city destroyed by the *galla* might well have been its undoing. Every family directly connected to the Khaskem line lived on estates neighboring the royal palace. If any survived, they traveled with the survivors toward Saggara and wouldn't waste a moment making themselves known to Brishen once they arrived.

She traced the column of family names, those who'd challenge each other for the right to rule if the House of Khaskem fell completely. Djehutim, Petomi, Serames. The three most powerful houses who could claim Djedor as a direct blood relative. If none within those families survived, others with weaker claims did— lesser nobles who lived beyond Haradis and a few within Saggara's province.

Ildiko's stomach had flipped at her first sight of House Senemset on the list. Only a catastrophic event enabled a house that far removed from the direct line to have a chance at ruling

Bast-Haradis. The *galla* attack was catastrophic. The Senemset matriarch had already sent a message that she, her married son and three unmarried daughters were traveling to Saggara seeking sanctuary. A possible queen with both male and female heirs to inherit from her. And no matter where in the blood line one stood, uniting with the last remaining Khaskem ensured the strongest claim to the throne for any family with aspirations to rule.

Despair seeped into her bones, weighing her down. "Oh Brishen," she said softly. "The prince of no value has become the most coveted Kai in all of Bast-Haradis." She, on the other hand, was worse than valueless. She was an obstacle either to overcome or destroy.

She gathered up her notes, blew out the candles and left the library. The manor house was a hive of activity, with servants scurrying this way and that, preparing the great hall for the evening meal. All the tables were set and the benches pulled forward to seat the greater number of guests staying at the redoubt.

Ildiko almost missed Brishen's arrival, catching sight of him only as he strode through the throng toward her. The hard cast to his expression warned of a dark mood, and people scattered out of his way with quick bows and worried glances. He motioned to her, indicating she follow him to the smaller, private study where he met with visiting councilors and vicegerents.

She closed the door behind her, pitching the room into perfect blackness. The clink of ceramic against pewter let her know he had made his way to a table near the shuttered window and poured himself a dram of whatever throat-scorching libation filled the bottle.

Even if she knew where the candles were, she couldn't light them. The hearth lay cold and unlit. She shivered in the darkness and waited, silent at the door.

"Forgive me, wife. I'm distracted." Brishen's voice carried a wealth of apology before he threw open the shutters, allowing in streams of moonlight that bathed him and part of the chamber in silver light. Their shadows stood in sharp relief on one wall, while other shadows flowed across the floor to huddle in corners and under the table.

Brishen's throat flexed as he tilted his head back and downed the goblet's contents. He gasped and coughed before pouring a refill. He raised a second goblet and met her questioning gaze with a singular one of his own. "Did you want one?"

She shook her head and crossed the room to stand in front of him. His bicep was tense under her touch, quivering beneath the layers of leather and fabric he wore. "What happened?"

He tossed back the second goblet before dropping it to the table with a careless thump. The heady fumes of fermented Dragon Fire drifted between them. Brishen's voice was clipped, despite his having imbibed enough of the Fire to make most people incoherent and likely senseless if they drank so much at once. "We scouted the Absu south of Escariel until we reached the town itself. Victims of the *galla* are littering the banks. What's left of them." This time his fingers wrapped around the bottle's neck and lifted it. "The first one ended up wedged between a pair of trees. Half a horse with even less of its rider still trapped in the saddle."

Ildiko gasped, tempted to ask him to share the drink once he finished the healthy swig he tipped into his mouth. The image his words conjured made her stomach lurch. "Are you certain it was *galla?*"

He wiped his mouth with the back of his hand and set the bottle down. "As certain as I can be without seeing them myself." His nostrils flared. "The corpses have a smell to them. Nothing as pleasant as decay."

His face was gaunt in the silvered dark, aged beyond his natural years not only by the horror he'd seen but the horror he would inevitably face. Ildiko laced her fingers through his and led him to one of the chairs. He threw himself into the seat, pulling her with him until she perched on his lap.

She rested her hands on his shoulders. "I'm sorry you saw that. Sorry for that rider and the others."

Warm breath drafted across her jaw where he nuzzled her cheek. "I've seen death," he murmured against her skin. "Dealt it myself. But nothing like this. This was...unclean, soul-sick. It seemed like even the river tried to flow away from the corpses." He shivered in her arms. "The malevolence trekking toward Saggara with the Haradis survivors is unlike anything any Kai warrior has ever faced in this age."

His words terrified her, and she wasn't the one plagued with memories of the grotesque images he briefly described. "How do you kill *galla?*"

"I don't know that they can be killed. Not with steel at least, and I can't begin to imagine how much magic it would take to cage them, much less destroy them." He leaned his head back against the chair's top rail and exhaled a long breath.

Ildiko straightened in his lap. "But the Kai have done it. Your histories record that a Kai shaman named Varawan trapped a dozen and banished them back to the void during the Age of the Red Seas."

The grim set of Brishen's mouth relaxed for a moment into a wan smile. "Raiding the library, were you?" He twined a curl of her hair around one claw. "I know the story. Every Kai does, but the Red Seas was a long time ago when the magic of the Kai wasn't faded as it is now. And this is more than a dozen *galla*. It's a horde, a *hul galla*. A nation of shamans can't defeat such a force. All we can do at the moment is keep the rivers and streams between them and us."

Ildiko pictured the Absu, the settlements, both Kai and human, perched on both sides of its flow. One side now the open maw of death, the other a chance at sanctuary. "Water is more valuable than gold now."

A gust of frigid night air hurled itself through the open window, whipping strands of Brishen's hair across his face. He scraped them away with an impatient swipe of his hand. "Half my garrison will spend its time keeping the waterways flowing and free of debris that might block them. The other half will be put to controlling the Kai who'll descend on Saggara from every holt and dale, not to mention those fleeing Haradis."

"All those Kai gathered in one place." They'd need three times as many storerooms and barns bursting with food to prevent a famine. Ildiko clenched her teeth against the swell of panic threatening to choke her.

"We'll be a beacon to every demon spilling out of the void." His next words, spoken in a voice strained with helpless anger, encapsulated her every fear and shot it skyward. "Gods, this is a disaster." She squeezed his shoulder but didn't reply. What was there to say? He was right.

"If I didn't think the journey too hazardous to take, I'd send you to Gaur for safety."

She scowled at him. "I'd refuse to go if that were your reason to send me."

He tilted his head to one side, considering her. "Then what would convince you to go?"

"If you sent me to act as ambassador or envoy. I could ask for aid from Gaur. They are your allies now, not just Bast-Haradis's uneasy neighbor."

It was his turn to frown. "I don't see how they'd be much help. If Belawat got wind of Gaur sending an army to support Bast-Haradis, they'd declare war on us both so fast, we'd be on the battlefield by dawn of the next day."

She escaped his lap to stand in front of him. "As you said, steel doesn't work against the *galla*. You don't need an army of soldiers but one of mages. The Kai aren't the only ones graced with sorcerous power. Some humans are born with it as well. Hedges witches, court magicians, tribal shamans and holy monks. They can wield it with various levels of skill. Gaur can employ such people. Belawat does. The raiders who captured you had a battle mage with them. Remember?"

He folded his hands across his belly and stared at her with one glowing eye. "Were you Gaur, with a diseased kingdom next to you, would you give up your sorcerers?"

She shrugged, undeterred by his reasoning. "I might if I thought their help solved a common problem, and I have a difficult time believing the horde will only linger within Bast-Haradis.

They have no understanding of borders. Prey is prey, no matter where it resides. They'll cross into Gaur, into Belawat. Wherever they smell magic and blood."

"I'm sure they already have by now. Gaur's safety is that most of its territory sits between the Absu and the ocean, but its outland settlements are vulnerable on the wrong side of the river and any place there's a break in the river's flow." He shook his head. "I'd be mad to send you on such a journey. You'd be safe once you arrived. It's getting you there that's the challenge."

It would be dangerous, but if they hugged the river or even sailed it where the rapids weren't as treacherous, they had a chance. "Don't rule it out, Brishen. You can send a Kai, but who in this entire kingdom knows the Gauri court better than I do? The king is my uncle. I can at least beg for safe haven for Kai exiles. Temporary refuge. We have to tell Gaur something anyway if they don't already know. This isn't a secret that can be kept, and it will be better if revealed by me."

Brishen rose to stand in front of her. He wore riding leathers instead of his heavier armor, and there were tears in the vest and water stains splashed across his front from chest to knees. A cold draft sneaked in under the door to rifle her skirts, revealing damp spots from where she'd sat in his lap earlier. He'd been at least waist-high in the river at some point and was still drying off.

"You haven't considered something, wife. If my scouts return with news of my family's fate that confirms the messenger's, then our roles will change. The Kai won't allow their new queen to leave the kingdom."

The despair that had earlier nailed her to her seat in the library returned in a conquering tide. "I think they will" she said softly, remembering the list of noble houses related to the royal Khaskem and those that weren't but with daughters of acceptable bloodlines and the ability to bear heirs.

She was saved from explaining her answer by a sharp rap at the door. At Brishen's call to enter, Mesumenes opened the door. "Your Highness, you have visitors."

Ildiko groaned. "More? We've had them all evening. Your devoted steward is being run to death trying to find accommodations for everyone." Mesumenes touched his forehead and bowed in her direction.

"Who are they?" Brishen asked in a dull voice. Ildiko patted his arm.

Mesumenes's own voice was a study in contrasts to Brishen's, filled with wonder and surprise. "*Kapu kezets* from Emlek. Three of them. An *Elsod* and her *masods*."

Ildiko's eyes widened at Brishen's reaction. His back snapped straight, losing its exhausted slump, and his voice now echoed Mesumenes's in its amazement. "Are you sure?" The steward nodded and threw the door wide as Brishen strode towards him. "Where?"

"Great Hall, my liege."

Brishen practically bolted from the room, Ildiko and Mesumenes hurrying behind him. She pummeled the steward with questions as she chased after her husband. "Explain," she commanded. "What is a kapzetet, a elsie person and their *masods*?"

Mesumenes jogged beside her. "*Kapu kezets* are the memory wardens of Emlek, guardians of the mortem lights housed there.

The principal *kezet* is the *Elsod*. Her apprentices are *masods*. An *Elsod* always has two."

He got no further with his explanations. They both almost cannoned into Brishen when he abruptly halted at the doorway leading from the corridor to the great hall. Ildiko settled next to him, her jaw dropping in disbelief at the sight before her.

The hall was full of people, crammed together like bundled cordwood. They might have held each other up with ease except for the fact every last one of them had fallen to their knees. Their expressions were as slack-jawed as hers as they stared at the three people in the hall's center. Ildiko rubbed her eyes to assure herself she wasn't delusional, but no, there was sha-Anhuset, almost prostrate herself next to an equally humbled Mertok.

A space had opened up around them, a near perfect circle of what had seemingly become sacred ground. Right in the middle of Brishen's fortress.

An ancient Kai woman, her silver hair woven into complicated braids, faced Brishen in regal silence. She wore robes of green and indigo, and her face and arms were heavily tattooed. Two younger Kai, a man and woman wearing similar robes and skin markings stood behind her, as silent and almost as regal as their elder.

Brishen's stride was far more measured than the earlier headlong flight down the hall. Like everyone else, he fell to his knees before the old *kezet*. Ildiko did the same, even though she had no idea why this woman, despite her commanding presence, earned the willing supplication of every Kai in the building.

Brishen raised his hands, palms cupped upward as if to present some invisible gift. "*Elsod*, it is an honor. I extend all of Saggara's hospitality to you."

The *Elsod* placed her knobby hands in his, her black claws caging his fingers to curve around his wrists. "Rise, Interrex. King between kings." A collective gasp went up at her words. "We humbly accept."

He rose to stand once more. Ildiko hesitated, at a loss as to what protocol demanded in this situation. She stood more slowly and only when the rest of the hall's occupants gained their feet.

Brishen reached for Ildiko's hand. His fingers were warm against her icy ones. "Forgive my lapse of decorum. This is Ildiko, once of Gaur. My wife and *hercegesé*."

Ildiko bowed briefly, still marching blind through a nest of unknown rules of etiquette. "It is an honor...*Elsod*." She mimicked Brishen. The gods only knew if she addressed the memory warden correctly.

She must have done something right or else not terribly wrong, because the *Elsod* nodded in return. "The pleasure is mine, Your Highness."

The gravid silence in the hall grew more pronounced when the *Elsod* turned her gaze back to Brishen. "We've come to speak with you regarding the *galla*."

The proclamation carried all the harsh dissonance of a widow mourning at a grave. She might as well have said "We've come to tell you it's time to die." Ildiko was certain she heard more than one person choke back a despondent cry.

Brishen had grown pale, but his voice remained even. "Of course, *Elsod*." He caught Anhuset's and Mertok's gazes. "Clear the hall."

The two leapt to do his bidding and soon the hall was empty except for the *kapu kezets*, Ildiko, Brishen and Anhuset. The *Elsod* stared at Anhuset standing guard at the door. "Do you want her here?"

Brishen waved Anhuset over to them. "Sha-Anhuset is my cousin and my second. Nothing happens in Saggara that she isn't aware of it."

The warden acquiesced. "So be it." She raised her hands and sketched invisible patterns in the air. Ildiko sucked in a breath as her ears popped. Brishen and Anhuset shook their heads and tugged on their ears. The *Elsod* dusted her palms together. "That should do it. Now I will tell you how you might rob your people but save your kingdom in the doing."

CHAPTER FIVE

B rishen tried not to reveal his shock at having Emlek's *Elsod* standing in his house. The memory wardens, as sacred to the Kai as Emlek itself, had not left the holy island since Brishen's grandfather had married. Even then, it had been a party of *masods*, the second-tier wardens, and not the *Elsod*, who attended that wedding. Only circumstances of the gravest nature would coax the oldest *kapu kezet* out of Emlek. He supposed a *galla* horde overrunning the land qualified. The ringing in his ears had nothing to do with the *Elsod*'s silencing spell and everything to do with the realization for why she was here.

"My family is dead," he said abruptly. Ildiko gasped, and Anhuset scowled.

The *Elsod* eyed him for a moment. "And what makes you so certain?"

"Because my mother always coveted one of you as a captive. To plunder the mind and memory of a *kapu kezet* would be like drinking wine made by the gods. You would never have left Emlek's shores were Secmis still alive."

Her eyes, faded to a pale yellow, flickered for a moment. "You knew your mother well." He flinched at her remark. "The Scrying Wheel revealed the fate of Haradis. None survived such a plague. The *galla* engulfed the palace and devoured all inside."

Her voice softened. "We of Emlek offer our sympathies. The king is dead. Long live the king."

She didn't kneel before him, but his wife and his cousin did, as did the *masods*. Brishen's heart kicked hard beneath his ribs. Her news didn't surprise him. He had waited for the scout's return to tell him what he'd known at gut-level. He was the last of his line. No longer the spare, the prince of no value.

He bent to grasp Ildiko's hand and coaxed her up beside him. Her icy fingers entwined with his. "Rise, all of you." He tried not to think of his brother's lost children or their dispirited mother. He had never coveted the throne, happy to relinquish it to Harkuf and the offspring Tiye bore him. To gain it through such tragedy filled him with guilt. He happily laid the blame for their deaths at his mother's feet, yet he too shouldered a sense of responsibility.

Every gaze in the room remained fixed on him, waiting for him to speak. "Why did you address me as Interrex if you knew my line was dead?"

Ildiko, not the *Elsod*, answered him, and he swore her hand grew even colder in his. "Because now is the worst time for a permanent transference of power. Those alliances in place will stay in place because many believe at the moment that Djedor or Harkuf, or both, may yet still live. None want to jeopardize positions hard-fought for and earned. If it's confirmed you're king, those old alignments mean nothing and new ones must be forged, whether through secretive bargaining, threats and extortion or outright warfare. Not only will you have all of Haradis camped on Saggara's lands and *galla* on our doorstep, but factions of the surviving nobility clawing at each other for power and influence."

Brishen blinked at her, stunned, as did Anhuset whose eyebrows had climbed up her forehead during Ildiko's speech.

"You understand the machinations of court and power very well, Your Majesty." The *Elsod*'s voice hinted at her amusement.

Ildiko paled at the address. She glanced at Anhuset before settling a long stare on Brishen. "Warfare isn't always played out on battlefields or fought by soldiers with sword and shield. It's court where rulers truly rise and fall."

His fragile, human wife. Any Kai older than a decade could break her in half with little effort. But behind those strange, sometimes disturbing eyes lay a mind sharp as a blade with an innate sense of strategy honed by years of surviving in the Gauri court. In his lifetime, he often depended on his cousin's sword arm and battle worthiness. Now, he'd lean hard on Ildiko, as skilled in her way as Anhuset was in hers.

He executed a short bow. "I will need your counsel in such things, Ildiko. Now more than ever." He turned his attention back to the *Elsod*. "You didn't come all the way from Emlek to tell me what the Wheel revealed. What did you mean when you said I'd rob my people but save my kingdom?"

They dragged chairs from the high table and set them in a makeshift circle. Ildiko brought the memory wardens goblets of water and wine. Brishen leaned toward her after she took the seat next to him and whispered in her ear. "Thank you, Ildiko." She nodded and squeezed his arm.

The *Elsod* settled into her seat and began a rhythmic tapping on her cup with her nail that set Brishen's teeth on edge. "The Wheel showed us the destruction of Haradis as it happened. Emlek holds the memories of Kai nearly as ancient as the Gullperi.

We left for Saggara while the Haradis Kai still clung to the Absu's safe shores. We believe there's a way to defeat the *galla* and banish them back to the void from which Secmis summoned them."

Rage surged inside him to do battle with a burgeoning hope. "Then my mother was responsible for this mess we're in."

"Yes."

Anhuset gave a low whistle and shot him a revealing look as if to say "This is bad."

It was bad. If it was made known. "You possess powerful information, knowledge that could plunge Bast-Haradis into civil war and collapse the kingdom faster than any demon horde on a rampage," he told the *Elsod*.

Her stern features, wizened and tattooed, softened a fraction. "That is something we want to avoid at all cost. We're history keepers, Sire, not kingmakers. With Djedor's death and the deaths of your brother and his children, the line of succession belongs to you. We wish only to help you save our country so you may rule more wisely than your parents before you."

That was some relief. Ildiko's statement regarding the machinations of ambitious nobles weighed heavily on him as it was. All he needed was the newly elevated peerage planning an impromptu regicide because of Secmis's colossal mistake. "What is this plan you have?"

"Every necromancer who has summoned *galla* paid the price of their foolishness with their lives. No one can control those creatures. Your mother was no exception."

One of the *masods* spoke then. "When the queen died, there was no one to stitch close the barrier she tore open. The *galla* first freed are joined by more spilling through the breach. The horde is growing as we speak."

"Like a disturbed hive of hornets." The fear in Ildiko's voice made Brishen's stomach turn. He was as frightened as she was, but it seemed somehow worse to hear the proof it in her words.

The *Elsod*'s expression turned even grimmer. "If only *galla* were as gentle and pleasant as angry hornets."

He was growing impatient. If there was a way to kill *galla*, then he wanted to get on with it. "We have very little time then. How do we close the breach?"

Ildiko fetched more wine when the *Elsod* raised her cup for a refill. Brishen tried not to tap his foot too obviously while she drank. When she finished, she set the cup aside and gave him a knowing look, as if completely aware of, and amused by, his fretfulness. He wasn't in the least amused.

"Have any of you heard of the Wraith King?" She continued when they all replied they hadn't. "Because we've never before seen a *hul galla* emerge, I brought forth Emlek's oldest mortem lights and drew out their memories."

The oldest mortem lights were ancient, from when the Kai were barely civilized and the Gullperi held sway over the lands. Brishen wondered how strange it must have been to reach that far back and see the memories of a time long forgotten.

"The Wraith King was a Gullperi turned necromancer," the *Elsod* said. "Immensely powerful with the ability to raise and control the newly dead—those spirits who had not yet moved beyond this world's tethers. To do it, he split himself into distinct entities. An earthly body that slept and a mirror image made of spirit and magic. An eidolon with physical presence who couldn't be harmed or killed by normal means and who could force the dead to do his bidding."

"Why do I get the feeling this plan is going to reek worse than the back end of a breezy mule?" Anhuset's sour expression reflected Brishen's own growing concern.

Where in the gods' names was he going to dig up a necromancer? And one not so warped and malevolent that he would actually help instead of harm?

Despite his misgivings matching his cousin's, he couldn't have her flaunting disrespect to the *Elsod*. He gave her a warning frown. "Sha-Anhuset." She returned the expression but fell silent.

Instead of taking offense at Anhuset's remarks, the *Elsod* cackled. "She's right. We searched for something else, an alternative that might work. This is the only one with a chance of success."

Beside him, Ildiko stiffened in her seat. That thread of fear in her voice was no longer as distinct as earlier, but still undiminished. "What terrible thing about this plan would make you seek another alternative?"

"*Galla* can't be killed, but they can be contained, herded and banished. By the dead and their king."

Brishen exhaled a frustrated sigh. "*Elsod*, it all sounds reasonable when you say it, except for the part where I have to find one of these Wraith Kings. I'm not a necromancer, and even if I were, we're speaking of a *hul galla*, a horde. We don't just need a few dead. We need an army of them. Thousands. And they'll be as bad as the *galla*. Angry, vengeful, outraged at being summoned back. The living can't control the dead any more than they can control demons, and I don't think I want to ever cross a necromancer who can, if such a one existed."

The *Elsod* stood, and suddenly she seemed almost twice her height. Her faded eyes burned bright and hot, as if a fire had suddenly ignited inside her and cast its glow throughout her body. Even the markings etched into her skin shimmered. "No such necromancer lives in these times that we know of, Your Majesty. You must become one. A Wraith King."

"Oh gods, no." Ildiko looked as if she would faint.

Anhuset joined her, far more strident. She jerked from her chair and kicked it out of the way. It slid across the floor and toppled. "No! This is madness, Brishen!"

Brishen cut a hand at her in a silencing motion, never taking his gaze off the memory keeper. "How does one become a Wraith King?"

"You must be killed, then remade as eidolon."

Ildiko shuddered beside him, trying her best to swallow back the horrified cries he could hear trapped in her throat. He wanted to comfort her, but his own shock kept him frozen in his seat and his eyes locked on the *Elsod*. A small part of him congratulated himself on the calm timbre of his voice when he spoke.

"There's always a high cost to these things, isn't there? And it's usually a life."

The *Elsod* tilted her head as if to puzzle out his character and the iron control he maintained in the face of such bleak news. "I said you'd have to be killed. You won't have to die, at least not fully."

Brishen scowled. He wasn't in the mood to appreciate clever plays on words. "I've always been under the assumption that death is a one-time, encompassing event."

"Why would you ever think that?" she said. He growled low in his throat. "The ritual I mentioned—if we read the memories and the attendant texts correctly—offers a way to turn you eidolon for a short time before returning your spirit to your physical body, neither one permanently damaged by the ordeal."

"How?" Ildiko stood now, pale as milk and her hands curled into fists as if daring the *Elsod* to lie.

The old woman returned to her seat. "The ritual calls for separating the person into three entities: a weapon, the physical body and the eidolon. To do so, the weapon must be infused with the power of a particular spell. It must then taste the lifeblood of its wielder with a killing stroke. The spell then works to split the spirit from the body. All three are separated but still tethered together. The eidolon bears his weapon into battle while the body remains behind, protected until it can be reunited with the spirit."

"Wait." Ildiko's eyes were huge in her face. "What about the wound made by the sword? There's no body to come back, only a corpse emptied of blood." Her features went even paler as she spoke the words.

"The eidolon is infused with both magic and life. It can heal the body to which it's tethered."

Brishen dropped his head into his hands. An odd memory came to him, one from childhood, when his beloved nurse Peret entertained him on a makeshift swing. He remembered the soaring feeling, both exhilarating and terrifying, certain one moment he'd be flung into open sky to crash to the ground, sure the next he'd sprout wings and fly. That's what this conversation had been thus far. Sheer terror interspersed with moments of euphoria only to be cast down again into despondency. It was exhausting.

He raised his head and folded his hands under his chin. "Again, that all sounds straightforward and simple. Except it will require far more magic than I possess. Than even you possess."

"More than any single Kai possesses," she agreed.

"Then we're at an impasse."

"No, we're not." The *Elsod* said no more after that, only did her best to burn holes into Brishen with a gimlet stare as if trying to force him to read her thoughts.

Her earlier words echoed in his mind. *"Now I will tell you how you might rob your people..."*

He surged out of the chair. "No! There must be another way."

She shook her head. "There's no other way. You must if the spell is to succeed.

Ildiko and Anhuset gaped at them with confused expressions before Ildiko asked "What is the way? How do you make the spell work?"

"By stripping every Kai with even a spark of magic of their birthright," he snapped. "Am I right, *Elsod*?"

"Unfortunately, yes. Were we as strong in our sorcery as our ancestors, such a ritual might only require the strength of a large convocation. Now, for the spell to work, we will have to bleed the magic out of the Kai except for the young who haven't yet come into their power."

Anhuset recoiled as if Brishen had thrown something at her. Her eyes burned bright, and her lips curled back, exposing her sharp teeth in a snarl, as if to warn him off. Sickened, he turned away from her.

He dropped his gaze to the floor. "We will lose the ability to harvest any mortem lights." His throat closed at the knowledge, and he had to clear it twice before he could speak once more. "At least three generations of Kai memory will be lost forever. My dear, treacherous mother," he breathed. "What have you done?"

Except for Anhuset's clipped breaths and the thunder of his own heartbeat in his ears, the room fell silent, its occupants awaiting his decision. He scrubbed his hands over his face before seeking out Ildiko. "I'll need to call a *sejm*—a council. Most of my ministers and vicegerents are here already. They'll support you while you act as my regent during my absence."

She hugged herself, fingers digging into her arms. The muscles in her jaw flexed as she clenched her teeth but remained quiet. Her answer to his announcement was a quick nod and wide, frightened eyes that threatened to roll in panic.

"Anhuset," he continued. "You'll guard her while I'm gone."

His cousin slapped her hands on her hips and thrust out her chin. She looked ready to leap the space between them and pummel him. "Stop! Did you miss the part of the *Elsod*'s explanation where you'll be run through with your own sword?"

"I would prefer my favorite axe." No one laughed at his feeble joke, including him.

"You can't do this," Anhuset practically snarled at him.

"Then offer me another solution because if we don't turn back the horde, this kingdom, this world, will be scoured clean of life," he snapped back.

"And if you fail?"

"I will have already failed if I sit here and do nothing."

Anhuset turned to the *Elsod*. "I'll do it. I'm battle-tested and have led armies. I doubt troops of dead soldiers are any more troublesome than troops of live ones, and I'm eager to rip apart a few *galla* along the way." She smacked her breastbone with a fist. "This is my duty. I consider it an honor to shoulder this task for my king."

His order for her to stand down hung on his lips, but the *Elsod* spoke ahead of him, admiration in her voice. "You are a credit to your position and your king, sha-Anhuset, but it must be Brishen."

"Why?" Anhuset and Ildiko asked in chorus and glanced at each other.

The *Elsod* ignored them, her gaze steady on Brishen. "You know the rumors about your mother. The whispers about her beauty, ageless and unchanging though she should have been even more wrinkled and bent than I am."

He shrugged. "She was always a vain creature. When she wasn't planning death and world domination at her mirror, she was manipulating magic to hide her age."

She crooked a gnarled finger at him. "Come closer. The woman who bore you is much older than you think." Brishen knelt at her feet and closed his eyes as the rough pad of her finger traveled up his forehead, the tip of her claw grazing his scalp. "Behold," she said.

Images flooded his mind, superimposed over his surroundings. Instead of a room inside Saggara, he looked upon a moonlit village. Humble houses lined a main avenue that was nothing more than a grassless path trenched by wagon wheels and horses' hooves. A young girl played a game of ball with other Kai children of similar age. Not only did she play, she manipulated the game, slyly tripping a runner, distracting a kicker, tipping the ball. All maneuvers that ensured the team on which she played won.

Brishen recognized her. Secmis. The promise of extraordinary beauty already defined her features, along with a cunning no amount of beauty would ever mask.

The image changed, replaced by others that showed his mother as she aged into the spectacular, vicious queen he knew. She danced at grandiose balls in Saggara's great hall, hosted by a monarch Brishen didn't know but who seemed vaguely familiar. He startled when he finally recognized the king on the throne. Mendulis, who ruled Bast-Haradis five generations earlier. His statue stood among those of other Kai kings and queens in the palace's throne room.

He jerked away from the *Elsod*'s touch, and the images vanished.

"What did you show him?" Ildiko asked her as Brishen gained his feet.

"Memories of those who knew Secmis when she was a bead-maker's daughter raised in a holt not far from Saggara."

"When Saggara was nothing more than a patch of ground on an open plain," Brishen added. "I knew her to be older than my father, a few decades at most. That was common conjecture she never denied."

"She was born before your grandfather's grandfather." A hint of admiration flickered in the memory warden's faded eyes. "Intelligence, beauty and consuming ambition, combined with strong sorcery, and the woman with humble beginnings rose to become queen of the Kai kingdom."

Anhuset, in her typical fashion, kicked the pedestal out from under that admiration. "So she was unnaturally old and foul and probably bathed in the blood of innocents to stay alive. Tell us something we didn't already know, like what does that have to do with Brishen being the only one who can become this Wraith King?"

The *Elsod* laughed outright. "A Wraith King isn't only a general leading the dead. He will be the vessel that contains and controls the power which makes him wraith. That much magic concentrated in one spot requires the strength of a sorcerer with more magery than you possess, sha-Anhuset."

Brishen finished the explanation for her. "If the *Elsod* is right, then the magic I inherited from Secmis is from five generations earlier. At least. Thanks to her, I'm the only living Kai strong enough to withstand and manipulate the force of that much power."

"And only for a short time," the *Elsod* warned. She slumped in her chair. "There's more."

"Of course there is," Brishen said flatly. It had started badly; it turned worse and hinted at becoming ruinous. Then again, he had just agreed to die in order to become a ghost, raise the dead, and fight demons. Never again would he complain about herding cattle as a living Kai, especially when he was about to herd *galla* as a dead one. A bubble of gallows laughter hung in his throat, threatening to choke him.

Ildiko spoke up, her voice soft. "Enough for now, *Elsod*. You and your *masods* have traveled far. We may reconvene after you've rested. I'll have my chamber prepared for your use."

The old woman rose from her chair, shrugging off her *masods'* help. "That isn't necessary, Your Majesty."

"It is my privilege. I'll simply share with my husband."

Brishen edged closer and murmured close to Ildiko's ear. "You steal the blankets."

A small smile cracked her grim mask. "And you always tuck your cold feet under my legs," she countered.

He caressed her back with one hand. Leave it to his wife to lift his mood.

Anhuset poured herself a goblet full of wine, only to stare into the liquid, scowling. "Gods, I need a real drink. Not this weak swill."

Ildiko bowed to the *Elsod*. "I'll find Mesumenes or Sinhue, have the chamber prepared for your needs and a repast sent up unless you'd rather eat in the hall." She then bowed to Brishen. "By your leave, Sire."

In no time, she had a small army of servants, commanded by Mesumenes, who surrounded the *kapu kezets* and guided them out of the chamber. Ildiko joined the entourage, her features solemn as she nodded to Brishen before closing the door behind her.

As soon as she left, Brishen searched out a dusty bottle from a nearby cabinet, opened the cork and splashed drams of clear liquid into a pair of goblets. Anhuset abandoned the wine she held but hadn't yet drunk. "Here," he said, offering up the new goblet. "We both need it."

They tossed back the libation at the same time, gasping and sputtering afterwards. Anhuset shook like a wet dog. "That's more like it," she wheezed in a thin voice. She smacked the goblet down on the table surface and glared at him. "I can't believe you're even considering this crazed plan, much less agreeing to it." The wheeze was gone, her voice once more sharp and disapproving.

What choice did he have? "As I said, offer me another solution, and I'll gladly put this one aside."

"Let me do it."

"You heard the *Elsod*. This is my burden. Were Harkuf still alive, it would be his. As Secmis's son, he also inherited her power." He tried not to think poorly of the dead, but his brother had been a weak-willed sort, and Brishen suspected this task might have yet fallen to himself even if Harkuf had lived. "Either way, it can't be yours. Besides, I need you here to watch over Ildiko while I'm off herding *galla* into their pen. I'm a pathetic drover, and *galla* make the worst kind of cattle." He'd take a hoofprint on his leg any day over this.

Anhuset snapped her teeth at him. "Stop joking. None of this is funny. You can't make the *hercegesé* your regent, Brishen. The Kai will accept her as your consort but not as their ruler. They want a Khaskem on the throne, but not one who comes by the name through marriage and isn't even Kai. Besides, they may turn on you, not because of your wife, but for the worst act of thievery ever committed in the history of the Kai people."

"Then keep your tongue behind your teeth about it," he snapped back. "I'm still trying to reconcile how stripping my people of their heritage is somehow the brave and honorable thing to do. All I need is for word to get out about that little detail of the *Elsod's* plan, and I'll find an axe planted in my skull before I'm given the chance to save us."

She pinched the bridge of her nose between thumb and forefinger and closed her eyes. "This is a disaster."

He'd lost count of the times he'd said or thought the same thing ever since the Haradis messenger arrived half dead from exhaustion at Saggara's gates. "Promise me you'll keep your eyes open and your ears sharp, and if things turn sour in Saggara in my absence, you'll take Ildiko safely to Gaur."

Anhuset nodded. "I promise, but you already knew that." She glanced at the door. "I have to leave. I'm to meet Mertok at Lakeside to coordinate the increase of patrols around the lake and at the dye houses. If we're to host all of Haradis and half the countryside over the next week, I don't want slippery thieves with quick fingers and an eye for opportunity to make off with barrels of amaranthine."

Ah, his fierce cousin. Militant, overly protective, devoted not only to him but to the well-being of all Saggara. The stigma of illegitimacy prevented her from rising in station to inherit from him or even to act as his regent, and she'd balk at both ideas even were they possible. Still, she'd make a fine queen in her own right.

He held out his arm, and she grasped it firmly with her hand, their forearms pressed together. "It's an honor to serve with you, sha-Anhuset. My trust in you is absolute."

Her eyes narrowed to sulfuric slits. "If that was some kind of botched up final goodbye, I will knock your teeth down your throat."

He laughed. "When you see Ildiko, tell her to meet me in my chamber. Our chamber for now."

Anhuset bowed. "Your Majesty." She pivoted and strode out the door, slamming it behind her hard enough to make the goblets rattle on the table. One splashed drops of Dragon Fire onto the surface where they smoked on the wood.

Brishen lost his grin. *Your Majesty. Your Majesty.* He never imagined the title might become his, and he hated it. Not an address of authority or power, but a malediction laid upon him every time someone uttered it.

CHAPTER SIX

Kirgipa, the infant queen and their protectors made good time after separating from the main body of Kai fleeing Haradis and traveling during the day. The roar of the river now overrode the gibbering shrieks and wails of the *galla* that had clotted the opposite shore. Only a few had paralleled them as they put greater and greater distance between themselves and the others.

The weather was a questionable blessing. It was cold, with the damp seeping into their clothes and the scent of snow in the air, but the sky domed gray above them. Sunlight filtered through heavy clouds in feeble beams. At least daylight hadn't bludgeoned them into near blindness, and for the most part they journeyed without shielding their eyes.

Kirgipa's gaze surveyed the suspiciously empty opposite shore. "Are they gone?" She kept her voice low. Even with the river's boisterous voice drowning out anything less than a shout, she didn't dare risk drawing the *galla* back to them. Necos shook his head and quickly pointed out the futility of her precaution.

"See? There." He gestured to a spot across the water, where the forest hugged the shoreline, leaving a strip of rocky shore no wider than a hair ribbon in spots. Within the evergreens' thick darkness, lurked a deeper black. It coiled, sinuous and serpentine, around tree trunks, draping into the higher branches. Pinpoints of red winked in and out of shadows thicker than cold ink.

She shivered, as much from the knowledge the *galla* still stalked them as from the cold. "How long do you think they'll follow us?"

Necos had taken the queen from her, and the child nestled in the makeshift sling hung across his chest, amusing herself with a pinecone he'd gathered nearby. He patted the baby's bottom with one hand, as much at ease with child-minding as he was with fighting. His gaze scanned the opposite shore before settling on Kirgipa. "They'll follow us for as long as it takes them to figure out how to reach us and eat us."

Beside him, Dendarah hissed. "Don't soften the blow, lad. It isn't as if we're scared enough."

He bristled. "Well it's true."

"We know it's true. No need to pummel us with the knowledge." She edged closer to the water to peer down the river's path one way, then the other. The writhing blackness raised a hungry whine on the other side. She ignored it. "We should have spotted a boat or ferry by now. I've never seen the Absu this quiet."

Kirgipa hadn't noticed the lack, but now that Dendarah pointed it out, the river seemed eerily empty of traffic. "Word must have reached Saggara and the outlying dales. The *herceges* probably ordered a halt of all sailing on the river."

"Maybe." The palace guard didn't sound convinced.

They traveled along the shore, wading into the shallows when the land sheered sharply upward and became too difficult to climb. Kirgipa paused in one spot, her skirts eddying around her in the freezing water. The Absu was a clear river, with a sandy bed free of silt. Fish were easy to see and catch in the translucent water, and they'd supplemented their travel rations with a daily meal of trout.

Now the fish swam hidden beneath waters that ran dark and red past her legs in bright crimson waves. She gasped, stumbling back from the liquid streams swirling around her. "Blood. Gods, is that blood?"

Necos scooped up a palm of water. He sniffed before letting it spill through his fingers in pink droplets. He showed the two women his hand, stained pink. "Not blood. Amaranthine."

She blew out a relieved breath, one cut short by Dendarah's reply. "Dye in the water. A shipwreck maybe?"

He shrugged, his shoulders tense as he echoed Dendarah's earlier actions, staring long downstream and upstream as if to catch sight of a boat. "Maybe." He crooked a finger at Kirgipa. "Keep walking, girl. The quicker we're back on land, the quicker we'll warm up."

They stayed silent, wading through water that flowed pink, red and magenta, until they reached a half-moon shaped oxbow. Kirgipa slogged out of the water, grateful to once more reach dry land. She gestured for Necos to hand her the baby now fretting and squirming in the sling.

"She's wet," he warned.

"Aren't we all?"

He grinned at her quip, and for a moment she forgot their peril and her exhaustion, the memory of her mother's death and worry over her sister's safety. She liked this fierce, resolute soldier. A dull sound interrupted her musings. She opened her mouth to question its source and was stopped when Dendarah put her finger to her lips. "Shh."

The baby's fretful snuffles and the river's ceaseless rumble didn't give them complete silence, but they still managed to hear the rhythmic thumping noise, as if someone beat a plank of wood with a cudgel.

Necos and Dendarah exchanged glances before Dendarah nodded. "I'll go. If I don't come back, don't come looking," she warned.

Kirgipa's stomach tied itself into knots at her words. She glanced at Necos who watched Dendarah's retreat. "Change the baby, Kirgipa. We need her peaceful as much as possible." His voice was cool, calm, but she heard the tension, the unease as he split his attention between Dendarah and the *galla* across the water.

She fished a scrap of dry cloth out of her ragged pack, folded it and swaddled the queen's bottom before tucking her back into the sling along with a small piece of *tilqetil* cake to gnaw on. The soiled cloth, rinsed clean in the river, was now pink from its washing.

Except for strands of his hair that had come loose from its leather tie, Necos was stiller than a monolith, listening. A piercing double whistle made Kirgipa almost leap out of her shoes, but Necos only exhaled, his shoulders slumping in obvious relief. He grasped one of Kirgipa's hands. "Come," he said, pulling her gently along beside him.

Her pleasure in his touch evaporated the moment they came upon Dendarah and the source of the sound. Dendarah's features were drawn into harsh lines and hollow spaces as she stared at the riverbank across from them. The Absu narrowed here for a short run, thinned by a moraine of boulders that made boat navigation a challenge for even the best steersman.

There was no steersman on the listing barge that ran partially aground with her pounding herself into splinters on the boulders. Barrels, cut loose of their lashings, piled on top of each other in the low corner, threatening to fall into the river with each bump against the rocks. A few had cracked, spilling amaranthine into the water.

Kirgipa hugged the baby to her at the ominous sight of bones scattered across the pitched deck, as if thrown by the hand of a giant shaman reading fortunes. Some lay in dark, viscous pool, and she feared those crimson puddles weren't amaranthine.

"Anyone?" Necos asked softly.

Dendarah shook her head. "None alive. Humans sailed this barge I think. Loaded with cargo from Saggara." She pointed to the barrels. "The cargo is stamped with Saggara's seal. I'm guessing they were Gauri."

Kirgipa licked lips drier than dust. "How did the *galla* get to the crew? I thought they couldn't cross water." Please dear gods, let that still hold true.

The other woman shrugged. "If I were to guess, I'd say they docked for a short time. Maybe needed to make a repair. The last sailor to die probably lived long enough to release the barge's mooring in a bid to escape."

They each fell silent then. Kirgipa wondered if her companions thoughts were as filled with the grotesque imaginings of the humans' deaths as her own were.

Necos worried his lower lip with his finger. "This isn't good. If *galla* attacked a barge this far up river and away from the Kai, then they're spreading beyond the Absu's shores, hunting for more than the prey on the opposite shore."

As much as Kirgipa didn't want to go near the carnage littering the barge's deck, she still hoped for some small blessing that would speed their journey to Saggara quicker and safer. "Can we sail it to Saggara?"

Necos sighed. "I wish we could, but no. See how she's listing in the water? There's damage to her hull somewhere below the waterline. She's sinking too fast, and we've nothing to patch her."

"And we'd need more than just the three of us to steer a vessel that size upstream," Dendarah added. "Even if she was undamaged."

Something flew through the air, glancing off Necos's shoulder before clattering to the ground. A leg bone, broken at one end, with strips of flesh still hanging from it like tattered rags. Kirgipa screamed, startling the baby who wailed her fright. The sounds echoed back to them, ghastly, warped and unearthly, bellowing from the sullen things slinking and slithering across the barge's bow where it lay beached on the shore.

Another bone sailed through the air, followed by a third and accompanied by mad laughter, as if a crowd of malevolent children taunted and teased by slinging their ghoulish toys at them.

"Move," Necos snapped and shoved Kirgipa further away from the river toward the oxbow's edge and the thin sanctuary of a cluster of trees.

The laughter changed to enraged howls as the *galla* lost sight of their prey, and Kirgipa bit back sobs at the sound of bones striking ground and tree trunks.

"We wait here until they tire of their game," Dendarah said. "Then we'll walk again. You might as well get some sleep while we wait."

"How can any of us sleep after that?" Kirgipa hoped she wouldn't be sick.

Necos tucked her next to him, his body slowly warming hers. "We can because we must. You're safe, Kirgipa. Dendarah and I will keep watch."

Another time, she might have pulled away, conscious of propriety and their roles in the Kai court. But this wasn't court, and the rules no longer applied. She settled against him, the now quiet baby a comforting weight in her arms. She looked to Dendarah who sat opposite her, her proud features highlighted in profile by the pale winter light. "How much farther to Saggara?"

The guard flicked a quick gaze at her before returning her attention to where the angry *galla* writhed and screeched. "An eternity."

CHAPTER SEVEN

Ildiko paused outside of Brishen's bedchamber—hers now also since the *Elsod* and her *masods* guested at Saggara— and leaned her head against the door for a moment. The echoes of a conversation she'd overheard in the kitchens earlier plagued her mind, validating the fear she carried with her the moment she left the library with its scrolls and revelations.

A servant standing at one of the hearths stirred the contents of a large kettle and chatted with another who cut vegetables. "Do you think the old king is dead?"

The other raised a shoulder, her cleaver hacking away at the heap of produce in front of her. "Who can say? The rumor is no one in the palace survived. That makes the *herceges* king now." Firelight from the hearth winked off the blade. "This isn't bad. Brishen Khaskem will make a good king."

"That may be, but who will come after him once he dies? The *hercegesé* can't bear him children."

They both went silent when the cook, wearing a thunderous scowl, suddenly appeared in the doorway that led to the kitchen gardens. "Stop gossiping and get back to work," she ordered.

Though the servants didn't say anything Ildiko had not already told herself, her gut still churned. She blinked away the gathering of tears in her eyes and knocked softly on the door before opening it to peek inside.

Brishen stared back at her from his place by the hearth, puzzlement flitting across his features. "You don't have to knock, Ildiko. You're always welcomed in here. Besides, it's your chamber too."

"I didn't want to wake you if you were sleeping." He gave a disbelieving snort. Ildiko doubted he'd slept for more than an hour at a time since the messenger arrived from Haradis. She closed the door behind her and took up a perch on the edge of the bed. "The *Elsod* is resting, and the *masods* are keeping watch over her. They have food and drink as well."

He reached for the fireplace poker and stirred the burning coals to brighter life. The last time *kapu kezets* ventured forth from Emlek was for my father's coronation."

"I'd think they'd attend his wedding to your mother."

"Too dangerous. I imagine my mother never forgave them for it. Not only did she miss the opportunity to take one of them captive, their refusal to attend was a humiliating insult. An unspoken message that Emlek disapproved of the union and would officially record it in the *Elsod*'s memory."

Gaur had no equivalent to memory wardens. Humans didn't know how to capture the mortem lights of their dead. The Kai's ability to do so was unique, and Ildiko remembered the awe and esteem in which the Saggaran court held the *Elsod*. She was an important dignitary. Her absence at the wedding of Brishen's parents would have been noted and discussed to death. Secmis must have seethed. "Many others witnessed the ceremony. Their mortem lights hold the memory."

Brishen left his spot by the hearth to stand in front of her. "But they weren't *kezets*. Besides, with the *galla* razing Haradis, I suspect only a few are left alive who remember that day."

She sighed. "Part of me wishes the wardens had never come here. They're like ravens, harbingers of bad news and death."

He caressed her hair, loosening a pin or two with his claws. "The *Elsod* didn't tell us anything we didn't already know, Ildiko."

"We didn't know about this horrible ritual. Surely, there's another way."

"Maybe, but it would take time to find it, and we don't have time. If the *Elsod* is right—and what she said makes sense—then *galla* will continue to pour out of the rupture between worlds. They will empty their prison and fill our lands until there is nothing left alive. Even if I were only interrex or regent without my mother's power, this task would still fall to me."

She stared up at him, into the firefly eyes with their swirls and flickering shades of yellow. "Are you afraid?"

He didn't hesitate to answer. "Yes. You?"

"Terrified. And angry." Helpless and frustrated. She could extend the list far beyond those words, but Brishen carried a heavy burden. She refused to add her complaints to the weight.

He sat next to her. "You're not alone in that. If I'm not careful, I'll choke on my own rage." He exhaled and fell back on the mattress. "Was it not only months ago that I was of no value? I'd give much to have those days back." His fingers toyed with the laces of her gown, tickling her back. "You will make a worthy queen."

She bolted off the bed. "Brishen—" A knock at the door interrupted her, and she was torn between the need to screech her frustration and the temptation to faint in relief.

Brishen was less forbearing. He came off the bed in one fluid motion, eyes narrowed and mouth thinned. "This is relentless. Are we not to have even a moment's peace? Enter!" he snapped.

The door eased open, and a servant peeked cautiously around its edge. "Forgive the intrusion, Your Highness. Three more families have arrived at Saggara. Houses Amenirdis, Duaenre and Senemset. They seek your counsel."

Ildiko closed her eyes for a moment. The Senemset matriarch must have packed her family and departed only minutes after sending her messenger to Saggara. Thin as their ties were to the Kai royal house, they, like Ildiko, obviously understood their change in status if it was confirmed that Brishen was the sole surviving Khaskem.

Brishen muttered something under his breath before straightening his tunic. "Tell them I'll be there." He held out a hand for Ildiko to accompany him. "Madam."

She shook her head. "I'll catch up. I want to check on the *kezets* once more to make sure they have what they need. The *Elsod* seems frail."

He didn't argue, only caught her fingers to brush them with a quick kiss. "Then I'll see you when you're done." He bowed and left to follow the servant. Ildiko stared at the door, seeing not the wood grain and strap hinges, but lines of Kai succession sketched in ink on old parchment. She rubbed her eyes.

The *Elsod* greeted her as if expecting her visit. She reclined in Ildiko's bed, propped up by a backrest of pillows. Blankets and furs were piled across her legs, nearly swallowing her thin frame. One *masod* stood sentry by the bed, ready to serve any of the food and drink laid out on a nearby table. The other *masod* waited by the door.

"You've come with questions, Your Majesty." The memory warden motioned for her to sit in the chair closest to the bed.

Ildiko ignored the gesture. She was far too agitated to sit peacefully and chat. She was here with a purpose. "What is this 'more' you spoke of earlier?"

"The king should be here."

While Ildiko appreciated the other woman's prudence in relaying information, they didn't have the luxury of keeping Brishen tied down to glean more facts. "He'll return soon. He's busy trying to hold together a kingdom on the verge of collapse."

The *Elsod* inclined her head, surrendering to Ildiko's insistence. "What do you know of the Kai?"

An odd question, but she answered readily. "I studied a little about you before I married. Mostly the language so I could communicate and understand without relying on the Common tongue. Learning about Kai culture and history is an ongoing task. Your politics though are similar enough to Gaur's to be familiar."

"You know about the mortem lights?"

The sublime memory of a gathering of Kai who blessed their fallen and took up their memories danced in her mind's eye. "Yes. I witnessed a mortem ceremony. Brishen carried the light of a young Kai soldier named Talumey back to Talumey's mother so she could take it to Emlek."

The *masod* standing sentry by the door spoke. "I remember his mother Tarawin. Talumey's light rests safely in a place of honor in our halls."

Ildiko smiled briefly. "Thank you for telling me. The king will be glad to know it."

The *Elsod* plucked at her blankets with claws grayed with age. "You've seen the spirits of our dead rise and leave their bodies. However, they don't leave this realm completely at first. For a short span of years, usually no more than one or two, they linger, tethered by their loved ones' grief or the sense of business unfinished."

"Wraiths?" Ildiko shuddered at the thought. The wandering dead. Restless, lost, frightening.

"Not quite," the other woman assured her. "They don't haunt or plague the living. They simply wait until the last thread of an earthly life breaks, and they pass beyond this world forever."

"These are the dead Brishen must lead to defeat the *galla*." What a terrible fate for those who simply bided time before moving beyond the reach of the world's sorrows.

"Yes, but they aren't enough. There are more *galla* than there are wraiths. Were we at war or suffering from plague, this wouldn't be a problem. The king will also have to raise the human dead, and those won't follow a Kai leader."

Ildiko scowled. "Why is it that 'there is more' always heralds something worse instead of something better?"

The memory warden shrugged. "You insisted I tell you. The king will have to reach out to the human kingdoms and find those willing to help him in this endeavor."

She made it sound easy, as if Brishen were only planning to send out missives requesting horse tack for his favorite steed. "That means whoever aids him will also die violently only to be resurrected and battle demons?"

"Yes."

She rolled her eyes, taking some small delight as the others gasped. "I'm sure we'll have a line of volunteers stretching from the great hall to the gates."

Obviously not hearing the snide tone in Ildiko's voice, the *Elsod*'s eyes widened. "Truly?"

"No." All three Kai frowned at Ildiko. Her face heated. "Forgive my facetiousness, *Elsod*. I'm just...dismayed by the news."

The *Elsod* scrutinized her more closely now, as if realizing there was more to Brishen's human *hercegesé* than she first assumed. "You will tell the king what we've discussed?"

How she would love to, but she recognized her weakness—the safety of her husband. "I believe it best if you did. I'm afraid my first instinct is to try and talk Brishen out of this madness altogether. I understand what's required. I hate it. And fear it."

The lines carved into the *Elsod*'s face softened. "You love him very much."

"He is everything to me." *And in the end, I must give him up.* She inwardly recoiled from the thought.

She excused herself from the *Elsod*'s presence to join Brishen in the great hall. A small crowd of people surrounded him. Ildiko noted each person, especially the women, and tried to guess which were the Senemset family. She didn't have long to ponder.

A stately woman settled a haughty gaze on Ildiko as she approached. Behind her stood a cadre of younger Kai—a man, and four women. Ildiko would have wagered half her dowry that this was House Senemset and its widowed matriarch, Vesetshen.

They all bowed when Brishen introduced her. "Welcome to Saggara," she said in clear bast-Kai, noting a few starts of surprise and wary looks. She suppressed a smirk. They had assumed she wasn't learned in the native tongue. They'd have to watch what they said now. Ildiko might have laughed if the air wasn't so thick with tension. Human she might be, but this household was as loyal to her as they were to Brishen. Even if she hadn't known a word of bast-Kai, the servants would be quick to relay everything to her in the Common tongue—in detail.

The arrival of a messenger from High Salure saved them from the excruciating small talk. Ildiko was spared watching the political maneuvering that came with matchmaking the members of influential houses. That Brishen was already married didn't matter. Even if he kept his human wife, the role of concubine held its own considerable power.

Brishen begged their leave and sent them off with Mesumenes who showed them to chambers located on the manor's first floor, rooms that had once been for storage and were converted for guests.

The messenger, dressed in Serovek's coat of arms, handed Brishen a letter and waited silently as he broke the seal and read.

Ildiko held her tongue until curiosity got the best of her. "What does it say?"

He stared at the missive. "*Galla* have been spotted in Beladine territory, and Serovek requests an audience." He nodded to the messenger. "Tell his lordship his presence is always welcomed at Saggara, and I look forward to meeting with him at the first opportunity."

The Beladine courier bowed and left, not lingering to take food or drink before returning to High Salure.

Brishen massaged the back of his neck with one hand and passed the note to Ildiko. "We'll be fair to bursting with people in a few days and the Haradis Kai aren't even here yet."

Ildiko scanned Serovek's sweeping scrawl. "Brishen, if Belawat knows of the *galla*, and Gaur discovers you've kept this information from them, they'll assume you're planning something nefarious with the Beladine." That's all they needed, war with their allies over a wrong assumption.

"I know. I'd hoped for more time but at no point since this disaster began have I been granted such a boon."

"I can still travel to Gaur as your envoy," she said. "I know what to say and how to say it. My uncle will grant me an immediate audience, if only for curiosity's sake."

He stiffened. "I'd be...displeased to say the least if he kept the Kai queen waiting." His mouth curved into a wan smile. "Two days ago, I might have said yes just to see you safely out of Bast-Haradis. Now it's too dangerous. I'm risking the lives of my messengers as is, and they're fast and light on horseback. I won't risk my wife."

"I can be a fast traveler," she argued.

Brishen gathered her close. "I'm sure you can, but I want you here. I need you here." His words simultaneously warmed and frustrated her. "There's nothing stopping you from writing the message to be delivered. If you believe you know the best way to impart this news, then do so. You're Gauri; I'm not. I trust you to know what to say. Just do it in writing."

He growled softly when Mesumenes approached and bowed to Ildiko. "My lady, a word if you please."

Brishen rested his forehead against hers for a moment. "Go. I must ride out with Mertok anyway. We're clearing all the homesteads on the western side of the Absu and sinking wells in preparation for more people. I'll find you later."

She watched him leave before turning to her overworked steward. "Now what fires need putting out?"

The hours flew by, and she didn't see Brishen again until they met for hurried changes into more formal clothing for supper. The great hall was full of people, the benches crowded with diners from the provinces under Saggara's control.

Brishen leaned in to whisper in Ildiko's ear. "How empty are my larders now?"

She scanned the sea of Kai from her spot at the high table. "Still fairly full for now, but that won't last if we feed this many people every night."

Brishen spent the majority of the meal answering questions between quick bites of food. Ildiko listened and stayed mostly silent, observing how the various lesser nobles and vicegerents employed tactics and strategies worthy of the most complicated battle plans to place themselves high in Brishen's esteem. Kai women didn't flirt the way Gauri court women did, but she understood the intense scrutiny to which Brishen was subjected. Those women, widow and maiden alike, with an eye on the throne in even the smallest way, judged him as a potential mate or lover. They judged Ildiko as well, but as an adversary and obstacle.

Supper was interminable and lasted for centuries in her estimation. She almost cheered when Brishen stood and called an end to the evening. He escorted her out of the hall and up the stairs, exhaling a relieved sigh when they found themselves alone in the corridor leading to their rooms. "Thank the gods that's over. And lucky us. We get to do it every night." His words carried the razor edge of bitter sarcasm.

She couldn't agree with him more and regretted that she'd halted their celebratory escape. "You still need to talk with the *Elsod*. Remember, she had more to tell us."

He groaned. "I forgot." He laced his fingers with hers. "Let's get this over with."

The *Elsod* had exchanged the bed for a seat by the fire. She sat swaddled in a blanket and made to rise when Brishen entered the room. He motioned for her to remain seated and dragged another chair close to sit opposite her.

Ildiko retreated to a corner to listen as the memory warden repeated to him what she'd told her earlier. When she was done, Brishen leaned back in his chair, expression haggard. He looked to Ildiko. "Make sure your letter includes a generous dose of groveling and flattery. I don't see Gaur being too quick to give up one of its valuable generals to help us. We'll likely end up with some luckless stable hand, if Sangur the Lame bothers to send anyone at all."

"And Belawat?" the *Elsod* said.

He rose to pace in front of the hearth. "I'm friendly with the margrave of High Salure. I can ask him to exert whatever influence he might have with the Beladine court." He paused as if considering whether or not he wanted to ask his next question. "Is there anything else?"

"Yes."

The faint slump to his shoulders revealed his weariness. "Of course."

The *Elsod* straightened in her seat and shrugged off the blanket, looking as if she prepared for battle. "You are the only surviving member of the royal house of Khaskem. The throne of Bast-Haradis now passes to you as does the duty to ensure succession of your line and the continuity of the monarchy. You must provide the kingdom with heirs."

Ildiko's hands fisted in her skirts. She had dreaded having this conversation with Brishen. Now it seemed the *Elsod* would do it for her.

He whirled on the old woman, teeth snapping together in annoyance. "Are you jesting? I think we all have enough to worry about at the moment that's far more important than who gets to play king after me."

She didn't back down. "This is no small matter. It's as important as defeating the *galla*, and you must consider it now. You are married to a human woman. The Kai will accept her as a powerless *hercegesé*; they won't accept her as a Kai queen. And she cannot bear you children. As the Kai sovereign, it's your duty to give the country heirs."

The temperature in the room noticeably dropped. Ildiko glanced at the windows, certain someone had thrown open the shutters to let in the winter wind. They were latched shut, with nary a draft to disturb the lit candles set about the room. Instead, an icy fury poured off Brishen. Normally sanguine in his affections and temperate in his emotions, he now practically vibrated with rage. "Considering what I'm about to willingly embrace, don't presume to lecture me about duty to crown and country," he bit out in scathing tones.

This time, the *Elsod* paled. Her eyes dropped to her lap, and her voice softened. "Forgive me, Sire, but I have to tell you honestly. You must renounce Ildiko of Gaur, dissolve your marriage and marry a Kai woman."

"No!"

Everyone flinched at his bellow, including Ildiko. She caught the *Elsod*'s eye. "Surely, this could have waited. His burden is heavy enough already."

It was the wrong thing to say.

Brishen stilled, staring straight ahead before he slowly pivoted to face Ildiko. She tried not to cringe further into the corner. Her husband's features settled into a blank mask. Only his eye blazed, no longer yellow but white as a summer sun at noon.

Her teeth chattered, and she hugged herself for warmth. A whine hummed up her throat as he padded toward her. She didn't fear him. He had never hurt her, and she trusted he never would. But she had hurt him. The shock of it lay behind the blank look and swirled in his eye.

Forgive me. She desperately wanted to say the words, but they fell to ruin on her tongue, leaving her to stare silently at him until they stood nearly nose to nose.

The tension threatened to suffocate them all. Brishen clasped her hand, turned and pulled her wordlessly toward the door that connected his chamber with hers. He ignored the *Elsod* and the other wardens, striding without pause until they were over the threshold in his chamber and the door closed behind them.

He dropped her hand as if it scorched him and as quickly gripped her waist to hoist her in the air. Ildiko gasped and clutched his shoulders, staring down at his face. The mask cracked and bled away. Brishen's features stretched tight along his cheekbones and sank under his eye sockets. A muscle flexed in his jaw, and she braced herself for an ear-pinning.

None came. Instead, he stared at her for a long moment. When he spoke, his voice was quiet, flat. "Had I sent you to Gaur for safety, would you have come back when it was over?"

Her vision blurred. Had he cut the sentence short before "when it was over" she could honestly answer in the affirmative. To abandon him during these dark days was unthinkable. But that wasn't how he asked the question, and the flicker of knowing in his gaze revealed he was aware that how he couched his words determined how she answered him. Oh how she wanted to lie.

His fingers flexed against her sides, claws pressing lightly into her gown's heavy fabric. "Would you have come back when it was over?" he repeated in those same dead tones.

Tears trickled down her cheeks. "I would have wanted to."

He lowered her until she no longer dangled midair and dropped his hands. The empty expression settled over his features once more. "So my reward for defeating the *galla* is to lose my wife and be put out to stud."

Ildiko wiped her face with her sleeve. The horrid, deathly calm he embraced knotted her insides. "You are the king of Bast-Haradis and will very soon assume the throne. Whether or not we dislike or disagree with the circumstances, the *Elsod* is right. It's your duty to provide your country with a legitimate heir to the throne Just as your father did, just as your brother did. You must have a Kai queen."

He froze her in place with an unblinking regard. "Do you want me to renounce you?"

"It doesn't matter what I want. It doesn't matter what you want either. Our wishes and desires come last here. You're no longer simply Brishen Khaskem of Saggara. You are Bast-Haradis."

"Answer my question, Ildiko," he almost snarled. "Do you want me to renounce you?"

"No!" she cried. "Never." She massaged her aching throat where more sobs gathered to choke her words. "I also don't want you to suffer through that ritual or fight *galla*. But you will because you must. And you must renounce me."

He snatched a goblet from the table next to him and hurled it against the door. "I am king!" he roared, the thin veneer of calm burned away by rage. "I will do as I wish, and I will keep my wife!"

Ildiko ventured to touch him, a light glide of fingertips on his arm. He shivered but didn't move away. He breathed hard, as if winded from a long run across the plains. Sorrow warred with pity to see her valiant husband struggle under the yoke of kingship. "Privilege," she said gently, "gives the crown its shine. Duty gives it its weight. It's because you are now king that you can't do as you wish. The person you are—honorable, brave—will do what's required."

"I'll abdicate."

Her knees buckled at his declaration, and this time her fingers dug into his forearm. "Oh my gods, Brishen. You can't abdicate! You'll plunge this country into civil war."

He snatched her to him, and her feet cleared the floor for a second time. "I will not give you up," he vowed between clenched teeth. "I will suffer the ritual, gladly. Let it rip me apart and put me back together again. I will rob my people of their magic and fight the *galla*. I will not renounce my wife." He shook against her, burying his face in her neck. "Don't leave me, Ildiko," he implored. "The burden is only bearable because you're here."

The gasping sob that escaped her lips rendered her speechless for a moment. She hugged Brishen with all her strength, feeling his powerful body shake in her arms. She caressed his thick hair. "I will stand beside you through all of this," she said when she could finally speak. "And welcome you home with gladness when it's over, and you return triumphant."

He raised his head to once more pin her with that singular lambent gaze. "Promise me."

"I promise." And she didn't lie. She would remain in Bast-Haradis, as wife, as regent, as succor and sanctuary in the bleak days to come.

"I will not renounce you," he repeated and once more sought solace in the curve of her neck and shoulder.

Ildiko didn't argue, only continued to stroke his hair and silently grieve over the inevitable.

CHAPTER EIGHT

Brishen pulled his cloak hood forward, shielding his eyes from the bright morning sun and waited at the main gates for his guest's arrival. Sleep was a forgotten luxury. Even when Saggara quieted and slumbered in the daylight, he had lain awake next to Ildiko and counted the strands of a spider's web spun high in a corner of his bedchamber. When he wasn't counting, he watched his wife sleep.

Hers wasn't a peaceful rest. She mumbled, clawed the blankets and turned back and forth. Her pale eyelids fluttered ceaselessly, the eyes themselves shifting from side to side under the translucent skin. She frowned often and reached for him, growing still when her hand found his arm or chest, as if assuring herself he was still there.

He tried not to dwell on their conversation from two nights earlier. The remembered words still made his guts roil as did the look on her face when he asked her if she intended to return to Saggara if the *galla* were defeated.

"*I would have wanted to.*"

Such a mournful utterance, as if she'd already said farewell to him in spirit. The sense of betrayal kicked him in the chest so hard he forgot to breathe. Then came the backdraft of fury.

Until then, he'd accepted the monumental task before him with relative equanimity laced with a touch of bitterness. He'd carry the burden that to save his kingdom, he'd strip generations of Kai of their birthright. And he might not return home alive. All of that he accepted as part of his duty as Bast-Haradis's newest king.

The *Elsod*'s insistence that he put aside Ildiko in favor of a Kai wife had ignited the helpless anger simmering below the surface. Ildiko's agreement and staunch defense of the warden's argument fanned it to a bonfire. It had taken every last drop of control not to shake her, shout at her and ultimately grovel at her feet and beg her to stay.

A cry went up, signaling a small contingent of riders had been spotted turning onto the main road leading to the redoubt. Brishen shook off his grim thoughts and listened for the next alert confirming the riders were Beladine from High Salure. The gates opened, and he stood to the side, listening to the growing thunder of hoof beats drawing close.

Anhuset drew next to him, her head bare, silver hair fluttering in the wind. She used her hand to shield her eyes from the sun, and her breath steamed from her nose and mouth in vaporous clouds. She reminded him of a dragon waking from slumber. His lips twitched.

"What?" Her squint deepened with her growing scowl.

He shrugged. "Nothing of import. Good morning to you, sha-Anhuset."

She huddled inside her heavy cloak. "Nothing good about it. I should be sleeping instead of standing out here half blind and freezing my arse off, waiting for his lordship to arrive. Not only are humans ugly, they're inconvenient."

Her peevish expression only intensified when a dozen horses cantered into the bailey, wheeling to an abrupt halt that sent mud spraying in all directions. The rider on point swung easily from the back of a heavy-boned courser. Brishen instantly recognized the commanding height and shoulders wide as a battery wall. The margrave of High Salure pushed his hood back, his grin friendly as he strode to Brishen.

The two men clasped forearms in greeting. "How was your journey?" Brishen said.

"Interesting. We passed one of your scouts. Looked like she was headed to Gaur and in a hurry." Serovek's gaze settled on Anhuset. He inclined his head in greeting. "Sha-Anhuset," he said in a voice that might have coaxed bees from their honey.

Brishen was sure Anhuset's backbone made a snapping sound as she stiffened. "Lord Pangion," she replied in clipped tones.

His smile widened even more, flashing square, white teeth. Different from a Kai's. Much like Ildiko's. So human. Brishen's chest tightened.

The lord of High Salure gazed beyond Brishen's shoulder to the bailey crowded with wagons, horses and row upon row of tents. "It looks like you're quartering half of Bast-Haradis here."

Brishen turned to survey the scene. Displaced Kai families slept in those tents, homeless for now until an army of resurrected dead could purge the *galla* from Bast-Haradis. From the world altogether. "That's probably accurate," he said. "Come. I'm guessing you're parched from the road."

"I'll see to quartering your men and getting them fed," Anhuset said. She glared at Serovek when he thanked her in honeyed tones. Brishen, watched, fascinated as his cousin strode away, Serovek's stare steady on her back. Ildiko had once told him that

Anhuset had beguiled the Beladine. He had a difficult time believing it. It seemed he was wrong.

Ildiko was still awake and greeted Serovek with a wide smile and outstretched hands when he entered the great hall. "Welcome, my lord! It's good to see you at Saggara."

He caught her hands in his and bowed. Wavy dark hair spilled down in a curtain, hiding his face and Ildiko's fingers. Brishen went rigid. This man had rescued him, and Brishen owed him a life debt, but he found it hard to squelch the jealousy rising within him or the suspicion that behind the hair, Serovek might have kissed Ildiko's slender fingers.

Serovek straightened. "The fair *hercegesé*," he said. Brishen's hand flexed briefly on the hilt of the knife sheathed and belted at his waist. "How are you, my lady?"

"I'm well, Lord Pangion." Her cheeks flushed the delicate pink Brishen once associated with the amaranthine mollusk. "I'll take my leave of you for now and see to that refreshment. Please make yourself at home in our hall." She turned to Brishen, and her expression sobered. "Is there anything you need before I leave, my lord?" The rose in her cheeks faded. "Leave for the kitchens," she amended.

This sudden awkwardness between them, fueled by fear, sadness and his own sense of betrayal, hung between them like a dark cloud. "I'm fine, Ildiko," he said and watched her figure until she disappeared through the doorway leading to the kitchens.

He returned his attention to Serovek, whose measuring gaze questioned. Brishen had no intention of explaining. He gestured to a pair of chairs. "Your message said you sighted *galla* in your territory. Are you certain?"

Serovek shrugged out of his cloak and draped it across his chair before sitting, long legs stretched out before him. "Quite certain. I didn't see them myself, but a thane of mine did. They attacked a small estate near where your borders touch mine. Three *galla*. Fortunately for the family, the thane's brother was visiting. He's some kind of sorcerous monk and trapped them within a rune circle inside the house. It didn't hold them for long but long enough for the family to escape, warn the neighbors and flee to High Salure." He stretched his hands out to the fire to warm them. "I'll risk a guess and say you've dealt with a few of those things yourself the past couple of days."

Brishen shook his head. "Not personally. Just the results of their ravages. I'm glad you're here. For all that I'm reluctant to reach out to Belawat for help, I don't have much choice. And I view you first as a friend and second as a Beladine." He glanced at the doorway where Ildiko had disappeared. Don't make me change that opinion, he thought.

Serovek whistled. "This must be bad."

"Worse than you can imagine."

A pair of servants delivering a carafe of wine and plates of cold food interrupted them. Serovek ate while Brishen recounted the attack in the Kai capital and the bodies they'd recovered from the Absu near the town of Escariel.

Serovek poured himself a second goblet of wine. "How do you kill these creatures?"

Brishen finished his own wine. "You don't, but they can be banished back to their place of origin."

"How?"

"Ah," Brishen said. "That's where I need the aid of both Gaur and Belawat. There's someone here at Saggara who can tell this tale better than I can. She's upstairs."

They finished the wine and food, and Brishen led Serovek to Ildiko's old room.

The old warden once again occupied the largest chair in the most coveted spot by the fire. Her faded eyes followed the two men as they entered, Serovek's impressive size shrinking the space.

"*Elsod*," Brishen said after a brief bow. "May I present Serovek, Lord Pangion, Margrave of High Salure. His territories border mine. He was instrumental in my rescue from my captors many months ago."

The *Elsod* tilted her head, gaze running Serovek's length. "A Beladine saving a Kai from the Beladine," she said in the Common tongue. "Interesting. More than a neighbor then. A friend. You've succeeded where your father failed, Sire."

Serovek jerked and leveled a surprised stare on Brishen.

"I'm the last legitimate Khaskem. None of my family survived the *galla* attack."

Serovek stepped away to bow low before Brishen. "Your Majesty," he said in the most solemn, formal voice.

Brishen sighed inwardly, suspecting the casual camaraderie that had always existed between them was now a thing of the past. The costs of kingship were both great and small.

The warden repeated the plan she'd presented earlier to Brishen, leaving nothing out. Serovek listened without interruption until she finished, and remained quiet for moments afterwards. "So you need a human Wraith King to lead the human dead."

Brishen nodded. "Indeed. Ildiko has drafted a missive we've sent to her uncle. That was the scout you saw. We've sent a copy by pigeon. Ildiko believes he will find someone suitable and willing, but I have my doubts. I've no additional trade to offer beyond the amaranthine and no military support to give. We're cut off by the *galla*, and I need every fighting Kai here to defend us."

Serovek huffed. "You'll probably have worse luck with the Beladine court. King Rodan wouldn't send you a bucket of rancid horse piss after your father signed that trade agreement with Sangur the Lame. Unless you breach the agreement."

"There'll be no breaching agreements. Gaur makes a more powerful ally than Belawat makes an enemy.

Serovek pointed to Brishen's empty eye socket. "I'm surprised you'd say that, considering."

He shrugged and touched the scarred ridge of his cheekbone. "This is of no consequence in the scheme of things. You know that Belawat's only interest in Bast-Haradis is as a means to attack Gaur. As long as the trade agreement stands, Gaur won't let your people invade my lands. It's in Belawat's best interest to help us. Gaur's rivers and coastline protect it far more than the mountains cordoning Belawat. Water, not rock, stops *galla*.

"If your *Elsod* is right..." Serovek paused to offer the warden a quick bow. "There's no time to deliver a message to Rodan and wait for a reply. Even if there were, he'd probably tell you to shove your plea for help straight up your—"

Brishen cut him off. "Understood."

"I'll do it," Serovek declared. "I'll stand with you against the *galla*." He grinned. "But you knew I would, didn't you?"

Brishen returned the smile, lightheaded with relief. "I hoped. And prayed. What about High Salure and its governance?"

The other man waved a nonchalant hand. "I'll take care of it."

"You realize this has a whiff of treason about it."

"I don't see how. Belawat hasn't declared war on either Gaur or Bast-Haradis."

Brishen wasn't nearly as insouciant. "Yet."

Serovek snapped his fingers. "Exactly. There's no treason. I'm not allying myself with a declared enemy. I'm helping a neighbor and defending my territory just as I did when we tracked down the raiders who were killing my farmers and stealing livestock. The fact they held a Kai *herceges* prisoner was incidental."

"A fortunate coincidence for me then," Brishen agreed. He sought the *Elsod*. "Can we control the dead as is? Just the two of us?"

"I don't know," she said. "The *galla* are many; the dead will have to be even more. It will be difficult for only two of you to control them."

Again Serovek waved away their concerns. "Eh, I've faced worse odds."

Brishen stared at him doubtfully. "You have?"

"No," the other man readily admitted. "But that's no reason to hide under the bed. Or forego a good drink. Tell me you've tapped a barrel of Dragon Fire in preparation for my visit. We've much to plan and I'm still thirsty."

They took their leave of the *Elsod* and were in route to Brishen's smaller council chamber when a vicegerent crossed their path, followed by two young Kai women.

The vicegerent introduced the two women as his daughters. Both greeted Brishen with graceful bows and calculating smiles, along with their names and ages. Their gazes flitted briefly to Serovek before sliding away on a shudder. The Beladine's soft snort of laughter followed them as they bid farewell and continued down the corridor.

"I see the vultures are already circling," Serovek said. "Are you certain they don't know yet that the throne is yours?"

Brishen lifted one shoulder in a half shrug. He was wearied of such machinations. He'd been introduced to more unmarried and widowed women in the past two days than he had in the past twenty years. Names and faces were already blurring together. "I'm sure they do. I just haven't confirmed it yet. The *Elsod* will announce it and preside over some thrown-together coronation. I'll summon a war *sejm* after that."

"And Ildiko?"

Brishen's jaw clenched at Serovek's familiar use of her first name. "She'll act as regent while I'm off fighting *galla*. She isn't prepared for it but will do it. What choice is there?"

"The Kai won't like it."

Considering the threat every last Kai and human faced, their dislike was the least of Brishen's concerns. "They don't have to like it. They just have to accept it."

They entered the council chamber, and Brishen closed the door behind him. He gave it a half minute before someone planted an eavesdropper on the other side. To thwart them, he incanted the same spell the *Elsod* had used earlier to muffle his conversation with Serovek.

The other man shook his head and flexed his jaw to pop his ears. "Useful magic, that," he said. "Annoying though." He declined Brishen's offer of a chair. "If your ministers are anything like the pack of wolves always circling the Beladine court, they'll spend their time planning your wife's assassination, your overthrow, and the elevation of a favored puppet to your the throne."

Serovek wasn't telling Brishen anything he hadn't already planned for. "Then they'll be in for a surprise. The councilors I choose for the war *sejm* will benefit more if I stay on the throne. Anhuset will remain here also."

Serovek winced. "I'm sure that went over well."

"About as you might expect. But she's more useful to me here, guarding Ildiko and supporting her. Mertok will stay too, so it isn't as if I'm singling her out. The first hint of sedition that rears its head, and that person will be put to the sword. Ildiko may be human, but she isn't weak. She'll do what's necessary to hold the throne until I return."

"If we return."

"I can't afford to think otherwise."

Serovek and his company had traveled through the night to reach Saggara by morning. He assured Brishen several times that High Salure would be secure without him for an extended period. He left the hall to see to his men, refusing one of only three small chambers left in the main house, preferring a pallet in the garrison barracks.

Brishen climbed the stairs and eased quietly into his chamber. Ildiko huddled in the bed and didn't stir when he stripped and slipped under the covers to spoon around her. She was warm and soft and smelled citrusy from the orange water she'd requested their apothecary distill from the wild grove that bordered one side of Saggara.

Her hair tickled his nose, and he buried his face in the tangled locks. His garrison could now boast that nowhere else in Bast-Haradis did this many beautiful Kai women congregate. The lesser nobility had gathered in force, for safety, for influence and for the chance to show off their women folk to the king between kings. Ildiko's serene mask as she watched them vie for Brishen's attention on a nightly basis didn't fool him for a moment.

He pulled her closer into the curve of his body. He regretted not telling her he had no more interest in them than the shade of whitewash painted on the walls. That she, above all others, held his heart and his soul. Maybe if he had, she might not have embraced the *Elsod*'s advice so readily.

Maybe. Ildiko was a pragmatic sort who understood the requirements of duty better than anyone. Better, even than he did. It was why she'd willingly agreed to marry him in the first place. Her arguments supporting the *Elsod*'s insistence that he renounce her had kicked him in the gut, and the pain of her betrayal nearly put him on his knees. A day of reflection and the memory of her agonized expression tempered his initial fury. She didn't want him to renounce her anymore than he did. They only differed in their sense of obligation to the roles in which they'd been suddenly and unwillingly thrust.

"You are my queen," he murmured into her hair. "And my queen you will remain."

She replied with a slurred "I love you, Brishen," and he exerted all his willpower not to crush her to him, meld her into his skin. Keep her safe. Keep her close.

The following evening the signal bells hung at each of the redoubt's corners rang repeatedly, summoning the permanent residents and those who bivouacked in the bailey and surrounding fields. They gathered outside the perimeter walls before a hastily erected platform, faces curious and hopeful as they gazed at the *Elsod* and Brishen beside her.

His mouth was dry as a plate of sand. These people looked to him to save them. If they learned how he intended to do it, they'd turn on him faster than a pack of magefinders and tear him apart.

The crowd went silent when the *Elsod* stepped forward and raised her arms. "The Scrying Wheel revealed a great tragedy," she announced in a powerful voice that belied her frail looking figure. "One verified by the scouts returning from the capital. Haradis has fallen to the *galla*." An anguished cry rippled through the gathering. "Those who survived the attack now travel to Saggara."

A lone voice spoke up. "The royal family? What of them?" The question hung in the air as all gazes shifted to Brishen.

"None survived," the memory warden replied. "Save one." Her pause deepened the breathless hush hanging in the air. She turned to Brishen, and with the help of her *masods*, sank to her knees before him. "The king is dead. Long live the king."

As one, the crowd of Kai genuflected before Brishen, some with grief stamped on their features, others with hope. The second made him flinch. "Stand," he commanded, and the shift of feet rumbled like far-off thunder. "We are a country at war." His voice carried on the frosty air, sure and resolute. "Not with the human kingdoms—they who live and breathe, bleed and die as we do." His gaze settled on Serovek and his troop, standing separate from the Kai. "Cherish their families and love their children and elders as we do," he continued. "We are at war with creatures who know nothing of these things, value nothing beyond the need to devour and destroy.

"We all know the stories of the *galla*, but we aren't defeated, not yet. There is a way to turn them back and send them once more from our world to the prison from whence they came." The crowd shifted and murmured among themselves. "But for it to succeed, you must unite. Put aside your differences, your petty ambitions and work together as one people. If you don't, we won't survive."

Brishen waited, allowing his words to sink in, allowing the Kai time to realize the challenge that lay before them. He spoke again, his voice building to a roar. "Long may the moon rise above Bast-Haradis! Long may the Kai thrive beneath her light!"

The Kai responded with shouts of their own. "Long live the Kai! Long live the King!" They surged the platform, and Brishen stepped down, instantly swallowed by bodies that pressed against him and hands that touched him reverently, as if he'd suddenly transformed from a nobleman to a god.

He caught sight of Ildiko still on the platform next to the *kapu kezets*. She held the *Elsod*'s elbow and gazed at the sea of cheering people, face pale and set.

More cheering erupted when Brishen returned to the platform, and the *Elsod* performed the simple ceremony of placing a plain gold circlet on his head. The applause wasn't quite as loud when Ildiko bent her head to accept the second circlet, and Brishen noted the faces of each noble family closest to him in rank. A few seemed genuinely glad; most wore calculating expressions and thin smiles that did little to mask their resentment at swearing fealty to a human queen. He could only imagine how they'd react when he named her regent in his absence.

For a few hours, the Kai forgot about the *galla* and the danger they posed. Brishen ordered the opening of wine and ale casks. Fires were lit, and musicians set to playing their instruments while others gathered for impromptu dancing. As coronation celebrations went, it was neither regal nor formal nor even dignified. Brishen didn't want it any other way.

He found Ildiko amidst a cluster of Kai women, all talking to her at once. She wore that falsely peaceful mask he was growing to hate. Anhuset hovered nearby, a grim guardian.

All conversation ceased when he waded into their ranks, with bland apologies for the interruption and whisked Ildiko out of their clutches. Anhuset's dour "Thank the gods that torture is over" made him grin and Ildiko chortle.

The manor's upper floors were deserted and blessedly silent. In the sanctuary of their chamber, Brishen removed Ildiko's clothes and his own until they both faced each other, naked and dappled in firelight. They exchanged caresses instead of words, kisses instead of conversation, and by the time they stumbled to the bed in a frantic rush, Brishen forgot—for a moment—the hollow chasm that yawned in the pit of his belly.

He made love to Ildiko through the evening hours, savoring her touch, the feel of her in his arms and the gasping sound of his name escaping her lips as he pleasured her. When they rested, she idly stroked the ridge of muscle that sculpted his stomach. He'd thrown back the covers to cool off, and her hand in the darkness glowed like a pearl against his own slate-colored skin.

"You've abandoned Serovek," she said and punctuated the remark with a kiss to his shoulder.

Knowing Serovek, he was in the thick of it—dancing, drinking, charming his way through the crowd of Kai and likely annoying Anhuset every chance he got. "I very much doubt I'm missed." He rolled her onto her back, his blood heated once more simply by her proximity. "And I couldn't care less if I were."

The following afternoon he finished the last touches to the instructions he intended to give his war council and left the first-floor study for the bailey. He slowed and changed direction when he spotted both Ildiko and Anhuset peering intently at something near the stables. A wagon blocked his view of the thing capturing their attention. When it rolled away, he arched an eyebrow.

Serovek was deep in conversation with one of the Kai stable masters. His horse, saddled and packed for the return trip to High Salure, grazed contentedly nearby. Brishen looked back and forth between the Beladine margrave and the two women before taking a circuitous path to where they stood. Neither sensed him lingering in the shadow of a stall gate. Serovek had disappeared into the stable's interior on the opposite side from where Brishen eavesdropped.

"Do human women truly find him handsome?" Anhuset's voice lacked its customary sarcasm. Her question held only disbelieving curiosity.

Ildiko chuckled. "I imagine so. He's blessed with good looks, a fine form and good character." Brishen's eye narrowed. Her praise seemed excessive. "And I imagine they don't call him the Beladine Stallion for nothing." He scowled.

Anhuset snorted and turned back to hoist a horse blanket over one shoulder. "Nothing but a bunch of bluster if you ask me. I'd want proof to believe that nonsense."

"Any time, any place, fair Anhuset." Serovek's sudden appearance out of seeming thin air made Ildiko jump and Anhuset snarl. He closed the distance between himself and the Kai woman until there was only a hand's length of space between them. Brishen feared the margrave courted imminent disemboweling. "Name it," he almost purred, "and I'll be happy to prove the title is more than bluster."

Ildiko eyes rounded. Anhuset didn't step back. Her eyes shone bright, even in the afternoon light. Quick as a striking snake, she cupped Serovek between his legs and pushed upward. He inhaled a sharp breath and went up on his toes, gaze drifting slowly down to where her claws caged his genitals.

Her wide, pointy grin guaranteed most human males would piss themselves at the sight. "You wouldn't survive me, horse lord."

Serovek wasn't most human males. After the first shock of surprise wore off, he relaxed into her palm and quirked a smile. "But I would die happy, and you'd regret killing me."

Her mouth slackened, and for a moment, her hand glided down the front of Serovek's trousers and back up again in a slow stroke before she snatched it away. Her low growl vibrated with outrage, and she stalked off without another word.

Serovek wasn't as unruffled as he wanted to appear. His knees sagged for a moment, and he wiped his brow with his forearm before focusing on Ildiko.

She crossed her arms and shook her head. "You risk more than your family line by teasing her like that."

He clasped a hand to his chest and blew out a gusty breath. "I can't help it. She is magnificent. And prickly."

Ildiko grinned. "Brishen should be here soon to see you off." Her features turned pink for a moment, a sure sign she remember the earlier hours in their bed. "I'm guessing he's trying to claw his way out of the net his vicegerents and the local gentry have cast over him."

She didn't exaggerate. Once he left the safety of his chamber, those honorable folks had descended on him like flies on meat.

Serovek reached for her hand and bowed and this time his forehead, not his lips, grazed her knuckles. He straightened, and for a moment his gaze went directly to where Brishen lurked in the stall's shadows. He shifted his attention back to Ildiko. "I'll return in two days. Take care of each other, Ildiko," he urged. "You are each the other's greatest strength in these troubled days."

Brishen stepped from the shadows to wish his friend and fellow Wraith King farewell.

CHAPTER NINE

K irgipa chewed listlessly on a bite of road rations. Her stomach rumbled in protest at the hunger pains, but she had little appetite. The journey to Saggara was wearing on her. Fear for the sister she'd left behind, the endless slogging through the cold Absu just as they dried off from a previous wade into the water, and the crawling sense of constantly being watched (and coveted) by the *galla* that tracked them—it all sapped her of energy.

Necos and Dendarah walked beside her, the latter with the baby nestled in her arms. Neither seemed affected by the long hours of travel or the cold or the damp. She supposed such stamina shouldn't surprise her. These were royal guards, chosen not only for their staunch loyalty to the royal family but for their prowess and toughness. She, on the other hand, had trained as a servant. The role required a certain skill set of its own, but slogging through rivers and forests wasn't one of them.

"Not much further, Kirgipa." Necos slowed his steps to match her and gave her an encouraging smile.

She didn't return it. "You said that yesterday, and it feels no closer." She sighed. "I'm sorry. I'm just tired of being wet and cold and blinded by the sun." And worried for her sister.

"You're not alone in that." He thrust his chin in the direction that Saggara lay. "Try not to think about what's left to travel and think about the leagues we've already covered."

"Still alive," Dendarah added.

Kirgipa wasn't much in the mood to embrace their optimism, but brooding over their current circumstances wouldn't make them any pleasanter. She jumped when Necos suddenly grasped her arm and pressed a finger to his lips, signaling silence. Dendarah had also stilled, both staring ahead at something Kirgipa couldn't see. Her heart galloped from her chest into her throat. Oh gods. Had the *galla* somehow found a way to cross the Absu?

A pair of bedraggled Kai, man and woman, emerged from the trees. Neither Necos nor Dendarah called a greeting. Dendarah passed the baby to Kirgipa before taking up a protective stance in front of her. Necos did the same, the two a living wall between Kirgipa and the newcomers.

The couple paused, and the woman raised a hand. "A fair day to you, friends."

Necos inclined his head. "A fair day." His voice lacked inflection, neither friendly nor hostile, and his shoulders remained stiff. Kirgipa peered around him for a better view at the unexpected travelers. They were the first they had come across since leaving the main body of Kai days before, and they came from the opposite direction, ahead of the path on which Kirgipa and her company journeyed.

The man accompanying the woman was odd. A blank expression set in a haggard face and yellow eyes that looked through those who watched him. The woman tugged on his arm, drawing him up beside her as if he were a young child guided by his mother.

She patted him on the shoulder before addressing Necos and Dendarah. "This is my brother Sofiris. I'm Nareed. We were hunting when demons attacked. They killed my sister-in-law. My brother and I barely made it to the river. We're traveling to Haradis to warn them."

Kirgipa's two guards didn't ease their protective stances, but Necos's rigid shoulders loosened. "They already know. The *galla* attacked there first. Those who survived are traveling this way, to Saggara, for sanctuary."

Nareed's skin paled to a gray the same shade as the winter sky. "Our father lives in Haradis," she said in a thin voice. She tugged on her brother's arm. "Did you hear that? We can either wait here or continue our journey and meet up with the those coming from Haradis. Yeta might be among them."

Sofiris stared into space, his blank expression unchanging. Kirgipa was tempted to offer a comforting hand when Nareed faced them, stricken. "He saw the *galla* kill his wife." Her breath stuttered past her lips. "If they corner us, I will kill him and myself before they take us. I don't want to die the way Iset did."

Necos and Dendarah exchanged weighted gazes before Necos shrugged off the pack he carried and dropped to his haunches. "Here's as good a place as any to stop and eat." He hefted the sharpened stick he carried, a makeshift spear he used to catch the fish swimming the Absu. "You're welcome to rest and share the catch with us."

Nareed accepted the invitation and settled her brother opposite Kirgipa and Dendarah. While Dendarah built a small cooking fire and spit rack, Nareed joined Necos in the river's shallows, bow and arrows in hand. In no time they had caught enough to feed everyone with scraps left over.

Sofiris ate automatically, placing bits of fish into his mouth as Nareed dropped them into his hand and coaxed his hand toward his lips. She wiped her fingers on her trousers, gaze resting first on Dendarah, then Kirgipa and the baby before settling on Necos. "You travel with your wife and daughter?"

He nodded. "My sister also." He gestured to Dendarah who passed a flask to Nareed. "We decided we'd cover ground faster to Saggara if we left the larger crowd."

"There's safety in numbers," Nareed argued.

"Not where *galla* are concerned. That much blood and magic concentrated in one spot? They're drawn to the Kai like moths to a bonfire."

He was saved from further conversation when Sofiris choked on the piece of fish he was chewing. Nareed thumped him hard on the back, and he spit the partially chewed mush into his lap. He didn't wipe it away or scrub his lips, simply stared into the distance.

His sister sighed and stroked his hair. "Come, brother," she coaxed gently. "Let's go to the river and clean you up."

Kirgipa watched them leave. "How sad. His wife's death has destroyed him."

"Grief can do that to some," Dendarah replied, breaking sticks into smaller kindling to feed the fire. She peeled off her boots and stretched her feet toward the flame. "You two might want to do the same," she said. "Or you'll have foot rot in no time."

Kirgipa followed her lead, sighing as the fire's warmth caressed her toes. Necos didn't move, his gaze steady on the pair by the shore. "Do you think they believed we're a family?"

He shrugged. "No reason why they shouldn't. Keep up the pretense. This baby isn't safe until we deliver her to her uncle."

"Vengeance again?" The idea infuriated Kirgipa. The person responsible for this disaster was dead from her own folly. Killing off her innocent relatives wasn't going to get rid of the *galla*.

This time Dendarah answered. "There are some families who would benefit if the House of Khaskem died out completely. It's a lot easier to assassinate an infant than a seasoned warrior like Brishen Khaskem."

Kirgipa bounced her knees up and down, joggling the baby in her lap. The infant giggled and waved her arms in the air. She was a good traveler, a lot better and less whining than many adults Kirgipa knew. "How many more nights to Saggara?"

"Three, maybe four." Dendarah reached out and stroked the baby's soft hair. "Once we get there, we'll have to find a way to reach the *herceges* without shouting to everyone within hearing distance that we have the Queen Regnant."

"That's easy." Kirgipa said, happy to contribute something useful to their trio other than baby-carrying and nappy-changing. "I served the human *hercegesé* when she was in Haradis for a short time. She took a Kai servant with her when she left for Saggara. I trained with Sinhue. She'll take us to the *hercegesé* or the *herceges*.

"I've also trained with sha-Anhuset in the past," Necos said, gaze still locked on the brother and sister. "That might help us.

I'll just be happy to get there. I'm sick of traveling with the *galla* attached to us like ticks on a..." He stopped abruptly and stood.

Puzzled by his sudden action, Kirgipa followed the path of his stare. The flitting shadows lurking in the trees across the Absu slithered toward the shore. They gathered together, congealing into an oily black mass that shifted into the vague shape of a woman.

For the first time since they'd met them on the path, Sofiris reacted. He spun toward the *galla*, his eyes no longer vacant and far-seeing. The sinister shape solidified even more. Still featureless, it formed long hair that floated in the breeze like waterweed and raised slender arms, reaching out to the brother and sister as if to embrace them.

Gibberish spilled in an eerie voice from an unformed face. Kirgipa recoiled, skin crawling at the hungry, yearning tone. Nareed screamed when Sofiris suddenly lunged into the river, crying out above the water's roar.

"I'm coming, Iset! I'm coming!"

"Holy gods," Necos said before bolting to the shore's edge. He plunged into the Absu, Nareed close behind him. Water churned as they swam frantically toward Sofiris and the *galla* waiting for him. The womanly shape lost some of its curves, sliding out of form into shapeless darkness before forcing itself back into the silhouette that lured a man to his death.

"They saved him!" Kirgipa turned to Dendarah with a wide grin, one that faded when Dendarah's gaze didn't turn from the river, and her scowl sharpened. Kirgipa looked back. "Oh no."

Sofiris fought his saviors like a beast gone mad. He bellowed Iset's name over and over, punching and striking at both Nareed and Necos until the latter got behind him and latched a muscled forearm around his neck. Sofiris writhed and twisted in his captor's unrelenting grip which tightened slowly, slowly, until Sofiris's eyes closed, and he slumped unconscious.

"You killed him!" Nareed shrieked, and the *galla* shrieked with her.

Necos shook his head and said something Kirgipa couldn't hear above the river's voice but which calmed Nareed. Between the two, they dragged Sofiris back to shore, leaving the *galla* to scream their frustration at losing their prey. The feminine silhouette had long dissolved into a sludge of shadow that boiled in a malevolent froth.

Kirgipa held the baby close and jogged with Dendarah to where the three lay on the ground. Nareed gathered her unconscious brother close, rocking him in her arms and crying. Necos hadn't killed him, only rendered him unconscious in a strangle hold.

Necos clambered to his feet, dripping water and blood from the numerous cuts and gouges Sofiris had inflicted on him during their struggles.

"You're bleeding," Dendarah stated the obvious in a dry voice.

He snorted and smeared a ribbon of blood across his neck with one hand. "Just a few scratches. I'm lucky. Had I been any slower, he would have laid my throat open with his claws."

Kirgipa unwound the sling and handed the baby to a surprised Dendarah. "Watch her. I'll tend to him." She didn't wait to argue, only grabbed Necos's hand and led him back to their fire.

They had only a few bits of dry clothing left. With his injuries and night falling soon, they should stay where they were, build the fire higher and let everything dry. She'd insist on it.

Necos followed her orders to strip down to his waist. She laid his wet, bloodied shirt on the rocks, while he sat and waited for her to tend him.

He was an easy patient, neither complaining nor flinching when she cleaned the deep gouges scored into his flesh from Sofiris's claws.

"We don't have any spirits to cleanse the wounds," she said. "And I don't dare forage for herbs. Pray that these don't poison. A fever will make it harder for you to travel."

His lazy smile sent heat rushing up her neck and into her face. "I could get used to such vigilant care by you."

She ducked her head and continued cleaning his cuts as best she could. Hard to do when his body was bared to her, all sleek muscle and smooth skin where the claws hadn't reached. To distract herself, she thought of the *galla*. "I hate those things," she declared. "It's more than just the hunger."

"It's the cruelty," he replied. They delight in pain and suffering. It's nectar to them."

She glanced at Sofiris, still senseless in his sister's arms. "He kept saying his wife's name. 'Iset.'" She shivered. "Poor woman. I don't want to die like that."

Necos's light touch on her chin made her pause and she looked into eyes bright as gold coins. "You won't, Kirgipa. I swear it."

CHAPTER TEN

"I can leave you to sleep longer, Your Majesty." Sinhue stood next to the bed, a robe draped over one arm as she waited for her mistress to stand.

Ildiko stifled a yawn with her hand. She had managed to crawl out of the covers enough to sit on the side of the bed. The effort to stay partially upright and gaze blearily at her maid almost defeated her. "I feel like I just closed my eyes."

Sinhue draped the robe across the bed. "Wait here, Your Majesty. Cook brews a tea every soldier suffering from drink-sickness swears by."

"I wasn't drunk." Although, as muzzy-headed as she was, one would think she'd been deep in her cups.

"It works to enliven anyone who's slept poorly," Sinhue assured her. "I'll bring you a cup."

Ildiko pitched sideways to recline once more on the bed. "Thank you, Sinhue. And bring a pitcher of Cook's brew, not a cup. I'll need it." She closed her eyes and listened as the servant padded out of the room, leaving her to solitary rumination.

Brishen had left their bed long before she awakened to disappear somewhere on Saggara's grounds. The demands on his time were many and unending, and she wondered how he managed not to crumple into a heap from sheer exhaustion.

She opened her eyes and stared at the stone wall opposite her. The pleasant ache coursing through her muscles reminded her of the previous hours. Brishen had made love to her throughout the day and into twilight and had done the same the day before, leaving her sated but exhausted.

Her husband was generous with his affection toward her and unafraid to display it in front of others. His passion scorched the sheets, and Ildiko savored every touch. These latest encounters though... She sat up once more, winced, and reached for her robe.

Grateful he hadn't withdrawn from her after their argument, she had almost sobbed when he wrapped her in his arms and loved her through the sunlit hours. She hadn't lost him, not completely, though a shadow of hurt still flickered across his features when he thought she didn't notice. It was those times when Ildiko squelched the temptation to fall to her knees, beg his forgiveness and agree that abdication was a sound idea. Anything to remain his wife.

The *Elsod*'s declaration and Ildiko's agreement had changed something fundamental between them, introduced a panic into their lovemaking that wormed its way between them. Insidious and subtle, it bled slowly into every touch, turning passion into purpose, desire into desperation.

Brishen spent himself inside her, kissed her and murmured endearments into her ear. And each time he rubbed her belly, hand gliding back and forth over her navel as if to incite some magic that slept there. Ildiko blinked back the sting of tears, fingers drifting across her abdomen. He could charm and bespell and fill her with his seed every hour. There would be no child of their union.

Sinhue strode into the room, a steaming mug of Cook's brew clasped in her hands. "For you, Your Maj..." She paused and frowned. "Are you all right, Your Majesty?"

Ildiko stood, summoning a wan smile. "Just tired, Sinhue. Thank you." She reached for the cup. "If this draught is as miraculous as you say, I'll feel better in no time."

The servant's dismayed expression didn't lessen. "You need more rest. You aren't sleeping."

That was certainly true. Ildiko sipped at her drink, surprised at its sweetness. Most draughts brewed for drink-sickness tasted foul. "I intend to sleep a fortnight straight when all of this is over," she assured Sinhue.

A quick bath and breakfast followed by a visit to inquire about the *Elsod*'s health, and Ildiko made her way to the pigeon house. "Any news from Gaur?" she asked the bird keeper.

"None, Your Majesty. I can send another bird if you wish?"

She refused the offer. Gaur had not yet responded to either the message sent via rider or the one sent by carrier pigeon. Sangur the Lame should have gotten one of them by now. She agreed with Serovek that Rodan of Belawat wouldn't raise a finger to help, but she hoped that Gaur would. They were trade partners and allies after all, even if the enemy was no longer a human neighbor but an otherworldly demonic force.

The most loathsome part of her evening had yet to start—time spent socializing with the newly elevated nobility who rejoiced at their change in rank, even if it was accomplished through dire circumstance.

"Still not used to the waking hours of the Kai, Your Majesty?" Vesetshen Senemset threw down the first gauntlet the moment

Ildiko stepped across the northern solar's threshold. "I saw His Majesty this morning and inquired after you. He said you were resting and would be available later."

The chamber was crowded with women at various tasks. At Vesetshen's question, and its implied criticism, their conversations halted. Weary and not particularly tolerant of the not-so subtle jibes the matriarch had tossed out on numerous occasions since her arrival, Ildiko claimed her seat nearest the fire with its bright light and warmth and shuffled through the papers Mesumenes had left her to review.

She dipped her quill in the inkpot and paused, letting the room's expectant hush grow and Vesetshen's impatience with it. "I'm used to the different hours, madam." She met the other woman's gaze, poisonous as an adder. "I'm not always used to His Majesty's ardor, which often results in little sleep for either of us."

Choked laughter and a few coughs broke the tension. Vesetshen's face darkened to the shade of wet slate, and her lips thinned to reveal the ivory pickets of her teeth. Ildiko shrugged and went back to reviewing her lists. Vesetshen's ambitions spelled trouble, but Ildiko had faced down the Shadow Queen of Bast-Haradis in her own court. This upstart was nothing more than an annoying gnat by comparison.

She was in the kitchens reviewing the dwindling larder when Mesumenes appeared at her side. "Another harvest wagon has arrived, my lady. Half a barn's worth maybe, but it's better than nothing."

He escorted Ildiko out to the bailey, now dangerously overcrowded with people and livestock. A wagon stood parked near one of the bailey walls, piled high with wheat. Ildiko surveyed the yield, mentally calculating how much bread or gruel it might convert to once it was threshed, winnowed and milled. "How many do you think our stores will feed now if we ration and encourage people to eat soup instead of a haunch of meat?"

The dismal number Mesumenes gave her had them both frowning at each other. "I wish it were different, my lady," he said.

Ildiko worried her lower lip with her teeth, ignoring Mesumenes's aghast expression. "We could feed the current population for a few months if we counted every spoonful. With the Haradis survivors coming, we'll be lucky to make it a month, even with strict rationing."

"One meal a day," he replied. "And if necessary, one meal every other day. It might work if we did that."

"It will be hard on the younger children."

His brief smile lifted her spirits. "Kai children' aren't like human children, my lady. They'll weather the deprivation much better than you think."

That was a small relief at least. "Find out what the mollusk bed in the lake is like right now. How extensive."

The steward gaped at her. "Your Majesty—"

She understood his shock. Eating an amaranthine mollusk was like eating gold. That, and they weren't called bitter mollusks for nothing. "A last resort, Mesumenes, but I want to be prepared just in case."

The two spent the remainder of the night traveling through the camps, talking with the displaced Kai, hearing their complaints and fears, their hopes and plans. All were frightened and homesick. Sometimes the fear took the form of aggression, with both Kai men and women offering up their services as soldiers for the garrison. Others begged for tasks to keep their hands busy and their minds distracted. Ildiko sent the first group to Mertok. With their population swelling at such a rapid pace, Saggara needed to strengthen its military ranks with more bodies. Mertok would assign some menial but necessary work, something that helped the Saggaran troops but lacked the power to influence or turn loyalties.

She dealt directly with the second group, enlisting the steward's help to delegate chores that ranged from digging cess pits to working the grain mills, forge, washhouse and the makeshift kitchens set up to dispense hot meals to those in the tent city. There was more than enough work for everyone; there wasn't nearly enough food.

"They will riot when there's nothing left," Mesumenes said softly.

"Pray the *galla* will be defeated before that happens," she replied.

The sky was fading from black to indigo when Brishen returned from patrol to Escariel. He found Ildiko counting elixir bottles and spice boxes in the large cabinet to which only she and Mesumenes possessed a key.

Ildiko's welcoming smile faded at her husband's severe expression. "What happened? Another half of a horse?"

He shoved his hair back from his face. "No, but the *galla* have arrived in Escariel. I don't know how many, and I'm certain it's not the horde's main body. We could hear them in the trees. Some venture out to torment the Kai on the safe shore."

"What do they look like?" She'd grown up hearing stories of the *galla*. Vile and ancient, they were the monstrosities that haunted the nightmares of every child threatened by a nurse or parent for misbehavior.

"Like shadow and sickness combined. As if plague took form and stalked the land, red of eye and drunk on cruelty." His brow furrowed. "It's not how they look so much as what they are. Unnatural. Abomination. Malice distilled into its purest state." He shook, as if to slough off their taint.

She caressed his forearm, hand gliding over his gauntlet. "Have you eaten? The kitchen fires are still lit…"

He captured her fingers. "Not yet," he said and pulled her along behind him toward the stairs and upper floors. Once inside their room, he kicked the door shut and set to untying the laces on her gown. "I hunger for you, wife," he said in a voice thickened with lust.

Ildiko flattened his hands against her, halting his movements. The moment she dreaded had arrived, far sooner than she liked. "No, Brishen."

His claws skittered across the clasps that closed the front of her tunic. "We won't be long, and I don't mind cold food." The first clasp snapped open under a persistent claw.

This time she swatted his hand, hard. "Stop it." He recoiled as if she'd bitten him, and gawked at her, face slack with surprise. She gentled her tone. "Do you not see what you're doing?"

If anything, he looked even more flabbergasted by her question. "Trying to make love to my wife."

Ildiko snapped the clasp closed and took a bracing breath. Her knees were like water, and the words thick as wet wool on her tongue. "No, Brishen," she said as gently as she could. "You're trying to sire a child." She almost retracted her words at his expression—stunned, confused, hurt. Much as it had been when she defended the *Elsod*'s proclamation that he set her aside.

"I love you," she continued. A tear tracked down her cheek when he retreated a step from her. "I love that you desire me. I hope you always will. I feel the same for you. But this isn't lovemaking. It's breeding, and we're doing it, not out of love, but out of fear and misguided desperation." She reached out to him, begging for his understanding. "I feel it too, but this is wrong."

"What are you saying?" His question was hardly more than a croak, and he'd gone ashen.

Ildiko lowered her arms and crushed her skirts in her fists. "You've had me under you, on top of you, in front of you. I think I've forgotten what it feels like not to have you inside me. I can't walk from one room to another without you lifting my skirts. But no matter how often you spill your seed within me, it won't catch." Thinking the words made the fact real. Saying them hammered them home in a painful strike. "I will never conceive. You know this."

His eye color lightened, a sure sign of a Kai's agitation. He crossed his arms, his biceps flexing in involuntary twitches as if he physically restrained himself from breaking the furniture. "That's what you think?" he said in the same dead, icy voice he'd used on the *Elsod* earlier. "That I'm using you like a brood mare? I never guessed your poor opinion of me."

She forgot to breathe. "No! You're twisting my words, their meaning."

"Am I?" His eye blazed whiter with each passing second, and his lips stretched tight across his teeth. "You refuse me because you say this is breeding. What part of that can be misunderstood, Ildiko? What made me so diminished in your regard that you'd think such a thing?"

Tears poured down her cheeks, and she let them drip to the floor. She'd done this all wrong, wrecked something precious between them in a staunch but misguided bid not to mislead him. "It isn't you who is diminished, Brishen. It's me. To your people, I'm lesser because I can't fulfill the one task that is vital to my role as your queen. Making love to me a dozen times a day won't change that, no matter how much either of us want it to. You have a human wife, and all the limitations that come with such a mate."

He stared at her for long moments, his gaze piercing, distant, as if he measured her and wondered how he might have been deceived into loving her. "Did you never think that maybe I sought solace in the one person who could make me forget this madness for a few short hours? Even minutes?" She cringed at the hollow flatness of his tone. "Give me hope when it feels hopeless?"

She wanted to throw herself at him, plead for his understanding and his forgiveness, swear she never meant to be callous. "I'm sorry I hurt you. You are the last person I'd ever want to hurt, but I don't want to give you false hope."

"Sometimes false hope is far better than no hope." He pivoted and left her without another word, closing the door behind him with a soft click of the latch.

Ildiko stared at the expanse of wood, blurry in her vision. She sank slowly to the floor, rested her head against her bent knees and sobbed into her skirts.

CHAPTER ELEVEN

Serovek returned to Saggara almost as soon he left, this time with a companion. Brishen met him in the stables as he unsaddled his mount. "Change your mind, yet?" he asked. He didn't think the margrave would, but Brishen certainly understood if he did.

Serovek surrendered tack and horse to a waiting groom with an arch stare. "I have many weaknesses; indecision isn't one of them. We spotted the Haradis survivors on our journey here and the *galla* that followed them. Wolves tracking a herd, ready to cull the weak and unwary. More than half the kingdom of Bast-Haradis is about to descend on Saggara."

"So my scouts have reported. We can hardly feed the ones already here." His gaze settled on the silent newcomer standing behind Serovek. "Who is this?"

"A bit of good news in the midst of the bad." Serovek motioned, and the other man stepped forward. "The monk I told you about. This is Megiddo Cermak."

Slender as a stripling lad next to the bigger, powerfully built Serovek, Megiddo possessed a gravitas woven into every fiber of his bearing. From his stance to the elegant construction of his facial features, he wore dignity like a second skin. That he was a cenobite in service to a god didn't surprise Brishen.

The monk executed a graceful bow. "It is an honor, Your Majesty," he said in measured tones.

"Welcome to Saggara..." He paused, wondering how the follower of an unknown religious order was addressed.

Megiddo's lips tilted as if he heard Brishen's thoughts. "I'm called by my birth name or my designation, *macari*."

"What does '*macari*' mean?"

Megiddo shrugged. "Monk."

Serovek grinned. "Not ones for poetic imprecision, these monks."

Brishen laughed for the first time in days. "An admirable trait." He motioned for them to accompany him back to the manor house. "Come. You can break your fast and satisfy my curiosity as to how something as simple as a rune circle trapped *galla*, even for a short time."

They settled into the ground floor study, which had become the central hub of planning and discussion for anything involving Saggara's defenses and ability to offer sanctuary. A tray of bread and thinly sliced cold meat was brought in, along with pitchers of warm ale. Brishen leaned back in his chair, claw circling his goblet rim as he observed his guests. Serovek tucked into the food without hesitating while Megiddo declined.

"What gods do you serve, Megiddo?"

The monk sipped at his ale before setting it aside. "A single god only. Faltik the One."

Serovek dunked a piece of bread into his ale before pointing it at Megiddo. "Megiddo's a heretic," he declared blithely, ignoring the other's disapproving side glance. He popped the bread into his mouth and washed it back with a swallow of ale. "A foreign faith that's gained hold in Belawat." He stabbed a slice of meat with his eating knife. "Its practitioners don't hawk their beliefs too loudly. It isn't sanctioned by the king."

Brishen, intrigued, wondered what moved a worshipper to put all their faith into a single, solitary god with no pantheon behind him. He refilled Serovek's goblet. "You do like to cultivate risky associations, my friend. Do you follow this Faltik?"

Serovek snorted. "Hardly. I prefer to hedge my bets. If one god won't listen to my prayers, I can always appeal to a dozen more."

Even Megiddo's solemn features relaxed into a half smile at Serovek's irreverent philosophy. "So sayeth the blasphemer," he uttered in that calm voice. Its timbre made Brishen think of a still lake, barely rippled by an insect's glide or the whisper of wind over its surface.

"Tell me how your rune circle worked. Magic tends to only whet the *galla*'s appetite." An idea had teased the edges of his mind since Serovek first described how Megiddo had saved his brother's family from the demons.

"I think that's why it worked." Megiddo drew an invisible circle on the tabletop. "The circle is a demon trap, one taught to third-year *macaries* in our order. It served more as a distraction than a cage, was more appetizing than we were. I think they fed on it while we escaped." He paled. "Do you think it made them stronger?"

Brishen shook his head. "Gods, I hope not. They're feral and powerful enough as it is." Still, a rune barrier to encircle a city... He scowled. It would have to be enormous and fueled by an unimaginable amount of magic.

Serovek broke through his musings. "Could the Kai do something similar? Create a greater barrier around Saggara? Your magic is easier to come by than ours since you're all born with a measure of it."

Not for long, Brishen thought. But he'd take that secret with him to his grave as would the handful who shared the knowledge with him. "Maybe, if there were fewer *galla* and less land to cover, but this is a *hul galla*; a horde. And getting bigger all the time. And I don't think I'd circle Saggara." The idea continued to gnaw at him. Not Saggara but maybe destroyed Haradis.

"Have you heard anything from Gaur?"

"No, nothing." He had hoped Sangur the Lame would at least confirm he'd received the message, even if his answer was a refusal to help. They'd sent a Kai messenger and a carrier bird. Neither had returned yet, and they couldn't wait any longer.

Serovek rubbed his hands together. "Then the good news I mentioned earlier will improve your day. Megiddo has volunteered to join you in fighting the *galla*. He's willing to become one of your Wraith Kings."

Brishen eyed the monk across from him. How ironic that those who came to help were not of Gaur, Haradis's ally, but of Belawat, the uneasy neighbor. "Did Lord Pangion tell you what this involves?"

"Yes. I saw those things up close." Megiddo's expression remained untroubled, though a sharpness edged his voice now. "My order has fought demons. It was part of my training. But the galla...they're like nothing I've ever encountered. Unclean isn't a strong enough word to describe them. I'm not sure if you set the whole world on fire it would be enough to cleanse it of their stain.

As a member of the Jeden Order, I took a vow to hold sacred all that Faltik created, by sacrifice or sword. All earth is hallowed ground to Faltik. It's my duty to rid it of these creatures."

Not so much a man with a purpose but one on a crusade. Brishen didn't usually approve of such men. The fire of belief often crossed the boundaries into the scorched earth tactics of the fanatic. Megiddo didn't seem that type despite an obvious and powerful sense of duty to his god. "A noble cause," he said. "But you're a monk. What do you know of battle?"

"*Macaries* are trained for combat to protect ourselves, our elders and our temples. The monastery I serve was given an estate in the Lobak Valley to farm. The warlord Chamtivos seized the valley to establish a prefecture. My order fought his troops and won it back."

Serovek refilled all three goblets with ale. "I've heard of Chamtivos. A tough enemy to engage, much less defeat. Too bad the *galla* didn't spring up in the middle of his camp. Would have gotten rid of that festering boil in no time." He clinked goblets with Megiddo and Brishen.

Brishen admired the monk's courage, but he also needed an experienced fighter who had engaged in warfare. Training for it was one thing. Engaging in it, another. "You fought in this battle?"

"Yes."

Serovek spoke up once more. "I've seen him handle a sword. He's adept and a skilled rider too."

Brishen stared at Megiddo, who stared back, unflinching. "If you do this, there will be no fame or glory. No wealth or status. Not even a guarantee you'll return home alive or whole. If we're lucky, we'll come back, intact, to the loved ones we fought for." *Will you be here if I return, Ildiko?* he wondered. She had promised once already and still he doubted. Shame rode hard on the back of that doubt.

Megiddo's gaze never wavered. "Why else fight?" he said.

Silence reigned in the chamber for a few moments before Serovek raised his goblet. "Well? Are we three or two?"

Brishen raised his goblet as did the monk. "We're not much better off with three, but it's more than two." He inclined his head to Megiddo. "You have my gratitude and the gratitude of all of Bast-Haradis."

Serovek helped himself to the uneaten portion of bread on Megiddo's plate. "I also took the liberty of sending a message to the mountain clans wintering at the base of the Dramorins. I trade with them. They have as much to gain or lose from joining this fight as any of us."

That bit of news surprised Brishen. The nomadic clans who wintered on the plains in Belawat territory and summered in the mountains were almost as insular as the Kai. Unlike the Kai, they were human, and he doubted a people closed to others would help their human neighbors much less the non-human Kai.

"I hope you trade with a friendly chieftain who owes you a favor," he said. "And pray to your troop of gods that he says yes and arrives soon. We leave for Saruna Tor tomorrow. Three of us or four, we can't wait any longer."

Megiddo's gaze drifted as if he looked inward. "Gul Hill. I remember my mother telling me about that place. She said it was cursed."

Brishen smiled briefly. "That's what we Kai want you to believe. It keeps humans away from Kai sacred ground."

They spent the next hour making plans for their travels and exchanging ideas for how to move their armies of ghosts to herd a horde of demons back to their birthplace. It would be the most terrifying cattle drive Brishen had ever participated in. He only hoped he was better at herding *galla* than he was at herding cows.

Again Serovek declined his offer of a chamber in the manor house, and Megiddo echoed him. "Nothing personal, Your Majesty." He uttered the address around a sly grin. Brishen winced, still unused to the title. "This is a fine abode indeed, with all the comforts of a woman's touch added to it thanks to your lovely queen. But you're up to your ears in courtiers, bureaucrats and parasites in fine silk and velvet. Human or Kai, it doesn't matter. I'll suffocate in that air. Give me an open field and a warm blanket any day over this."

"Good luck finding an empty field around Saggara these days," Brishen said in a dry voice. "A place can be made for the two of you in the barracks, like before. Or the stables."

Megiddo was quick to choose. "Stables."

Serovek was slower to decide. "Barracks for me. I like my horse well enough, but there's far more interesting company among your soldiers."

Brishen had no doubt the margrave thought of Anhuset. Either she'd accept Serovek's courtship and swive him until she killed him or simply split him open with her claws or sword. One way or the other, he'd be dead, and Brishen hoped she'd at least wait until they got this Wraith King business behind them first.

They parted ways in the great hall with promises to meet again later for a more formal meal and a council meeting with Brishen's newly appointed *sejm* and regent.

He spotted her crossing the bailey, Mesumenes by her side, as was the usual thing these days. They waded through ankle-deep mud and the sludge of melted snow, deep in conversation and oblivious to the crowds of Kai eddying around them. The steward scribbled on the top page of a sheaf of parchment, nodding or shaking his head at whatever Ildiko told him.

Her red hair shimmered in the torchlight, bright and fiery as a hilltop beacon among the Kai with their black or silver locks. Even Serovek and Megiddo, both dark-haired and tanned by the glaring sun, blended more easily with the crowd than she did.

His soul ached at the sight of her. Ached for her. She had emasculated him in their chamber, human tears streaming down her cheeks as she did it. Brishen wielded knives that could never be as cutting as the words she uttered then.

"*...this isn't lovemaking. It's breeding...*"

Had she carved any deeper, he would have bled out in front of her. The shock of her accusation had rendered him speechless at first. He'd barely gotten over the realization she'd sacrifice their marriage for the security of his throne, and now this. His fury didn't boil hot. Instead, it settled in his gut, colder than a lump of ice that refused to melt, spreading to freeze every other emotion inside him. He hadn't gone near Ildiko for two nights and days since then except at the more formal suppers in the great hall, and those interactions were torture of the acutest kind. He didn't dare touch her, and he didn't let her touch him. If either happened, he'd break, and kings did not break.

She persevered under the cloud of his resentment, wearing that placid mask he so utterly loathed now. The mask only fell away when she saw Serovek again and met Megiddo for the first time. Then, her entire face lit with a smile.

Brishen bent the stem of his goblet nearly in half. Across the hall, he caught Anhuset's gaze. Piercing. Concerned. Ildiko was even more skilled than he at hiding the turmoil between them from those guesting at Saggara, but neither fooled his astute cousin. She eyed him and Ildiko every time they crossed in their daily tasks. Anhuset never asked, and Brishen didn't volunteer, but he knew she wondered.

He remained secure in his knowledge that no one except Anhuset had guessed there was trouble between him and Ildiko until Serovek pulled him aside. "Is your wife ill?"

Brishen stared at him for a moment before answering. "Why do you ask?"

His question came out more belligerent than he intended. Serovek stiffened, and his mouth turned down. "Because she wears the look of a woman either sick or sorrowing. The last time I saw such an expression in a woman's eyes, I was returning her husband's body to her after he fell in a raider's skirmish."

The lump of ice filling his chest and spreading slowly through his limbs, disintegrated in a sizzle of steam. Brishen clamped his teeth together and counted the breaths he inhaled and exhaled through his nostrils. "I can't interpret such things in a human's eyes," he said in a guttural voice.

Serovek's stern features didn't soften, and his gaze set hard on Brishen. "Then you aren't looking close enough, Your Majesty," he said before bowing abruptly and melding back into the crowd of Kai to chat and socialize as if they were lifelong friends. As if they were human or he was Kai himself.

At supper, they sat side by side but either spoke to others or ate without comment. Tension pulsed between them so thick Brishen imagined he could hack through it with his axe.

Ildiko, dressed in black, reminded him of a red-beaked magpie. She presented a cool facade to the rest of the diners, but she quivered in her chair, perched on its edge and ready to fly away if he even twitched toward her. Surely that wasn't fear of him? He'd done nothing to incite such an emotion in her. He was on the verge of abandoning the supper and escorting her out of the hall to hash things out between them when one of his justiciars approached the table, wife and daughter in tow.

Cephren was one of Brishen's favorite ministers, a man whose judgments in his provincial court were known far and wide to be fair and sometimes merciful. Brishen wanted him on his war *sejm* for those reasons and was heartily glad to see him arrive safely with his family at Saggara.

Cephren bowed. "My liege." He bowed a second time to Ildiko. "My lady queen." He gestured to the two women with him. "You may remember my wife, Lady Hemaka and my daughter, Ineni."

"It's good to see you, Cephren," Brishen said. "There'll be no leisure here for you, I'm afraid. I've reserved a place for you on my council, and there's much work to be done."

The justiciar beamed. "I'm eager to assume the tasks awaiting me, Sire."

Cephren coaxed his daughter forward. An attractive young woman with a direct gaze and a proud tilt to her head, she reminded him of Anhuset. Not as fierce but not easily intimidated either by an audience with her sovereign. "Ineni has an idea she wishes to present to you, Sire."

Brishen held up a hand, curious as to what the girl wanted to tell him. "Please do," he said. Exquisitely tuned to his wife's every movement, he sensed her sharpening focus. She leaned forward to listen, as if Ineni were about to reveal a secret of the ancients.

"Sire, there's a minor stream three leagues north of Akoris Dale. Fed by the snows which melt off the Dramorins in the spring."

He nodded, intrigued. "I've ridden by it before while on patrol."

Ineni grinned, warming to her subject. "Years ago, a wind dike was built there to protect a neighboring field of dream flower from the flood waters. I go there often. Forgive me if this seems impertinent, but if you brought in a crew to remove the dike, the stream can flood the field."

Cephren's smile became pained, but he stayed silent.

Brishen imagined the stream as he remembered it. "It would create a shallow lake."

Her honey-yellow eyes almost glowed. "Knee-deep at its deepest point."

"Easily crossed by the Kai and a wider barrier against the *galla* than the stream by itself."

Ineni laughed, a sound of pure delight. Beside Brishen, Ildiko drew a sharp breath. "Yes!" the girl said. "And you wouldn't destroy a food supply by doing it."

Brishen turned his attention to Cephren who met his eyes with despairing ones of his own. "Not a food supply, no. Only your family's wealth. This is your field, isn't it, my friend?"

Cephren bowed his head. "Yes, Sire." Ineni's smile faded into a stricken expression. So taken by her idea and Brishen's approval, she forgot how it would affect her family's fortunes.

Brishen hoped he might offer his justiciar some comfort. "Your daughter has an excellent idea, Cephren." He nodded to her. "You're to be commended, and your father recompensed for the loss of the field." Cephren immediately brightened as did Ineni and her mother. Brishen motioned to Mertok who stood nearby. "Did you hear all that?" His master of the horse nodded. "See that it's done as soon as possible."

Ildiko spoke beside him. "Lady Hemaka, I would very much like to talk with you and your daughter and hear more of her ideas. Would you both join me for a goblet of wine after supper?"

Brishen's eyebrows arched, and murmurs rose from the Kai close enough to overhear the invitation. To be singled out by the queen for a social gathering was a high honor—one to garner both respect and envy. And no little resentment.

Hemaka blushed as did Ineni who gaped at Ildiko. Hemaka bowed low. "It would be an honor, Your Majesty."

Brishen turned slowly to stare at his wife. She refused to meet his eye. "*What are you up to, Ildiko?*" he wanted to ask but held his silence and finished the remainder of the supper in conversation with Serovek, Megiddo, and members of the *sejm*.

He stood to call an official end to the meal, halting when the doors to the hall opened, and a troop of Kai, led by Anhuset, entered. Behind them, a cadre of humans followed. Dressed in

calf length robes dyed in jewel colors and boots that laced above
the ankle with wide-legged trousers tucked inside, they strode
toward the high table. Six men, with their obvious leader on
Anhuset's heels.

Hair dark as a Kai's and skin the color of oiled walnut, he
approached the table where Brishen sat. Serovek had risen from
his seat, face creased into a wide smile. He leaned around
Megiddo and raised a hand to Brishen, thumb tucked against his
palm. "Four," he mouthed.

Brishen grabbed Ildiko's hand and coaxed her from her seat.
She didn't resist and accompanied him around the high table to
meet their newest guests. One could have heard a feather drop as
the Kai king and his human queen faced the nomads who
wandered the plains in winter and sheltered in the Dramorins in
summer. An isolate people of unknown origin and unknown
culture, they sequestered themselves away from other peoples
even more than the Kai. Serovek's charm had worked its magic
again to drawn them out long enough to parlay with Brishen.

He gestured for Anhuset to step aside. The nomad chief
reminded him of a predator bird. If a hawk could be transformed
into a man, then he stood here now in Saggara's great hall—
wingless, sharp-eyed and no less lethal. Brishen almost expected a
raptor's piercing cry when he opened his mouth.

"Your Majesty," he said in a low, clear voice. "I am Gaeres,
fifth son to the chieftain of Clan Kakilo of the Quereci. We
received word from Serovek of the demon horde and come to offer
our help."

As he had done when Megiddo arrived at Saggara, Brishen led
Gaeres and his entourage, along to the council chamber with

instructions to send for the *Elsod*. Before he left, he touched Ildiko's elbow. She bowed before he could say anything, her features somber. "I'll end the meal and send everyone off, Sire. Good practice for after you leave." She nodded to the chieftain's son and returned to her seat without looking back.

He put her from his mind simply so he could think clearly. Both he and the *Elsod* explained the ritual to the newest arrival, once more leaving out the part about stripping the Kai of their magic. Gaeres said nothing at first, his fingers tapping gently on the table's surface. Lamplight burnished his hair and winked off the small brass coins threaded in the length of braids woven at his temple and caught in a bone clasp at the back of his head. "When do we leave?"

It seemed almost too easy. Every person who lived and breathed had a stake in seeing the *galla* defeated, but the ones tasked with making it happen tended to find their motivation in additional things. Brishen had a kingdom, a throne and a wife to save. Serovek, his country and people. Megiddo responded because of a duty to the convictions of his faith. What moved Gaeres of the Quereci to offer himself up as a Wraith King? He didn't have to wait long for his answer.

"I'm the youngest son of a chieftain's third wife. I'm of low status and no importance." Brishen inwardly sighed, remembering with fondness when he held the same status. Gaeres continued. "I wish to marry later, but I must rise in my clan so I may attract a suitable wife willing to share her *hazata*—her home—with me."

Intrigued by the hint of social structure within the secretive Quereci culture, Brishen wondered why Gaeres didn't make his own tent. "Why not share your home with her?"

The other man scowled, as if such an idea was too preposterous to seriously consider. "Only the women own *hazatas*, along with the livestock, the blankets and the pots. Men own the ponies and weapons."

It was an interesting concept. While the men ruled the clans, it was the women who claimed ownership to most everything. And if it took something this monumental to woo a potential mate, Brishen wondered what a Quereci man had to do to gain a second and third wife.

Gaeres's frowned deepened at Brishen's silence. "Is my reason to join you unacceptable?"

Brishen hid a smile, doubting that the full force of a Kai grin would be seen as friendly. "Not at all. I can think of few things more admirable to fight for than the favor and affection of a fine wife."

As soon as the words left his mouth, something knotted inside him loosened, allowed him to breathe easier. He had such a wife, and he'd follow the wisdom of his own words. Ildiko was worth fighting for. Resentful of the *Elsod*'s insistence that he remarry, he turned a jaundiced eye on her. "We have four now. Is it enough to harness the dead?"

"It's better than two or three," she hedged.

He growled. She wouldn't be satisfied until he had a hundred Wraith Kings, and even then he doubted it was enough. Whether the memory warden approved or not, they were out of time. No word from Gaur had arrived, and they had four men willing and ready to suffer through the ritual that would allow them to fight the *galla* and maybe survive the battle.

It was after midday when he sought his bedchamber for the first time in three days. He stared at the closed door, imagining Ildiko sleeping in the bed they shared and in which they had found such joy. He hadn't shared it with her since she accused him of trying to breed her.

He flattened his palm against the door. It wasn't true. Not that at least. A child by his human wife would cause more problems than it would solve, even if she could conceive. The Kai wouldn't allow a bastard such as Anhuset on the throne, and she was a full-blood Kai. They'd revolt in an instant if anyone other than a legitimate Kai of pure blood sat on the throne. Ildiko didn't know that, and her remark that she was lesser to the Kai because she couldn't bear his heir was wrong. It didn't matter if she bore him a dozen children.

She was right in that he'd become ravenous and desperate. Brishen always hungered for her, dreamed of her when they were parted, eager to sink into her arms when he returned. It was a luxury he'd taken for granted—days, months, years to indulge in the love of his beautiful, ugly wife. Now, time slipped through his fingers, and with it the woman who meant everything to him. He fought the shackles binding him to a role and a throne he never wanted. His terror at the idea of losing Ildiko made him hold on to her harder in whatever way he could. With the affections of his body and the devotion of his soul. Somehow one began to overshadow the other, and Ildiko finally refused him in her mistaken belief that his desperation sprang from the want of an heir.

It still hurt, still gutted him, but he began to see past the anger and the pain to understand why she did it. Serovek was right. He needed to look harder.

He placed his other hand on the door and considered for a moment, wondering. The *Elsod* said he was the direct recipient of magic that had not suffered the fade of several generations thanks to a mother who probably bathed in and drank the blood of innocents to retain her illusion of youth. He'd been raised to believe his power was as diminished as the peers of his generation and never tested it beyond the spells he'd been taught were within the reach of his reduced capacity. He had never tried before. What if he stretched a little farther?

The spell to open the door whispered on his lips, the power flowing down his arms. He concentrated, imagining the grain parting like water sliding through his open fingertips. He almost lost focus when the wood softened under his palms, melting like hot candle wax, dissipating until it was no more substantial than revenant smoke from an old cooking fire.

Brishen took one step, then another, passing easily through the door. Once inside the room, he turned and watched the wood solidify. Strong, heavy planks and strap hinges that could withstand several strikes of a battering ram before giving way. Excitement surged within him, carrying regret on its back. The *Elsod* was right. He possessed a stronger, older strain of magic, and soon he would let it burn bright, burn hot and burn out, never to ignite again. Fate possessed a malicious sense of humor sometimes.

Ildiko lay as he imagined her, on her side with her back to the door, nearly buried by a pile of blankets and furs with only her red hair visible. The fire in the hearth had gone out, plunging the chamber into a sepulchral darkness easy for a Kai to navigate, impossible for a human.

He padded silently to her side of the bed and found a spot on the floor to sit, his back propped against the mattress, legs stretched out to the wall and crossed at the ankles. Brishen wanted to crawl in bed with her, haul her into his arms and hold her close. Just hold her. That was all. He hadn't done so in days, and his craving ran deep. But this separation was of his making, and he hesitated, unwilling to wake her. Unwilling to risk another rejection. He lay his head back on the mattress and closed his eyes, content to listen to her light, steady breathing.

Sleep had almost overtaken him when a rustle tickled his ear followed by a hesitant touch on his head. Ildiko's fingers glided along his scalp, teasing loose strands tucked behind his ear. Brishen didn't move, content to sit docile under her caress.

"I'm glad you're here," she said.

It was a simple statement but said with such warmth that he almost groaned her name. "So am I," he replied in a voice gone hoarse. Never before had they been this far away from each other, and he hadn't even left Saggara. She welcomed him back with gladness, as she always did.

Still cautious and afraid he might destroy this detente between them, he avoided the subject of their earlier argument. "What did you think of the Quereci chieftain's son, Gaeres?"

Her fingers paused in their combing of his hair before taking up their work. "My interaction with him was brief. I thought him proud and purposeful. Certainly unafraid."

Brishen couldn't agree more. He envied Ildiko's talent for sussing out a person's character in even the briefest of encounters. "He's agreed to do this because he wants to marry later."

Once more her fingers rested idle, this time near his nape. He shifted so they'd brush against his skin. "Good gods," she said. "A Quereci woman must be formidable indeed if a suitor has to fight *galla* to prove himself worthy of her hand."

They both laughed, and Brishen savored the sound of her laughter, something he rarely heard from her these days. "We're all moved by something we want more fiercely than anything else."

"Staying alive and not being devoured seems worthy enough to me," she said dryly.

"His reasons aren't as noble as Megiddo's, but I understand them better."

"I know nothing of warrior monks, but I liked Megiddo from the moment I met him." She traced the rim of Brishen's ear, making him shiver. "There's something regal about him, along with a humility you don't often see in people. I suspect the ways of a priest called out to him when he was still tethered to lead strings."

They stayed silent after that, Brishen lost to the feel of Ildiko's hand in his hair even as the cold from the floor numbed his legs and backside. He forced himself not to tense when she ended their quietude, her tone sharp.

"No reply from Gaur. I've checked with the pigeon keeper enough times that he now hides when he sees me. I'm ashamed of my homeland. Your ally offers nothing while the enemy that planned your capture and torture sends two of their own to help you." Her fingers tightened in his hair, loosening when he hissed. "Sorry, my love."

He forgave her instantly with those magic words. "In their defense," he said, "Gaur is still a distance, even for a fast bird. And Belawat doesn't know it's assisting me. I suspect when Rodan finds out, Serovek will have to answer for a few things. As for the monk, he may be Beladine-born, but his allegiance is very much aligned with his order. Were Belawat to declare war on that brotherhood, there's no question on which side Megiddo would fight."

An earlier suspicion reared its ugly head. Brishen hesitated in mentioning it, but he wanted nothing hidden between them, even when it was painful. "Why did you invite Cephren's wife and daughter for a private meeting after supper? The favoritism was obvious." And resented by others. Many disapproved of Ildiko as queen, but that didn't make her any less influential or her attention any less coveted.

She was quiet for so long, he didn't think she'd answer. Her hand left his hair to retreat under the blankets. He mourned the loss of her touch. When she finally spoke, her voice was guarded. "The Lady Ineni is educated, well-spoken and thoughtful. I'm told she's even skilled with knives and the bow. Her suggestion regarding the wind dike was brilliant."

She paused again. Brishen's gut churned in anticipation of her next statement. He knew what she'd say.

"She would make an acceptable queen, Brishen."

He surged to his feet to loom over her. "Stop it, Ildiko." Her eyes rounded, and she sat up. Swaddled up to her neck and down to her wrists in a heavy sleeping gown, she reminded him of a wraith herself—pale skin, pale gown, strange, haunted gaze. "Stop matchmaking me with every Kai woman who strolls through Saggara's doors. Last I checked, I still had a wife, one I'm more than happy to keep." He took a breath, striving to conquer his anger. "Are you that eager for your freedom?"

Her voice rose to match his. "I'm not a captive. There is no freedom to seek, only duty to fulfill." Her tense features softened, as did her tone. "You heard what the *Elsod* said."

"I don't care what that crone spouts! I refuse to accept such a fate! It's defeat, and I won't be defeated. Not by *galla*, not by politics nor the machinations of ambitious court parasites." He clenched his fists and strove for calm. "I will save my kingdom," he said quietly. "And my reward will by my wife at my side."

Slender fingers curled around his wrist and squeezed. Ildiko's eyes were glossy in the darkness. "Promise you'll return to me, alive and whole."

"Promise you'll be here for me to return to," he countered.

"I swear it."

He rested one knee on the bed and bent to place his hands on either side of her. "I'm not desperate for a child, Ildiko. I'm desperate for my wife. That's it. No matter what you believe, you aren't lesser. Not to me. You are all." Her eyelids fluttered down, and a small sob escaped her parted lips. "Lay with me. Give me the memory of your touch so I may carry it with me when I ride against the *galla*."

She lunged for him, wrapping her arms tightly around his neck and pulling until they both fell back on the bed together. Her gown and his garb soon landed in a heap on the floor. They lay beneath the covers, skin to skin as their hands mapped journeys over each other's body.

Ildiko cupped Brishen's face. "It's so dark in here. Except for your eye, I can't see you."

He kissed her, tracing her lips with the tip of his tongue, before sliding into her mouth to gently tease her tongue. When he pulled back, they were both gasping. "That's not true," he said between planting more kisses across her forehead, cheeks and nose. "Dark or not, you see me. From that first day in the gardens at Pricid— our wedding day—you've always seen me."

She held him close, with her arms around his shoulders and her legs around his waist. He rested in the hot cradle of her thighs, his erection pressed at the entrance of her body. "Forgive me," she implored. "I only meant to be honest with you. Instead I was heartless."

He shushed her. "No condemnation between us, Ildiko. Not here, not now. No demons to battle or memory wardens to obey. No thrones to defend. Just us for now." For always, he thought.

Later, he wondered that their lovemaking didn't set the bed linens on fire. As desperate as before, it was no longer tainted by his fear of her abandonment or her misunderstanding of his affections.

In the post-coital languor, they lay together, Ildiko drawing shapes on Brishen's chest and stomach with a fingertip. She sneaked in a kiss on his nipple, then blew a draft across its tip to tease him. He jumped and covered the sensitive nub with one hand. He glided his claw tips across her buttocks, not touching, but close enough to disturb the air and tickle her skin.

It was her turn to jump. "Stop that."

He kissed the top of her head, unrepentant. "Vengeance."

She nestled even closer against him, and her breathing slowly deepened. Brishen thought her asleep until she spoke in a drowsy voice. "What are you thinking?"

Within their peaceful cocoon, he was reluctant to speak aloud his grim musings. But she asked, so he told her. "That I can't fail in this endeavor."

"You won't fail," she declared, staunch in her belief. "And you will be revered. The great Kai king who saved a kingdom and possibly an entire world."

He sighed and hugged her, careful not to clutch too hard. If he held her as hard as he wanted, he'd break her. She settled into him and was soon slumbering, breath ghosting warmly across his chest. "I would have been content to live my life as just Brishen," he whispered into her hair. "Who was loved by Ildiko."

CHAPTER TWELVE

"Saggara is close." Kirgipa stared after a wagon that rumbled into the crowd, loaded with goods and people. Wheels creaked and the oxen in their traces snorted as they strained to pull the heavy cart down the rutted path that led from Escariel's docks to the town itself.

The noise was deafening. Across the banks, a black roiling wall of *galla* shrieked and gibbered its frustration at their inability to reach the prey in sight. The river sang back, taunting the horde. Livestock and transport animals bleated and whinnied, instinctively recognizing the too-close proximity of a deadly predator. Horses reared, fighting their riders, and more than a few people were almost trampled when a team of six overpowered their driver and raced through the town.

Kirgipa had surrendered the queen to Dendarah, whose warrior training made her a better child-minder in the dangerous chaos. Necos tapped his ear and shook his head. Kirgipa repeated her statement with a shout.

"Less than an hour on horseback from Escariel. No more," he shouted back.

They had reached the port town a few hours earlier, noting with alarm how the few *galla* following them had suddenly multiplied into another horde. There wasn't one main body of demons poisoning the land and tracking the Kai.

Hundreds of carts stuffed with both people and their possessions packed the main road. Soldiers on horseback wove through the crowd, breaking up impromptu brawls over wagon space and doing their best to keep order. Dendarah's gaze swept back and forth across the chaos milling around them. "Good luck trying to get such transportation," she yelled. "Even if we had coin or something valuable to barter, no one is giving up their ride."

Necos pointed to a wagon parked away from the main bustle. Still half empty, its driver leaned from his high seat, counting out the coins a Kai man pulled from a satchel. "Stay here. I'll try to get seats. At least one. You and I can walk while Kirgipa rides with the baby."

He returned, scowling. Dendarah looked beyond him to the cart, still with more than enough room for the three of them waiting. "Don't tell me he said there wasn't room?"

"There's room," he snapped. "For a king's fortune in fare. The people sitting in there now must have given up everything they own for a place."

Dendarah's expression darkened. "Take the baby. I'll talk to him. There are all kinds of ways to barter." Her hand on the hilt of her dagger promised negotiations would be neither friendly nor up for refusal.

Necos held her arm. "You know we don't want to draw attention to ourselves. Cutting off a cart driver's bollocks because he won't give us a seat isn't exactly the way to stay unnoticed."

"I hate thieves," she snarled, but released her grip on the knife and gave the baby a quick pat on the bottom.

Kirgipa shrugged. Her feet ached, and she had two blistered toes rubbed raw from her still damp shoes. She was so tired, she could lie down in the middle of the road and fall asleep, unaware of her surroundings until a horse stepped on her or a wagon rolled over her. A seat on a rickety cart sounded wonderful but not worth the trouble of securing one. "We've walked this far," she said. "And we can get there in less than a night if we go now."

The matter was settled, and they joined the mass exodus of foot traffic from Escariel. The moon hung high and bright above them, flanked by a retinue of attendant stars. The main road was a quagmire of mud, softened by melted snow and churned up by hooves and wagon wheels.

They were a trio once more. Nareed had refused to leave the riverbank with her broken brother when Necos declared it time to leave. Kirgipa had at first argued with him over abandoning the two. Necos's pitying gaze rested on Sofiris, once more conscious but still vacant-eyed.

"What choice is there, little maid? We can't stay, and we can't force them to come with us. If she changes her mind and catches up, they're welcome to travel the remaining leagues with us."

She couldn't argue that logic. They left the two sheltered by the riverbank, their shapes slowly disappearing behind a curtain of gently falling snow.

Kirgipa turned for a last look at the Absu and the screaming *galla* on the other side before putting her back to the scene and her gaze on distant Saggara. She prayed to whatever gods might still hear a Kai prayer that her sister lived and was herself not far from the redoubt's safety.

They were once again back in a throng of Kai, fleeing their hunters. Dendarah passed the queen back to Kirgipa. She and Necos took up positions on either side, using warning expressions and well-placed elbow jabs to keep others from walking too close to them.

The road widened once they left the town boundaries, easing the congestion. Those on foot spread out, drifting away from the road and the wagons that splattered mud on any unlucky enough to travel behind them.

Kirgipa and the guards caught up with a pair of Kai—fishmongers by the smell of them. One wore a faded red hat woven of yarn and oddly enough, fishing line. Bait hooks hung from the stitches in a glittering array, giving the hat an almost jeweled appearance. His companion's head gear was less flamboyant, though Kirgipa gawked at the dried fish tail he wore around his neck as either a talisman or charm.

She was so caught up by their appearance that she didn't notice her companions' attention until Necos caught her elbow to slow her down and let the two walk past them.

"I heard the king as left for Saruna Tor with the *kapu kezets*. His queen went with him as did the Beladine margrave and two others," Red Hat said.

Necos and Dendarah pretended their attention was elsewhere as they listened.

Fish Tail eyed his friend doubtfully. "Who told you that? And who's looking after Saggara?"

Red Hat punched him on the arm. "Are you deaf? The news is running through this crowd like fire. A war *sejm* is overseeing things, with that battle axe Mertok making sure none of them think to take the throne while the *herceges* is gone.

"You mean the king."

Red Hat whistled. "That will take some getting used to. The young prince as king. Never imagined such a thing. Not with all those children his brother sired. Every last one gone in a night."

"I can see it. Brishen always ruled Saggara and its territories with a fair hand. If he survives the fight with the *galla*, he'll make a decent king. I don't know if I'll get used to a human queen though."

A third Kai, walking close by, added her remarks to the conversation. "The queen of the Kai should be a Kai herself," she said. "Besides, who will rule once Brishen Khaskem is dead and no heir to succeed him?"

Necos casually lengthened his stride until he stood on Red Hat's other side. "Why is the king going to Saruna Tor?"

Fish Tail gestured at Necos and smirked at Red Hat. "See? Not everyone has heard this news."

Red Hat hissed at him and answered the question. "Rumor has it the *kezets* have a plan to drive back the *galla*. The Beladine margrave is helping him, along with a mountain chieftain and a monk. One Kai and a pack of humans. Never thought I'd see that either."

Necos thanked him and eased back into place next to Kirgipa. He gradually guided the two women away from the main body of traveling Kai until they gained enough distance to talk without being overheard.

Dendarah rubbed her eye, a gesture that revealed her fatigue. "Well, with everyone thinking the Khaskems of Haradis dead and

Brishen made king, no one will be actively looking for other survivors of the royal house. But the trip to the tor alters our plan if the *hercegesé* isn't in residence at Saggara. Is it possible her personal maid stayed behind?"

"I doubt it," Kirgipa said. "Sinhue would go with her. There'd be no reason for her to stay behind. Her duty is to the *hercegesé*."

Necos watched the crowd as it moved past them. Hundreds of displaced Kai who would join many more already at Saggara. "Then we continue as we have been. Find sanctuary at Saggara with my wife, my child and my sister. When the *hercegesé* returns, we'll seek her help.

Dendarah twitched a corner of ragged swaddling over the baby's bare shoulder. "Can you truly trust her?"

Kirgipa lifted her shoulders. "I hope so. I didn't know her long, but she was kind to me and Sinhue."

"And not every queen is like Secmis," Necos said. "Precious cargo is troublesome cargo. We must turn her over to her living relatives. She is the rightful ruler of Bast-Haradis."

Duty. Kirgipa sighed. It always came back to duty.

Dendarah's gloomy statement didn't lift her mood. "Let's hope there's still a Bast-Haradis for her to rule when this is done."

CHAPTER THIRTEEN

The camp lay within sight of Saruna Tor, its swell like the hip of a curvaceous woman rising from the flat plain that surrounded it. White menhirs decorated its peak, gleaming dully in the frosted moonlight.

Ildiko sat cross-legged on a thick horse blanket near the entrance of the tent she shared with Brishen. Sinhue sat on one side of her and Anhuset on the other, all three sharing a pot of hot tea as they watched the gathering of men at another fire across the camp. Quereci, Beladine and a single Kai crouched in a makeshift circle, passing flasks back and forth as they threw dice between them. Cheers alternated with groans as winnings and losses traded hands in unending bets.

Anhuset was the first to speak, keeping her voice soft so as not to disturb the *Elsod* and *masods* who slept in the tent nearby. "You still won't be able to hear them no matter how hard you stare."

Ildiko harrumphed and huddled deeper in her cloak. "I don't want to hear them. They're planning the details of their deaths and doing it as if they're betting on a horse race and picking the best odds. I think they've emptied a barrel of wine between them. And they're dicing!"

Their party had left Saggara and reached Saruna Tor in a day. Ildiko batted away Brishen's halfhearted suggestion that she stay behind and set to packing warm clothes for a long day's ride and a night spent out on the plains. Her hands shook as she and Sinhue folded and stuffed clothes into satchels. Soon, Brishen would transform into something otherworldly and ride to battle against something so loathsome it polluted the earth on which it roamed. She'd been queasy for hours knowing what loomed ahead.

Anhuset's questions pulled her from her thoughts. "How else would you have them do it? Sit there wringing their hands and tearing their hair?"

Why not? It worked for Ildiko. "I don't know," she said. "It just seems strange."

The Quereci, Gaeres, suddenly leapt to his feet and did an impromptu celebratory jig, cheered on by his men who had accompanied them from Saggara. Serovek slapped the ground with his palm, mouthing a scorchingly vulgar word even Ildiko, from her distant spot, could easily interpret.

Brishen's cousin snickered. "I'll wager the Stallion just lost a prized pony or saddle." She eyed Ildiko askance. "This is the eve of a battle. Of the four men who will face the *galla*, only two know each other as more than brief acquaintances. They'll have to depend on each other in the worst circumstances, trust that each will have the other's back against things that felled a capital and devoured half its citizens in a single night. This is a way for them to learn about their fellow warrior, build trust and assure themselves they aren't alone in this task."

Sage words from a seasoned fighter. Anhuset had always fascinated Ildiko, never more so than now. "How did you prepare before you fought?"

The other woman gave a half shrug. "Much as they're doing now. Diced for a treasure, drank good wine with friends. Swived a well-hung Kai soldier all night."

"I can't speak for the rest, but the only person Brishen will be swiving tonight is me." She grinned at Sinhue's choked laughter and Anhuset's startlement . The warrior woman matched Ildiko's grin with a pointed one of her own.

"Wouldn't it have been better to conserve your strength and rest?" Ildiko mused after a moment.

"I'll sleep long and hard when I'm dead. You defy death by celebrating life."

It was a down-to-earth philosophy to which Ildiko could relate. She sought out and found Brishen, bent to toss a handful of dice into the middle of the circle. He groaned while a smiling Megiddo thumped his chest with a triumphant fist. The nearby campfire planished his hair in flickering shades of deep red and silver. Her lingering amusement faded away. "Are you afraid for him?"

Anhuset didn't answer right away. Patterns of pale and dark yellow swirled in her eyes. "We've known each other all our lives. My first memory is of his face. My guts haven't stopped churning since the *Elsod* revealed what he would have to do to send the *galla* back."

"I wish I could take his place." She wouldn't have a clue about what to do, but she'd seen his broad shoulders bow at what lay before him.

"You'll carry your own burden while he's gone." Anhuset glanced at Sinhue who sat nearby, listening, and shrugged. "Bast-Haradis shudders in its death throes. It's only a matter of time before Belawat and Gaur start circling its carcass. You have to hold this kingdom together for Brishen so there's something for him to rule when he comes back." Her gaze, wolfish and piercing, froze Ildiko in place. "Do you think you're strong enough?"

How easy it would be to proclaim an absolute affirmative. Brishen had named her regent and put a *sejm* in place that, along with a military troop under Anhuset's and Mertok's command, was fiercely loyal to him. But such measures worked only temporarily, and rebellion often bred fast and hot under such circumstances, fed by those who thirsted for their own power.

"I hope I am," she admitted to Anhuset. "But I'll lean hard on you. On Mertok. On every Kai who owes their allegiance to Brishen."

Anhuset picked up a piece of kindling and drew symbols in the thin layer of snow at her feet. "That's a given. There isn't a Kai serving in Saggara who wouldn't die for him."

"I believe that, but it's me they'll see in Saggara's great hall, not Brishen."

"He's named you regent. In our eyes, you are Brishen Khaskem until he returns."

"What if I fail?"

Anhuset dropped the twig and swiveled to face Ildiko. "You can't fail," she said flatly. "Neither can he."

They fell silent, each lost in thought until Serovek looked their way and gave Anhuset a slow wink. Ildiko watched as the woman's spine went stiff as a broom handle. "He's enchanted with you, I think."

"He's annoying," Anhuset said on a growl. "And human." As if nothing could be more repulsive.

"I'm human." Ildiko pressed her lips together to hold back her laughter at the glare she received.

"You aren't winking at me or staring at my arse every time I walk past."

"Oh ho, you noticed that, did you?" Ildiko chose not to mention that she'd caught Anhuset eyeing Serovek's admittedly attractive backside more than a few times in return.

Anhuset gave a disgusted snort. "Brishen with both eyes patched would notice. His Lordship isn't exactly subtle."

Ildiko picked up the twig the Kai woman cast aside and scrawled a lazy design of her own in the snow beyond her blanket. "I'll wager," she drawled, "that if anyone could remind you about the celebration of life on the eve of a battle, it would be the Beladine Stallion."

Anhuset sprang to her feet in one lithe motion. "I'm going to check the horses," she said, a darker blush painting her high cheekbones. She gave Ildiko both a scowl and short bow. "By your leave, my Lady Queen." She stalked off toward the horses, corralled in a makeshift pen set away from the fires.

Ildiko watched her leave. Beside her, Sinhue spoke. "For all her bluster and prowess, she's an innocent in many ways."

Serovek suddenly rose from his seat amidst the betting crowd and sauntered away, toward the horse pen. Ildiko gave a low whistle. "A Gauri court maiden on the hunt couldn't have planned that better."

"Nor a Kai one," the servant replied. "Yet sha-Anhuset has no clue what's she's done." She and Ildiko exchanged smiles.

Ildiko stayed outside until her eyes grew heavy. They had ridden through the day, changing their sleep schedules to accommodate the larger human contingent in their party. Ildiko had enjoyed the winter sun on her face, the blue dome of sky above her. She rode with her hood down, ignoring how the cold made her ears burn.

Brishen, riding beside her, had smiled at her from the depths of his hood and reached over to gently tap the tip of her nose. "You look as if you've taken another dip into a dye vat. Red nose, red cheeks and chin."

Unconcerned by the stain of cold and sun on her face, she smiled. "The Mollusk Queen who married the Eel King." A mismatch if there ever was one, but for them, somehow, it worked.

Sinhue undid her laces before Ildiko sent her off to the tent pitched next to theirs. Their travel to the tor required speed, and they had packed light. Warm clothing, weaponry, armor and two tents—a small one for Ildiko and Brishen and a larger one for Sinhue to share with the *Elsod* and *masods* who accompanied them. Ildiko knew were it not for her presence, Brishen would have been perfectly content to sleep outside.

"I can sleep outdoors, Brishen," she had argued as they readied for their trip. "You can keep me warm enough."

"Indulge me, Ildiko." Brishen glided a hand across her backside as he passed her to retrieve personal items from a chest. "I'll welcome the privacy of a tent. I'd like to fondle my wife without a dozen pair of eyes watching." She didn't argue after that.

For now, she was alone in their temporary shelter and dove under the blankets, still wearing her woolen shift and thick stockings. She draped her heavy cloak over the covers for extra warmth and burrowed under the mound until she was completely covered. Sleeping under the stars in winter was madness. Thank the gods they had brought the tent.

She was still awake and poked her head out of her makeshift cocoon when Brishen entered the tent. "Tell me you didn't gamble away your horse and armor."

Their tent was pitched far enough away from the fire for safety, but close enough that its glow painted one canvas wall, illuminating the interior enough that she could see more of him than a black silhouette. He laughed and began unlacing and unclasping his own garb. "No. Though I lost a barrel of wine to Megiddo."

Remembering Anhuset's words about the building of trust, she asked "Do you truly think they can help you?"

He sat down beside her to remove his boots and shed his trousers. Ildiko admired the length of long, muscled legs, the sleek gray skin pebbled with gooseflesh. "Of Serovek, I have no doubts. The other two?" He shrugged. "Who can say? They have their reasons for being here, reasons that have nothing to do with the Kai. But they're committed to this task, and that's all I can ask of them."

Unlike her, he slid under the blankets, naked. Ildiko snuggled against him, shivering at the touch of cold seeping from his skin and through her gown. "You should wait until I warm up a little," he said.

She slung an arm across his chest and wrapped her legs around one of his, tangling them both in her shift. "I don't mind. You feel good."

He hugged her close, clawed fingers ghosting lightly down her back from shoulder to waist. "I thought you'd be asleep."

"So did I, but I'm not as sleepy as I thought I'd be." Dread of the following day's events kept her wide awake and edgy. "Brishen—"

She wondered if he somehow had learned to read her thoughts when he said "Shhh. Let's speak of something else. The time for the ritual will be here soon enough, and I'm sick of talking about it.

"What do you want to talk about?"

"How about our wedding day?"

She raised her head to peer at him. Obscured by darkness, his features were nothing more than the paling and deepening of shadow, offset by a single yellow eye that glowed bright in the gloom. "Which part?" she said. "When we thought the Gauri and the Kai would attack each other across the aisles? Or when your own people contemplated your murder after you commanded they eat Gauri victuals?"

A brief glimmer of ivory teeth before his smile disappeared into shadow. "Neither, though I'm lucky to still be alive after the wedding supper. I'd rather talk about when we first met in the garden."

This was indeed a much better topic to discuss than Wraith Kings. The weight pressing on her heart eased. "Ah. When I told you I would have bludgeoned you had I seen you in my room. Very romantic. At the time I fancied myself a most unfortunate bride. Marrying a stranger who wasn't even human." She kissed his shoulder. "How wrong was I, and how glad I am for it."

"But you aren't wrong, wife. I'm not human."

"You know what I mean."

A faint tug on her scalp told her he'd lifted a lock of her hair. "I recall you standing in the sunlight, pale as a bleached fish bone and this hair gleaming red. I thought your head was on fire."

She chuckled. "And I was sure someone had set loose a two-legged wolf in the garden, teeth and claws and yellow eyes. I think my heart stopped for a moment when you slid back your hood."

"That's because I'm breathtakingly handsome," he bragged in smirking tones.

Ildiko nipped his shoulder this time, making him twitch. "And obviously vain."

"The gods were surely laughing at my predicament. I know my mother did when my father announced I was to wed a Gauri noblewoman."

Ildiko tried to sit up at that, but Brishen held her in place. "That makes no sense," she said. "She was ashamed of my marrying into your family. She certainly didn't seem too jolly about the whole event when we met."

He continued petting her hair and stroked her leg and hip with his other hand. "Secmis always found delight in someone else's misery or discomfiture, even if she disapproved of what caused it."

"Well that female scarpatine under my bed linens certainly showed her disapproval." She frowned, picturing his mother poised on her throne like a spider waiting to ambush prey. "Didn't you say you wanted to talk about something more pleasant?"

He kissed her forehead in mute apology. "You'll never know how relieved I was when I discovered that the mollusk girl I'd spoken with in the gardens was the Ildiko I would marry."

"Oh, I have a fair idea. I felt much the same about you. Eel boy."

Brishen laughed, tickling her side until she squealed and begged him to stop. They quieted once more. "Want to know when I first fell a little in love with you?"

"When I didn't faint from fright after meeting Secmis?" She'd come close, practically falling into Brishen's arms when they escaped the throne room.

"That was impressive. No cowering subject before her, but no." He tugged the blanket over her shoulder where it had fallen away. "It was when you ate the scarpatine and declared it tasted nothing like chicken."

She sniffed. "Then you're easily impressed. I don't think I fell in love with you just because you choked down a potato. Granted, you didn't have to engage it in battle before you ate it."

"You're hard to please."

She thumped his chest above his sternum. "I am not."

"Ouch." He rubbed the injured spot.

She took up the thread of the conversation. "I'm certain I fell in love with you when you carried Talumey's mortem light back to his mother. It might seem a small thing to you, but you gifted a grieving woman with one last connection to her child and a chance to say goodbye."

That had truly been the moment when she realized how fortunate she was to call the Kai prince "husband." He had his faults, as did she, as did everyone, but the decision to subject himself to mortem sickness and carry back the memories of a fallen soldier under his command to his mother had given Ildiko a deep insight into his character, beyond courtship skills and martial prowess, beyond intellect and the status of birthright. He was a truly kind man.

Brishen suddenly shifted, rolling Ildiko until she stretched atop him. Strands of her hair fell across his face and stuck to his lips until she tucked them behind her ear. This close, and she could make out the angles of his cheekbones and generous curve of his mouth, the scarred socket where his left eye had once filled the space. She feathered kisses across the scars, over the bridge of his nose to his right eye which closed under her touch.

"If you were granted one wish, what would you wish for?" he whispered.

She pulled back to stare at him. For some reason the question frightened her, a desire spoken before a death sentence. "Why would you ask that?"

His brow furrowed. "Your heartbeat just changed. Why are you afraid, Ildiko? I'm only curious."

Ildiko lowered her head until her forehead rested against his chest. "It sounds final. So final."

He stroked her hair, tugging to coax her into looking at him once more. The yellow of his eye shone soft as candle glow, and a corner of his mouth curved upward. "It isn't. It will be a goal for me to attain." Both hands rested heavy on her back. "Tell me."

She swallowed hard past the knot of tears lodged in her throat and blinked hard to clear them from her vision. "I wish..." She inhaled and started again. "I wish for you to grow old with me."

He shifted a second time, sliding her beneath him until he lay heavy and warm on her from ankles to shoulders. "That's a good wish," he whispered in her ear. And I'll do everything in my power to grant it."

He kissed her then, the slow, careful teasing of lips and tongues that led to languid caresses and soon the frantic rustle of clothing and blankets. They made love in the waning hours, trading endearments and promises neither could guarantee they'd keep. She cried out his name into his palm and hugged him until her arms ached as he rocked against her and groaned wordless praise into her neck.

CHAPTER FOURTEEN

"Holy gods, look at all those people." Kirgipa stopped in her tracks to gawk at the sight before her. Kai in the procession from Escariel eddied around her in a steady stream as they made their way to Saggara's gates.

They joined what looked like thousands of their countrymen already camped on the plain surrounding the garrison as well as in the stand of young woodland at its entrance. The air itself was warmer from the mass of people huddled in such close quarters. Every blade of dropseed grass that once surrounded the garrison was flattened or dead, leaving behind a soggy morass continuously churned by feet, hooves and wagon wheels.

Necos nudged her. "Keep walking, little maid. We won't get to the gates by standing here."

"This many Kai gathered in one spot...they will have hunted out any game in the area by now and consumed whatever food stores the garrison keeps." Dendarah's gaze swept the field, her mouth turning down even more with each pass. "This isn't a good place to be."

"With *galla* roaming about, it's the safest place for now." Necos stared down at the bundle in his arms, smiled and bent to bury his face in the cloth. Gassy sounds erupted from the swaddling as he blew bubbles against the baby's belly. The infant chortled her delight, tiny fists waving in the air before she planted one in Necos's hair and gave a hard yank.

The guard's whole body jerked. "Ow!"

The baby's gurgling laugh rose even more as her fingers wove ever tighter into his hair until the side of his face was pressed hard against her. He froze in place, eyes squinted tight in pain. "Don't just stand there!" he ordered his two grinning companions. "Pry her loose!"

Kirgipa didn't bother stifling her giggles as she gently opened the infant's tight fist and unthreaded Necos's hair from an impressive iron grip. Once free, he straightened with a wince and rubbed his offended scalp with one hand. He scowled at his charge, still nestled in the crook of his arm. She cooed at him, and his face softened. "I might forgive you for that in a decade or two."

"You might want to consider braiding your hair like we do if you hold her again," Dendarah suggested.

Kirgipa nodded. She had learned that trick the first night she pulled nursemaid duty. There was still a thin spot on the side of her head where the infant queen had snagged a fistful of hair and come away with several strands as her prize.

"Dendarah? Is that you?"

The guard lost her lazy grin at the sound of her name. Her back stiffened, and she slowly pivoted in the direction of the voice. Wearing insignia that marked him as a member of the garrison, a Kai soldier approached them. He tapped his chest with a quick fist in greeting.

Dendarah returned the salute, her face wiped clean of expression, her gaze wary. "Amasis. Good to see you." Even her voice was bland. She maneuvered in such a way that as the soldier turned to keep facing her, his back was soon to Necos and Kirgipa.

Necos clutched Kirgipa's elbow, and gestured with his chin. They melted into the crowd, leaving Dendarah behind to distract her acquaintance with small talk.

"That's an example of the challenge we'll face until we can reach the *hercegesé*," Necos said. "People who recognize one of the three of us. Who know that we're not related by blood or marriage, and that you haven't recently had a baby."

"Should we stay on the edge of the crowd then?" Kirgipa hoped so. They were already packed like salted fish in barrels in the procession headed to Saggara's gates.

"I'm not sure. You can easily hide in a crowd this size, but it might be better to stay on the perimeter and keep to ourselves."

Kirgipa peered into the hive of Kai. "Do you think my sister is in there somewhere?"

She didn't bother to hide the wistfulness in her voice. Her heart ached at the thought of leaving Atalan behind with the main body of Kai refugees fleeing Haradis. She had done her duty to the royal house as any good Kai would, but that knowledge didn't lessen the guilt of not hunting for her sibling. She was desperate to see her again—to celebrate the fact they had both survived and to mourn their mother who had not.

A light touch grazed her chin. Necos's thumb glided softly on her skin until she raised her face to his. "The Haradis survivors haven't arrived just yet," he said. His expression was both gentle and determined. "Remember the promise I made. I swore I'd find her for you, and I will."

She sighed and closed her eyes, the hard ache in her chest lightening at little at both his words and his touch. "Thank you, Necos."

Dendarah caught up with them just before they entered the first set of gates into the bailey. She crooked a finger, and they separated far enough away from the line to not be overheard. "I think it's too risky for us to go inside the garrison together. Too many of Saggara's soldiers first served in Haradis, and they'll recognize one or both of us. That isn't a bad thing if we were alone. But two of us traveling with a young girl and a baby might make a few curious, and I don't want anyone curious about anything."

"What do you think we should do?" Necos surrendered the baby to Kirgipa. "I don't want to split us up." He nodded to Kirgipa. "They're better protected with both of us here."

"Agreed, but there are ways to look separate without actually being so. And one of us will have to hunt down the *hercegesé*'s personal servant, so we'll have no choice but separate at one point."

"Do you know what Sinhue looks like?"

Dendarah shrugged and glanced at Kirgipa. "I vaguely recall her, but it's you who know her best, and you she'll speak to if you approach her. Until she returns from Saruna Tor with her mistress, we just need to wait and make ourselves invisible as much as possible." Her gaze slid over the milling crowd passing nearby. "For all that no *galla* roam here, I suspect this child is in more danger now, and her enemies are her own kind."

CHAPTER FIFTEEN

When the sun finally cracked the horizon, Ildiko fell asleep only to awaken alone a few hours later to the smell of a cooking fire and the scent of more snow in the air. She threw back the covers to search for her discarded shift. A shadow paused at the tent's entrance, followed by a scratching noise on the canvas.

"Good morning, Sinhue." Ildiko gave the servant a quick smile of thanks when the woman bowed into the tent, immediately found the shift and passed it to her mistress. "I assume I'm the last to wake."

"We're all a little slower than usual, my lady," Sinhue replied diplomatically.

She was indeed the last to join their group, refusing the last bits of breakfast but accepting a mug of tea. Brishen stood to one side conversing with the *Elsod*. He was clad in brigandine and mail but without his pauldrons or vambraces.

Serovek, a big man in plain shirt and trousers, looked enormous in protective gear that was a combination of mail and plate, boiled leather squares and a long supple coat that swept around his ankles. Beside him, Megiddo had donned a calf-length mail tunic, strengthened with scale armor over a silk tunic embroidered in runic designs. Gaeres wore the lightest harness of hardened leather with baldrics criss-crossed over his chest to hold two back scabbards for a pair of swords. All impressive and intimidating, and Ildiko wondered why they had armored themselves to fight against shadow that couldn't die.

Anhuset came to stand next to her, unarmored but bristling with weaponry. "They're armored on the *Elsod*'s suggestion," she said as if Ildiko had voiced her musings aloud. "*Galla* can't kill Wraith Kings, but would you want something that foul touching your spirit form?"

Ildiko frowned, her stomach roiling. She tossed her cooling tea onto the ground. "Can this get any worse?" She sighed at Anhuset's deadpan stare. "I suppose it can."

Brishen left the men to join them. Anhuset spoke first. "We'll break camp whenever you're ready."

"We're ready," he said, his gaze steady on Ildiko.

Anhuset bowed and strode away to smother the fires and speak with Gaeres's retainers. The camp broke into a flurry of activity that eddied and swirled around king and queen. Brishen lifted Ildiko's cold hand to his mouth, turned it and pressed a kiss to her palm. She stroked his cheek. "You left me too soon this morning," she said.

He straightened and pulled her against him. "Had I choice, I wouldn't leave you at all." His lips brushed hers. "Grow old with me," he whispered.

Her fingers dug into the hard shell of his brigandine. "Come back to me and I will." Queen or concubine, mistress or scullery maid, she'd somehow find the means to remain with him.

Brishen's features, tired and gaunt in the morning light filtering weakly through the snowfall, drew even tighter. "I need to tell you this before we leave. If I don't survive..." He hushed her burgeoning protest. "If I don't survive this battle, you're to abandon Saggara and flee to Gaur. Anhuset will take you."

She jerked in his arms. "No! You made me regent, to hold the throne. I won't walk away."

He gripped her tighter. "Ildiko, if I'm defeated, there will be no throne to hold, no Bast-Haradis to save. We will fall, as will Belawat and the Quereci clans of the Dramorins. Everyone will fall, including Gaur. But her capital is near the sea, with islands that can offer sanctuary from the horde. You have a chance to live."

The horror of such a world, such a fate for him and everyone else, made everything inside her recoil. She wanted to argue, to protest that she wasn't a coward, that she wouldn't run. But it wasn't cowardice he was suggesting.

If the Wraith Kings failed to conquer the *galla*, kingdoms would fall, one right after the other with Bast-Haradis dying first. There would be those who would refuse to accept such an end and see Brishen's death only as an opportunity to seize power. As wife of a fallen king, Ildiko's status would plummet from regent to human outlander, an obstacle to be removed in the quickest way possible, and that way would be murder.

She stared into his strange Kai face, scarred, handsome, and so dear to her. "You're right," she said softly. "You cannot fail."

His body loosened, and he lifted her braid to kiss the tip. "No, I can't."

The camp was cleared and their gear packed in short order. The *Elsod* rode pillion in front of her male *masod* and gave a short bow from her seat in the saddle as Ildiko's horse came up next to hers. "Your Majesty, have you ever been to Saruna Tor?"

Ildiko's curiosity when she first met the memory warden had hardened to dislike. Unfair it might be to blame their circumstances on someone who had found a way to possibly save them all from the *galla*, but she couldn't help it. The dreadful plan seemed as dark and malevolent as those things it was supposed to banish. She couldn't find it within herself to feel anything other than resentment for laying this burden on Brishen's wide shoulders.

"No," she replied in cool tones. "We passed it on our way to Saggara shortly after I married Brishen, but I'd heard about it beforehand. The magic of the Gullperi is said to still linger there within the circle of menhirs."

It was why they traveled there to perform the ritual. Anything to strengthen the power Brishen would drain from the Kai people to fuel the spell used to create the Wraith Kings and the one that would raise and control the dead.

"You disapprove of this plan, don't you? Or is it that you disapprove of the king's new duties?" The *Elsod*'s voice lacked anything that might give away her emotions, but Ildiko wasn't fooled. Such a question, no matter how objectively asked, revealed its purpose. The time for planning had passed. Now it was the time to do. Ildiko knew she had some influence over Brishen; so did the *Elsod*. And now the *Elsod* wondered if Ildiko would try to dissuade him from this path of madness at the last minute.

She met the old woman's gaze, hardly bothering with politesse and not at all with a smile. "I disapprove of the first, most heartily. The second is an unfortunate consequence. Neither is avoidable and how I feel about it of no consequence. We are, each of us, duty-bound." The two stared at each other until Ildiko asked "Is there anything else you wish to know, *Elsod*?"

The *Elsod* did smile briefly at her. "Nothing else, Your Majesty." She inclined her head. "May your regency be successful and brief, to end with the safe return of the Khaskem."

Ildiko slowed her horse and let the *Elsod* ride ahead. Sinhue caught up to her. "Is everything all right, Your Majesty?"

Ildiko didn't turn her gaze from the warden and her *masod*. "I hope so, Sinhue. I truly hope so."

Brishen turned and motioned her to ride alongside him, and she gladly acquiesced. Around and behind them, the others had grouped together into pairs or trios. Gaeres rode with two of his clansmen while the others fanned out around their entire entourage with the memory wardens in the center. Megiddo rode between Serovek and Anhuset, and Ildiko had seen more than once the smoldering looks the Beladine margrave had leveled on the Kai woman. She stared straight ahead, mouth grim and downturned.

Were they involved in less dire circumstances, Ildiko knew she'd find Serovek's dangerous courtship of the lethal Anhuset entertaining. She'd deny it with her last breath and back it up with a swing of her sword if necessary, but the Kai woman was attracted to the Beladine as much as he was to her, and she chafed at the idea.

Ildiko wondered if Anhuset feared censure or ridicule by her people for the attraction. Surely, none would fault her. Serovek wasn't Kai, but he'd been instrumental in rescuing Brishen from his captors months earlier. He'd saved Ildiko and Anhuset from a pack of magefinders and their handlers and tended the arrow wound a raider had plowed into Anhuset's back with adept, gentle hands. What woman, Kai or human, could not help but admire such a man?

They halted at the base of the tor, and Brishen turned to address their party in Common tongue. "We need a few people to stay here and keep watch. Warn us if something untoward suddenly appears on the plain that we don't see." Amusement curved his mouth at Anhuset's immediate mulish expression. Ildiko suspected she wore a similar one. Brishen turned to Gaeres. "You'll want to bring one or two of your people with you to the top of the tor, but can the others stay here?" Gaeres nodded and lapsed into the language of his people. Four of his six men reluctantly nodded but didn't argue.

The *Elsod* spoke then. "The ritual is both powerful and fragile. It can't be interrupted once it's begun. If it is, I have no idea of the repercussions or if it can be started again. Whoever witnesses it must remain only that—a witness."

Ildiko didn't like that sound of that at all. Before she could demand the *Elsod* explain more fully, one of Gaeres's men gave a warning whistle and pointed south. A dark speck on the horizon grew bigger as it drew closer, becoming a single horseman approaching them at a gallop.

"And who might this be?" Serovek wondered.

Ildiko gasped when the rider was close enough to make out the barding on his horse and the crest of his shield. "I don't believe it."

Brishen turned to her. "Believe what?"

She shielded her eyes against the watery sunlight, trying to see their visitor better. "So kind of them to not only rush with their reply but to provide so much help in a single man." She didn't bother hiding her bitterness or embarrassment. Some ally Gaur proved to be. Her lip curled. "Of all the soldiers Gaur might have sent, I would have never guessed they'd send Andras the Forsaken."

Serovek snorted. "That's promising."

Brishen glanced back and forth between her and the rider. "You know him?'

"Not personally, but I know that family crest. It belongs to a nobleman everyone believed would die forgotten in exile."

Brishen arched an eyebrow. "Then his fate has gone from bad to worse if he's exchanged exile for this." He dismounted from his horse and awaited the newcomer's arrival.

The rider reined his mount to a stop in a swirl of snow and swung from the saddle. He removed his helmet with its concealing face shield, and they got their first glimpse of Andras the Forsaken.

Such weary eyes, Ildiko thought. Light gray, piercing, they took measure of her, Brishen and the others. She wondered what he saw. Brown hair hung to his shoulders in waves, and he carried himself proudly. His gaunt face, dominated by a prominent nose and sharp jaw, might have looked too harsh except for his mouth which was finely shaped. For now, it was downturned but Ildiko suspected, for reasons she couldn't explain, he smiled more often than he frowned.

His gaze finally settled on Brishen. "You are Brishen Khaskem? King of the Kai?" When Brishen nodded, he bowed. "I bid you salutations, Your Majesty. I am Andras Frantisek of Gaur." He bowed to Ildiko. "Lady Ildiko. I haven't seen you since we were both children."

He remembered her, but she didn't remember him. Childhood was a long time ago. "Lord Andras, tell me you're here because my uncle received my message."

"He did." His fine mouth quirked, and the tiny laugh lines at the corners of his eyes deepened. "When the king summoned me to court, I thought I traveled to my execution. Sangur the Lame had other ideas for my fate." He eyed the others in the crowd. "I read the letter you sent him and offer my service in Gaur's name. That is if you still need Gaur's help."

"We do," Brishen replied. "Though I'm curious why you agreed to this. Has Sangur the Lame threatened to punish you if you don't volunteer?" He scowled. "I need a fighter willing to serve, not one forced to."

Andras shook his head. "I'm more than willing." He tucked his helmet under his arm and settled in to give an explanation. "Your wife already knows this story, I'm sure. My father was a high-ranking general who started an uprising in an attempt to force Sangur off the throne. He was defeated and executed. I refused to join the uprising but also refused to fight against my father. For that, Sangur spared my life but banished me and stripped my family of all our lands. If I fight this battle, and we succeed, the king will award some of my lands back to me. Enough that I may dower my daughter when she's of marriageable age."

Silence followed his speech until Megiddo spoke. "Others have fought wars for reasons far less important."

"Indeed they have." Brishen held out a hand, and Andras grasped it in his. "Welcome, Lord Frantisek. We are grateful for your service." He introduced the other men who would become Wraith Kings and then Anhuset, the memory wardens, and

Gaeres's men. "Let's get on with it then," he said once the introductions were finished. "I'll explain to you what's ahead of us as we ride to the peak. You're free to go your way should you change your mind once you know."

Andras stiffened. "I'm no coward."

Brishen swung onto his mount's back. "No one here is. And you still won't be a coward if you decide to walk away."

He waited until Andras remounted and guided his horse to ride beside him. They started up the tor's slope, leaving behind Sinhue and four Quereci men Gaeres designated as guards. Ildiko split her concentration between guiding her horse up the treacherous pitch and listening to both Brishen and the *Elsod* explain the ritual and its purpose to Andras. Neither spoke of how the power to drive the spell would be obtained and Andras didn't ask. She glanced at Anhuset whose face and expression were hidden by her hood. Her white-knuckled grip on the reins told Ildiko she dreaded these coming hours as much as Ildiko did. Unlike Ildiko, she would be one of thousands pillaged of her magic.

As they climbed the slope, the horses began to fret, tossing their heads and snorting. After a short slide backwards, Serovek dismounted with a frustrated curse and scowled at the others. "Unless you want to take a tumble with your horse on top of you, I suggest we walk them the rest of the way up."

By the time they reached the top, Ildiko had forgotten the cold. Her hair clung to her heated nape in damp patches, and her gown hung wet and muddied from hem to knee. Except for the *Elsod*, the rest of their party didn't look any worse for the strenuous climb beyond taking a few deep breaths. The old memory warden used a fallen menhir as a bench, and her wrinkled face looked almost green in the weak sunlight. Her *masods* hovered around her like startled butterflies, patting her hand and asking questions until she shooed them away from her with a sharp slice of her hand through the air.

Ildiko drew a water flask from the pack tied to her saddle and took a drink before passing it to Anhuset. The others did the same, and quiet reigned until everyone had drunk their fill and caught their breath. The horses remained agitated, stamping their hooves in the snow.

"They sense the magic here," the *Elsod* said.

Megiddo tilted his head in puzzlement. "I can understand why Serovek's or the Quereci horses might balk, but not the Kai and not mine. I'm a minor spellworker, and the Kai are born with their magic, are they not? Those horses would be used to the presence of magic.

"True, monk, except this is the work of ancients, of spellcraft woven by the Gullperi. In some ways it's much like what clings to the *galla* since they were also made by the Gullperi. Can you not feel its otherness?"

Ildiko didn't feel anything except a faint vibration in the earth beneath her feet, as if the tor hummed a dirge or a lullaby in a voice heard more by the soul than the ear. "What happens now?" she asked.

"Now we die," Megiddo said.

That might have been better phrased. Brishen turned to Ildiko. "Are you sure you want to stay for this? I don't think it will be...pleasant to watch."

She circled around her horse until she stood in front of him, close enough that only he could hear her words. Her fingers traced the stiff plating of his hauberk. "It will be horrible to watch and even worse to experience. My place is here. If I could, I'd be the Wraith King instead of you."

His hand was warm at her waist, his lips soft on her forehead. "Not in a thousand lifetimes would I let you do this. I love you too much."

"You would have let Anhuset do it."

His mouth curved against her skin. "That's what she thinks."

She sighed before pulling away. His face was cool under her hands, his black hair whipped into a wild mane by the wind. "Prince of night, come back and grow old with me."

His mouth drooped at the corners. He glanced at the *Elsod*, then back to her. "I can't if you refuse to remain my wife. Will we not sacrifice enough for duty when this is done, Ildiko?"

He was right. Here on this high place built by a vanished race who had left their magic and their malice behind them, she finally understood something profound. While duty was the price of privilege, duty nobly fulfilled deserved requital. For what her husband was about to do, he had earned the right to keep the wife he wanted.

She cupped his face and pulled him down for a hard kiss. The brass studs on his brigandine pressed into her breasts and stomach as he held her tight and kissed her back, always passionate, always careful. They ended the kiss on a shared gasp. Ildiko stared into his face, once frightening, now beloved.

"It's more than enough," she said. "I will challenge anyone, *Elsods* and Kai matriarchs alike, for the right to remain your wife. Even you, should you change your mind."

She squeaked when he lifted her off her feet, arms tight around her back, and buried his face in her neck. He said nothing, simply inhaled and exhaled slow, deep breaths while she stroked his hair. He finally put her down, bowed low over her hand and kissed her fingers. "Woman of day, you have made me formidable again," he said.

I would make you invincible if I could, she wanted to say. Instead, she smiled and bowed in return.

During their conversation, the others had moved away to give them privacy. Even the *Elsod* had left her seat on the menhir. She drew closer now and motioned for Serovek, Megiddo, Gaeres, and Andras to join her. "Lay the blades you will carry into battle on that stone." She pointed to the menhir she'd sat on earlier.

They did as she instructed and donned what armor they'd left off until now. Fully harnessed except for his helmet, Brishen bent to the *Elsod* when she crooked a finger at him. "I give you the knowledge of the spells. The one to make you Wraith Kings and the one to raise and command the dead. I won't be here to reunite your body to your spirit. That is your task, to do for yourself and the others."

Brishen nodded and held still, eye closed, as she touched a fingertip to his forehead. He jerked once as a tiny arc of lightning flared from her finger and lit his face. His hand spasmed, opening and closing in repetitive clenches, and he swayed on his feet. Ildiko cried out and Anhuset leapt toward him, arms outstretched to catch him if he fell.

He kept his feet, shaking his head to clear it when the *Elsod* lowered her hand. "Do you know it now?" she asked.

He blinked at her slowly. "Yes. Though I don't know if I can shape the words when it's time."

"You will," she assured him.

She began the ritual in earnest after that. Ildiko gathered with Anhuset and the pair of Quereci warriors who accompanied their party to the edge of the menhir circle. The future kings grouped in the center with their horses.

The two *masod*s shadowed the memory warden as she approached the horses. Each held two bowls while the *Elsod* held one. She pulled a knife from her belt as she approached Andras's mount first. He lunged to stop her but was jerked still by Serovek. "It isn't sacrifice. Wait and see."

The *Elsod* nicked the neck of each mount, letting the blood trickle until it made shallow puddles in each bowl—one for the horse each king would ride. She then cut hair from their manes and added it to the blood.

Her blade glistened red in the sun when she turned to the five men. "Your horses won't let you near them once you change, nor will they abide the company of the dead. So you will ride *vuhana*, their blood shadows." She gestured to Brishen. "I need your blood as well."

He nodded, removed a vambrace and shoved up his mail sleeve and gambeson to his elbow. Ildiko hissed when the *Elsod* cut a crimson line across his forearm. He turned it and let the blood flow into the bowl contain his mount's blood and mane. The other four men followed his lead.

"Thank the gods you aren't sacrificing the horses for this ritual. I might have abandoned you over that," Andras said as he watched the scarlet stream slide down his arm to fall into the bowl reserved for his horse.

When it was done, the *masod*s scraped up earth from the tor, tossed it into each bowl and mixed until a dark sludge formed. The *Elsod* ordered the Quereci to take all the horses out of the stone circle. None of them moved until Gaeres gave a quick nod. Despite knowing the warden's command served to keep the horses from panicking during the ritual, Ildiko liked the fact that the Quereci didn't jump to do her bidding until they received confirmation from the one they considered their leader.

The bowls were set aside, and the *Elsod* looked to Brishen. "It's time," she said simply, and the bottom dropped out of Ildiko's stomach. Beside her, Anhuset growled low in her throat.

Brishen faced his cousin, his expression shattered. "Forgive me. I would have chosen otherwise." He turned his back, disregarding Serovek's puzzlement at the apology. His next words were neither of Common nor bast-Kai, but of a language neither spoken nor heard for centuries beyond count. Ancient and arcane, they summoned recondite power, pulling it from the air, from the trilling ground and from all the Kai who stood within the circle. All except Brishen, their wielder.

Anhuset gasped, and her eyes rounded. She clutched her belly and bent as if to hold in something doing its best to burst free. She snarled at Serovek who leapt toward her. "Stay away from me, human!" He halted, staring at her as she straightened and dropped her hand. His gaze touched on the *masod*s and the *Elsod*, all three holding each other tight, as if loosening their grip would cause each one of them to collapse.

"Do not stop this," the *Elsod* warned the Beladine. "You'll kill us all if you do."

Brishen chanted on, oblivious to the flurry behind him. He passed a hand over the five swords laid out on the fallen menhir. Blue light, shot with bolts of silver, cascaded from his palm in luminescent waterfalls. It spiraled toward the swords, gliding along pommels and grips, tangs and guards until it slid up the blades like blood through veins.

A low hum joined the cant of ancient words and the vibration of the tor, the song of steel made alive and aware. Ildiko jumped when Brishen went suddenly silent. The air within the circle crackled and sparked, and she wondered if they might all ignite if they moved.

No one burst into flame when Brishen faced them once more. He looked the same, scarred and yellow-eyed with tired shadows dusting the skin below his eye sockets. But there was something different. She took an involuntary step back, noting that everyone else did the same.

Ildiko didn't possess a drop of magery. She couldn't summon it, control it, nor, until now, sense it. But the power that emanated from Brishen might have been a beacon from a lighthouse and all of them ships in the dark. He practically pulsed with it.

Serovek's gaze darted between the drooping Anhuset and the equally languishing memory wardens. "What have you done, Brishen?" he asked, abandoning titles and formality.

"The unthinkable; the unforgivable," the other said, and Ildiko's eyes went blurry with tears at the anguish in his voice.

The *Elsod* shook off her *masod*s and shuffled to Brishen, her gait slow as if she'd aged a score of years since he started the ritual. "You must go on, Brishen Khaskem."

He nodded, slipped on his gauntlet and reached for the first sword—his. Ildiko swallowed down the moan rising into her throat.

"I'll do it," Anhuset said, slipping on her own gauntlet. The deadness in her voice sent chills down Ildiko's arms.

"No." Serovek blocked her path. "I will." He held up a hand when Anhuset made to push him out of the way. "Do you really want this memory between you?"

Brishen joined Serovek. "He's right, cousin." His eye flared bright yellow. "Unless you seek vengeance—and if so, I stand before you, arms wide—then let him do it."

The same confused look passed over Serovek's features at Brishen's remark. Neither Kai enlightened him, and Ildiko held her tongue. Only six people knew the one element of the ritual guaranteed to see Brishen overthrown as king of the Kai, and each had sworn to die with the secret. Only his knowledge of it might survive, and only if he allowed his mortem light to be reaped by the generation unaffected by the spell.

"There is no vengeance, Brishen, and no forgiveness," Anhuset said softly. "Because there is no wrongdoing."

He closed his eye for a moment and bent his head. "Thank you, cousin." He straightened and clapped Serovek on the shoulder. "All that trouble to save me from raiders and now you get to skewer me," he said with false levity.

Willing to play the game, Serovek gave a disdainful sniff at the sword Brishen held. "Don't you usually fight with an axe?"

Ildiko locked her knees to remain standing and shook her head to wipe free the gruesome image of Serovek using Brishen's axe on him.

"I do," Brishen replied. "But it seems there are rules about weaponry in ritual magic." He handed the sword to Serovek who gripped it in a gloved hand. "Are you ready?"

Serovek raised a brow. "Are you?"

He nodded. His features were less haunted though no less weary when he faced Ildiko. He reached for her. "Ildiko..."

She screamed when, quick as a striking viper, Serovek pivoted behind Brishen, wrapped an arm around his neck and impaled him on the sword. At such close range, the blade punched through armor and mail, piercing Brishen through the back until it emerged, blood-smeared, below his heart.

To Ildiko's horrified eyes, it happened in slow increments. The sound of Brishen's surprised grunt when Serovek struck, the exhalation of air from his mouth, the bulge of his eye as his back arched from the force of the stabbing. Ildiko's wail was a whisper in her own ears, competing with the hard thunder of her heartbeat.

"Brishen!" She lunged for him, only to be lifted off her feet and slammed back against Anhuset. Serovek jerked away, yanking the sword out of Brishen's contorted body. He caught him as he crumpled, and they sank to the ground together.

Ildiko twisted in Anhuset's grip. "Let me go!" She scratched at her captor's arms, wishing she possessed Kai claws to slice her way to freedom.

Serovek's face was washed clean of color as he held Brishen. He looked up, his gaze anguished. "Let her go, Anhuset," he ordered in a voice no longer strong or confident.

Ildiko burst free from the woman's loosened grip and slid on her knees in the snow to where Brishen lay. Blood covered his torso and hands, staining the ground beneath him in a growing patch of crimson. "Brishen," she sobbed. "Oh gods. Oh gods. Brishen." She placed her hands over Serovek's in a futile attempt to halt the font of blood that seeped through his fingers from her husband's wound. Brishen's face was a sickly shade of old ash. Blood stained his lips, and he mouthed her name around a spill of gore.

Behind her, Anhuset's voice rang sharp and venomous. "If you enjoyed any part of that, I will rip out your liver with my bare hands and eat it in front of you."

Serovek's blue eyes, brilliant in his bloodless face, burned hot. "Don't insult me, Anhuset," he snapped.

The *Elsod*'s voice rose above the rest. "Move away from him. The change has started."

He was changing. An iciness under her hands, not of cold, but of death. "Brishen..." She shrugged away Anhuset's tug on her shoulder.

His lips moved, and she bent closer to hear him. When he spoke, his voice was only an echo of a whisper. "Go, love. Changing. Can feel it."

She stared at him as the hideous cold froze her palms where she touched him.

"Now, Ildiko," Anhuset ordered and pulled her none too gently away from Brishen.

The same coruscating blue luminescence that spilled along the sword blade and illuminated Brishen's blood in its light now spilled from the wound Serovek inflicted. It spread across his body, purling back and forth until he was completely suffused. The light began to pulse, mimicking the beat of a heart, and its color deepened from azure crackled with silver to cobalt, to indigo and finally to black.

Ildiko's lungs threatened to burst with the need to scream, but she held silent, watching as light, which had become darkness, swallowed her husband whole. It spasmed and stretched before collapsing in on itself, only to extend once more as if struggling to break free of a shackle.

"That is how *galla* look." Megiddo's words dropped like boulders into the sea of quiet.

Ildiko whined softly before casting the *Elsod* a murderous look. If the old crone had turned Brishen into a demon, she'd carve her into pieces and feed her to him.

The shroud of black light suddenly heaved upward with an audible snap. Everyone leapt back, and Anhuset shoved Ildiko behind her. Ildiko would have none of it and tried to dart to the side, only to be efficiently blocked by her guard. "Let me pass, Anhuset!"

"No."

Brishen's body lay in the snow, unmoving, bloody. His face was no longer the dolphin-gray with its undertones of pink and blue, but ashy-white with jagged black lines that stretched from his neck into his scalp. Ildiko was almost knocked flat on her back when she reached for him only to run straight into Anhuset's outstretched arm.

The dark light, now a separate entity, continued its heartbeat pulse. It began to lighten, reversing in color to what it was before—black to indigo, to cobalt and finally azure. Its edges solidified, taking on hard angles and lines, a macabre butterfly emerging from its cocoon.

The luminescence dulled and lost its incorporeal quality, thickening from cloudy light to a true, solid form—one dressed in lamellar armor with long black hair and a single eye that glowed a preternatural blue, as if someone had dropped a torch into a vat of Dragon Fire and let it ignite.

"Wraith King." Gaeres's voice held both wonder and horror.

The *Elsod* edged forward and froze when the king's incandescent gaze landed on her. "What do you see, Your Majesty?"

"The soul of the Kai," he said in a hollow voice devoid of any warmth, any life. "Age beyond age."

Ildiko recoiled as bile threatened to surge from her stomach to her throat. Whatever this eidolon was, it wasn't the Brishen she knew.

The eidolon crouched next to the still body at his feet and reached out a hand.

"Stop!" Ildiko cried. She battled Anhuset's confining grip again and lost.

The eidolon paused. Ildiko shuddered as its cold gaze caressed her. "Peace, sweet wife. I mean no harm."

She was torn between rejoicing and vomiting at the sound of such an endearment spilling from his lips. He reached out once more and flattened his hand on the still body, covering the bloody wound. More of the blue light flashed and pulsed. When he withdrew his hand, the wound was gone, the only marker of its presence, blood stains darkening the brigandine and surrounding snow. His skin was still ashy, but the ugly black lines were gone.

Ildiko gasped when the body emitted a slow exhalation and began to breathe.

Spirit Brishen stood to face Serovek. The margrave stiffened for a moment, as if in preparation for an attack. When none came, he held out the sword to Brishen. "Your Majesty, your sword."

Brishen grasped the weapon and slid it into the sheath at his side. "Now you know," he said to the other four. "You can leave, and there will be none to stop you. None to judge you."

No one moved until Serovek strode past Brishen and lifted the sword he had brought with him to the tor. Like Brishen's and the others, its blade glowed blue, tiny bolts of lightning shooting up its length to spark off the tip. Brishen reached to take it, but Serovek held it out of his reach, shaking his head.

He approached Anhuset who leveled a scowl on him. "Vengeance," he said with a half smile and offered her his sword. "You know you want to, sha-Anhuset."

"You know no such thing," she spat and stepped back.

He lost the smile but didn't retract the offer. "I would be honored if you did."

She glanced at Brishen who only watched her with a radiant blue eye. "Very well," she said, and Ildiko sobbed quietly at the furious torment in her voice. The Kai woman grasped the sword grip with a gauntleted hand and centered the tip on Serovek's torso. Her lips curled back, revealing the sharp points of her teeth, and she glared at him with eyes hot enough to immolate him on the spot. "You would punish me for the kindness of your healing," she said. "What do you want from me, human?"

Serovek pinched the blade's tip between thumb and fingers, positioning it against an unprotected space where lacing created a gap between the armor. "Everything, sha-Anhuset," he replied with a faint smile and stared into her eyes. He pressed lightly until the blade tip indented his hauberk. "Here," he said. "The weakest spot."

She huffed. "I doubt it, though I don't think cutting off your head or your prick will help you become a Wraith King."

Were this a less awful scenario, Ildiko might have laughed.

His mischievous grin promised a retort to put Anhuset's back up, and he delivered. "When I return, you'll share my bed, warrior woman, and be very grateful you didn't slice off my prick."

Anhuset snarled and rammed the sword through armor, through flesh and muscle and the gods only knew what internal organs. Serovek bellowed and instinctively swatted at his attacker with a gauntleted fist. She dodged the blow and jerked the sword free. It fell to the ground, blazing bright, as she embraced Serovek.

His knees buckled, and he sagged in her hold. Had Anhuset been a human woman, he would have taken them both to the ground with his size. As it was, she staggered under his weight, half crouched, leg muscles straining.

Blood spilled out of his mouth to paint his chin. He gripped Anhuset's arms. "Help me stand," he said on a wet, wheezing breath.

She heaved him into a straighter stance, blood seeping into her clothes where she pressed against him. Megiddo stepped forward to help, and she snapped her teeth at him. "Back away."

He held up his hands in surrender and retreated. She and Serovek half staggered, half stumbled together to where Brishen's flesh and blood body lay breathing but unknowing. Serovek's eyes rolled back in his head before he fell into Anhuset.

She grunted but held her stance and lowered his limp body to the ground next to Brishen. Her clawed hand fluttered over his face, not quite touching. "I will never forgive you for this," she whispered before standing. The *Elsod* didn't have to issue a warning this time. Anhuset retrieved the forgotten sword, set it next to its owner and waited.

Like Brishen before him, Serovek's body bled out its lifeblood into the tor's sorcerous ground. The black lines spiderwebbed across his face and neck followed by the devouring light that rent his soul from his body.

When it was done, Serovek's eidolon picked up his sword and bowed low to Anhuset, his eyes changed from cold-water blue to that unearthly cerulean. Brishen laid his hand on Serovek's corporeal body and healed the fatal wound.

The two transformed kings turned to the three men awaiting their equally gruesome fate. Ildiko turned away, unwilling to watch such wretched, purposeful violence. The agonized gasps and smothered screams were more than enough to haunt her nightmares for years to come, and she covered her mouth with her hand to keep from adding her own horrified shrieks.

By the time the ritual was finished and all the kings transformed, Ildiko was beyond numb. She didn't even startle when each eidolon set the tip of his sword into the bowls containing blood and hair from both man and horse. The contents smoked, emitting the foul odor of burnt hair fibers. Ghostly tendrils swirled and gathered, mated to the light pulsing from the swords. They gathered together, much as the light had done over each king's body, becoming solid, bigger, and darker until five horses—*vuhana*—stood together, snorting and pawing the ground. Spirit replicas of their flesh and blood counterparts, they looked upon their masters with eyes that burned white, without pupil or iris.

"Is it over?" she asked.

"Not yet, but we can't remain here for that," the *Elsod* said. She addressed the kings then. "Like you, the *vuhana* will not tire or thirst, hunger or bleed. Unlike you, they are nothing more than transport, a soulless replica of your horses. When you no longer need them, they will simply fade."

"What will happen to our bodies?" Andras's eidolon motioned to where five bodies lay still on the ground, alive and yet not. Without spirit, without awareness or emotion. Nothing more than dolls with breath and heartbeat. Ildiko hugged herself and clenched her jaw against the urge to weep.

"They stay here," Brishen said. "The magic of the tor and the magic I wield will protect them until we return and are united."

One of Gaeres's men burst out in protest, an emphatic argument only his fellow Quereci understood, complete with scowls and sharp hand-waving.

Gaeres translated. "He says they refuse to leave our bodies to the crows and wolves."

"Then they will die." The Elsod pointed to Brishen. "The Khaskem will call forth the dead. Angry, vengeful dead. They'll be as quick to turn on your men as the *galla*. All of us not touched by a king's sword have to leave this place. Now."

"She's right," Brishen said. "We've delayed long enough. Twilight rises. The time of revenants. The time of the dead."

To Ildiko, he seemed far away, as if what made her love him remained behind in the sleeping body lying nearby. That was until he eliminated the space between them. He looked to Anhuset first. "Guard with your life that which is most precious to me."

"I will," she promised. "Don't dawdle. Bast-Haradis needs you."

Ildiko reached out with bloodstained hands to touch him. He stood so close, limned in ghostly light. He stepped away. "No, Ildiko. We're pariah to the living now." He closed his eye for a moment. When he looked at her once more, the bright gaze had dimmed. "I leave my heart and my kingdom in your capable hands, wife."

She inhaled a shuddering breath and cleared her throat. "I will hold and treasure both until you return, husband." She bowed.

"Pretty hag," he whispered for her ears alone. "I wish I could touch you, one last time."

His words jolted through her as if he'd touched her with one of his lightning-tinged hands. "Don't say that," she begged him. "Not a last time, just one more time. And many times after that when you come back."

Anhuset tugged on her arm. "We can't wait any longer, Your Majesty. We have to leave."

They joined the reluctant Quereci who held the horses and trekked down the tor's pitch, moving as quickly as they could without tumbling to the bottom. When they reached the base, Anhuset barked out orders in Common tongue. "Don't linger. We don't want to be even this close when they summon the dead. I've no interest in joining their ranks just yet."

They mounted and rode a short distance away before stopping. The tor glimmered under the rising moon, white and ethereal. A colossal pulse of light shot from her peak, spreading out in ripples as if someone tossed a stone into the middle of a motionless pond. It washed down the tor's sides, flooding the base in blue radiance.

Brishen's voice boomed across the darkening plain, low as a dirge, deep as a crypt vault, speaking a language that raised the hair on Ildiko's nape and set the horses to rearing and whinnying in panic. Once she controlled her mount, she sought out the *Elsod*.

"What did he say?" she demanded. "I know you can understand him."

The old woman's gaze remained frozen on the lit tor. "Rise," she said. "Rise and come forth, ye sleepers and ye wanderers. Come forth and prepare for war."

Ildiko's horse heaved under her as Brishen's command filled the air a second time. The *Elsod* translated.

"Rise, rise."

And the dead obeyed.

CHAPTER SIXTEEN

Brishen strode outside the circle to watch Ildiko, Anhuset and the rest descend the tor's slope. They were silhouettes to his altered vision, leached of color except for varying shades of gray, black and watery green. Ildiko didn't look back. Brishen hoped she wouldn't. If she did, he didn't think he could stop himself from tearing down the tor's side and dragging her off her horse and into his arms. Such a reckless act guaranteed her death. He was wraith now, made of spirit rent from flesh by a sword doused in blood and stolen magic and warped by necromantic spellcraft. To touch the living was to kill them.

He returned to the circle and the other Wraith Kings who stared at him with fulgent blue eyes. The *vuhana* gathered behind them. Shadow mounts unfettered by a fear of the dead or the demonic, they would carry their masters into battle.

"Brishen..." Serovek began, halting when Brishen held up a hand.

He walked to the five bodies laid out on the snow, side by side. They were empty vessels now. Healed of their wounds, they breathed while their hearts beat and coursed blood through their bodies, but they were no more aware than the straw men he butchered in the practice arena at Saggara.

The ritual had split each man three ways, and they lived as body, sword and eidolon. The magic of thousands of Kai surged inside Brishen's spirit form, along with a yawning emptiness. He had never been more powerful than he was now, and never more hollow.

He crouched beside his body and loosened the lacings of his brigandine at the neck. He found what he was looking for tucked beneath his gambeson—a silver chain upon which a recolligere was threaded.

Ildiko had given the memory jewel to him as a gift. A cabochon of citrine quartz, it was his most cherished possession besides the enchanted urn that held his long-dead sister's mortem light. He curled his hand around the cabochon and recited an old spell. The jewel disintegrated into a pale powder, and from it rose a pale spark to hover before him.

"A mortem light," Megiddo said in an awed tones.

Brishen shook his head, gaze on the transient light. "No. Just one memory from a woman still living." She'd given it to him to subsume if she died before he did. As a human, she didn't possess a mortem light, but a Kai jeweler had used a spell to help her capture one memory in a recolligere. She gave it to Brishen shortly after he healed from his capture and torture.

He caught the spark in his hand. It dissolved into his palm with a weak lantern-flare before going dark. He closed his eye. One memory, and it was of him on their wedding day. He entered the room where Ildiko stood with the Gauri queen and a troop of servants. He viewed himself through her eyes, nothing more than a tall shape backlit by the blaze of afternoon sunlight. An outlander Kai with gray-skinned hands tipped with claws. Then he had addressed Queen Fantine, requesting a moment of his bride's time.

"It's you," Ildiko had said in a voice so full of joy, it made him gasp.

The memory, brief in time, prosaic in context, carried all her hope and all her wonder. Hope that she'd marry someone kind. Wonder that she would marry him. "Ildiko," he whispered, and her name was both prayer and lament. Thanks to her and that memory, he carried within him a bulwark against the frightful memories of the past and those he would surely make in the future.

He rose, surveyed the bodies that once housed their spirits, and turned to the silent eidolons behind him. "Brace yourselves," he said. "When our army arrives, they will be hostile."

The words he called up to summon the dead were drawn from the mortem lights of Kai who had lived when Emlek was a thatched hut on an isolated island and first used by a Kai necromancer whose fear of his own death was greater even than Secmis's thirst for power centuries later. They scorched his tongue and filled the circle marked by the glittering menhirs.

Snow-covered earth groaned under his feet as a glow, bright as day, pulsed from the circle's center and veiled the entire tor. The light faded, and the wind rose. From a zephyr's whisper to a shrieking howl, the wind spun faster and faster around the tor until a whirlwind formed. It rocked and twisted, reaching skyward to blot out the stars above the menhirs standing in the calm eye.

The spinning coil darkened to a black smoke, shaping spectral faces that murmured and shrieked, cried and laughed. The deafening cacophony abruptly ceased, and the violent tempest collapsed, revealing sky once more.

"It seems we have company." Serovek's comment cut through the sudden hush.

He didn't exaggerate. Brishen slowly pivoted. The eidolons and their *vuhana* horses were hemmed in on all sides by a turbulent, black miasma. Phantom shapes formed in its depths only to dissolve as quickly as they configured.

A column of the revenant smoke separated from the main body, drawing closer to Brishen until it stood close enough to touch. Amorphous and featureless, it grew more defined until Brishen stared at a human male dressed in the garb of a peasant farmer.

"Why have you summoned and bound us, necromancer?"

Brishen couldn't tell if the man spoke in Common, bast-Kai or any other tongue. In this moment, the language of the dead was universal. Instead of answering, he asked a question of his own. "Who among you were victims of the *galla*?"

The tenebrous vapor swelled. A wave of wordless fury washed over him from the restless dead. More columns of smoke parted from the mass and took shape. Mostly Kai, with a few humans, they faced Brishen, their eyes as silvery-blue as his. He suspected many more Kai still lurked in the roiling darkness, including his parents.

One, an older Kai man, inclined his head. "Nearly all the Kai before you fell to *galla*. We tried to save who we could, give them time to reach the Absu."

Had his eidolon a beating heart, it might have fluttered against his ribs. Brishen eyed the revenant. "Are you General Hasarath?"

"I am."

Brishen went to one knee and bowed his head. "Your courage and your sacrifice are known and will be commemorated." He stood. "Step forward, those who held the line at the river."

More shades broke loose to stand before him. Brishen sighed when he recognized one. "Ah, Tarawin, I had hoped not to see you here." Sorrow sat heavy on his shoulders. Less than a year earlier, he had brought home her son's mortem light to her. He wasn't surprised to learn she had sacrificed herself to save others. The only blessing in this tragedy was that her son had been dead too long for the ancient spell to capture his spirit and bind it to Brishen. The shame of it was it had captured hers. "It's obvious from whom Talumey inherited his bravery."

"I'm honored to serve you as my son did, *Herceges*." Her ghostly voice held no resentment.

Hasarath repeated the human revenant's question. "Why have you bound us to you?"

"The living can't fight *galla*. The horde is loose in the world, ravaging Bast-Haradis and threatening the human kingdoms. I call you and all our brethren to help us vanquish the horde and force them back to the void which spawns them."

The human revenant's shape blurred and pulsed, agitated. "We don't follow Kai. We owe you no allegiance."

"Then follow us. We aren't Kai." Andras joined Brishen. "All our world will die under a *galla* onslaught. They don't care if we're human or Kai. We're nothing more than meat to them. Help us so your descendants may live to boast of their ancestors' bravery."

A deepening hush gathered inside the menhir circle. Brishen's gaze passed over the vaporous dead who filled the circle and spilled down the tor's slopes. The cares of the living were no longer theirs, but to be remembered well and praised in song...even death didn't fade such an ambition.

Hasarath ended the stalemate. "The Kai follow you, Brishen Khaskem."

"As do we," the human revenants said in chorus.

Relief surged through him as heady and powerful as the Kai magic. "Then we ride."

The dead parted before him until he stood in front of his sleeping body and the bodies of the four men who would help him. He'd seen Ildiko's gaze flick between his two forms, desperate, disbelieving, with a hint of revulsion when it rested too long on his eidolon. Unlike the *vuhana* horses, his eidolon was more than a simulacrum. Solid, strong, without the weaknesses inherent to his natural body. And that was the crux of it, the reason for the flicker of abhorrence in her expression. He was no longer just different; he was unnatural.

"I should have trimmed my beard before we left." Serovek stroked his chin as he stared at his body and the dark beard shadowing his jaw.

A chuff of hollow laughter from the monk sounded behind him. "I doubt anyone will show up here seeking your courtship." Megiddo led his *vuhana* through the crowd of waiting dead and swung onto its back. "Will they be protected while we fight?" he asked Brishen.

Brishen hoped so. He once more delved into the memories the *Elsod* shared with him. Ancient incantations built on the foundations of Gullperi magic. He incanted protection wards, touching each body as he walked a circle around them, leaving behind a ripple in the air that crackled with lightning.

"They—we—are as safe as I can make them." He nodded thanks to Gaeres who led his *vuhana* to him and handed him the reins. The simulacrum watched him with solid white eyes before giving an equine snort.

He was the last of the five to mount and found himself staring at a nebulous black sea of shapes and vaporous faces. Kai and human, they awaited his command.

"Which way?" Serovek asked.

"Escariel." According to scouts and witnesses, a portion of the horde had broken from the main body and reached the township. In his altered state, Brishen could smell them on the wind, like rot from a cesspit on a hot summer day.

The *galla* would linger there for a short time, confused by the sudden absence of tempting magic emitted by the Kai living in or near the township. It wouldn't take them long to hunt for its newest source—Brishen and his army.

"They're trapped by the Absu on one side. Are you familiar with double envelopment?" Serovek and Andras nodded, while Gaeres and Megiddo shook their heads. "It's a pincer movement in battle. Attack the enemy from the front, sides and back. You encircle them, then annihilate them. With the Absu acting as a wall, the dead only have to flank three sides. Once we block the *galla* in, we drive them toward Haradis and do the same to the greater horde we find further down river. Use your swords to cut down any that break free of the net."

Andras cocked his head. "I thought *galla* couldn't be killed?"

"They can't. A cut with the sword will simply send them back to the breach, where they'll come right back out until we close it." Brishen looked to each man. "Ready?" At their nods, he wheeled his *vuhana* around and raised his sword above his head.

"To me!" he cried and rode down the tor's slope on the fleet-footed mount, Wraith Kings beside and behind him, and a host of shrieking, howling dead flowing like black water around them. A macabre hunt illuminated by moonlight, they tore across the plain.

They reached Escariel before the dawn broke, a two-day ride accomplished in hours. The *vuhana* Brishen rode looked like his living mount, except for the eyes. The similarity ended there. This creature didn't gallop, it flew, ground rushing beneath its hooves.

Escariel was a husk of the town he visited days earlier. Empty of Kai and every other living thing that could flee the overrun township.

The midden rot smell buffeted Brishen's face as they galloped toward the Absu. Strange chittering screeches accompanied the rancid scent, and he got his first true look at the *galla*.

Agile, twitching things with bowed backs and bony fingers as long as his arm, they cavorted along the Absu's opposite bank, waving skeletal limbs and clambering over each other like rats in a feeding frenzy.

Their faces...

Brishen was an eidolon, a creature born of necromantic magic that controlled the risen dead, and even his spirit recoiled at the sight. If these were the twisted results of Gullperi ridding themselves of their malevolence to attain purity, it was no wonder their brethren punished them for the deed.

Anger fueled his revulsion. These things had fed on his people and threatened to devour everything in their path. They were an infestation to be burned out, scoured clean and utterly annihilated.

Their dissonant screams rose to a feverish pitch when they spotted the kings, some even separating from the legion to hurl themselves against the river's invisible wall. The dead answered, trilling their own challenges as they lined up along the safe side of the Absu in infantry lines.

Brishen guided his *vuhana* behind the line, calling out commands to the kings. Megiddo paired with Andras while Serovek rode with Gaeres. Brishen plunged into the crowd of revenant to face Hasarath and the human leader who first refused to follow him. Both bowed at his orders to split their company, and soon the army separated into two distinct units, one with the monk and exile, the other with the margrave and the Quereci chieftain's son.

Solitary, Brishen faced a *hul galla* that repeatedly smashed itself against the river's unyielding barrier in a frenzied attempt to reach him. He imagined he looked like nothing more than a sweet meat to a pack of starving wolves as his magic streamed off him like blood. He raised a hand and slashed downward. "Now!"

The dead surged across the river in a black wave, unencumbered by the impediment of water. They flowed around the edges of the *galla* mob, shadow grappling with shadow as the demons sought to avoid the tightening net, and the dead blocked their escape.

Brishen followed Megiddo as his *vuhana* raced along the perimeter. A pair of *galla* squirmed out of a break in the infantry's rampart. "Cut them down, Megiddo! Cut them down!" He slashed at a third that ran straight at his mount and leapt on Brishen.

The thing was a strangling, scratching serpent that tore at his armor and tried to drag him off the *vuhana*. Brishen peeled it away from himself long enough to stab it. The strength and rage bled out, leaving only a black dust that faded to nothing. Lightning licked down the blade's hamon line as if tasting the bitter flavor of a first kill.

Another charged him, and the *vuhana* sprang forward to meet it. Brishen's sword sliced through the *galla*'s torso, leaving sparks in its wake, and the demon disintegrated.

"They can't be that easy to kill," Megiddo shouted as he decapitated another escapee.

"Remember what I said," Brishen shouted back. "You're just sending them back to the breach." Where they would emerge again and again until he closed it off for good.

They fought until the sun was high above the horizon. The dead pressed ever inward, building an impenetrable wall around the *galla*, until the horde heaved and contorted against its restraints and screamed its rage.

Were Brishen still bound by his fleshly body, he'd be half dead from exhaustion. Instead, exhilaration, power, and horror hummed through him, as strong as the Absu's current.

Serovek trotted up to him. "Too bad we can't set them on fire and have done with it," he said.

"You don't know how much I wish that were an option." Brishen signaled for the other kings to join them. "I'm not much of a drover," he said. "So if any of you have that skill, speak up.

"I've been herding since I was old enough to walk," Gaeres volunteered. "Sheep, cattle, or *galla*, herding is herding."

Brishen nodded. "I defer to your knowledge for how to get these things down river and into Haradis." He turned to Megiddo. "Then I'll need you and your rune circle knowledge to trap them there."

"Whatever is required, Your Majesty."

Brishen surveyed their morning's work. A vast, roiling sea of demons and revenants darkened the plain. Haradis lay to the south, not far for a tireless *vuhana* to gallop, as distant as the moon for kings made drovers to lead the damned that had destroyed her.

CHAPTER SEVENTEEN

Ildiko returned to a Saggara bursting with displaced Kai and rampant rumors of demon battles in the empty streets of Escariel and along the Absu.

Tents, yurts, and other temporary shelters spread across the plain. A makeshift city had evolved from the refugee camp, swelling with more Kai. Horse herds dotted the grasslands and flocks of chickens flapped out of the way with indignant squawks as her party rode to the redoubt's gates.

Only she, Anhuset, Sinhue and the *kapu kezets* had returned to Saggara. The Quereci clansmen who accompanied Gaeres to the tor refused to leave.

Ildiko didn't argue with their decision. She was, in fact, grateful for it. Their insistence in remaining at the tor meant they would not only watch over Gaeres's body, but those of the other Wraith Kings. Even the threat of roaming *galla* or the returning dead didn't convince them to leave. She had ridden away with their assurances to guard the tor and Anhuset's promise to hunt them down if they made off with Brishen's favorite mount.

The journey back to Saggara was grim and quiet. Except for a brief discussion of where to camp and when to leave, they each kept their own counsel, and their evening camp had been more silent than a funeral procession. Ildiko had tried once to engage

Anhuset. "Are you ill?" As a human, Ildiko hadn't suffered the draining effects of the ritual that sucked away Kai magic.

Anhuset shook her head but didn't comment. Whatever lingering symptoms plagued her, Sinhue and the *kezets*, none of them mentioned it to Ildiko or each other.

The entire *sejm* appointed by Brishen met them inside the gate—nine men and women chosen from the ranks of his most trusted vicegerents, justiciars and military officers. It included Mertok and Cephren, whose daughter Ineni had caught Ildiko's attention with her clever idea of flooding her father's dream flower field to create a bigger barrier against the *galla*.

Mertok helped Ildiko off her horse amidst a crowd of curious onlookers. "Did it work?"

The same question was reflected in the face of each councilor. "It worked," she said. "We saw from a distance the kings ride toward the Absu with the dead accompanying them." The sound and the sight still made her shiver.

Quiet cheers and murmurs of relief greeted her statement, and she wondered if they sensed their magic drain away, or if it was a matter of proximity. The farther out from the tor, the lesser the effects? No one looked sick or panicked.

One of the vicegerents answered her unspoken question. He leaned into the impromptu circle they created around her and lowered his voice. "We must meet as soon as possible, Your Majesty. Many of the Kai have complained of sickness. If it's plague…"

She let the statement hang in the air and the others shuddered. Ildiko might have done the same if she didn't already know the source of this "illness." She slid a glance to the *Elsod* who leaned against her horse, a weary old woman made even older by what had transpired at the tor and the loss of her own considerable magic.

"Please see to the *Elsod* and her companions and give me time to wipe off the journey's dust. I'll meet with you all in His Majesty's council chamber."

Once in the bedroom she shared with Brishen, Ildiko shed most of her clothes and sent Sinhue to rest, promising to summon her if needed. Clad only in her shift, she raised the lid of the chest at the end of the bed. Brishen stored much of his everyday garb inside, and she plunged her hands into the neatly folded stack of shirts, tunics and trousers.

She brought one of the shirts to her nose and inhaled deeply. It smelled of him, cedar and the sachets of dried herbs and orange peel nestled inside the chest to ward off insects and freshen the clothing. His body lay far from her, within a circle warded with necromantic magic and guarded by nomads whose loyalty lay not with him but with the man who rode with him as eidolon.

Shivering, she yanked the shift over her head, replacing it with the shirt. Not as long as the shift, it still fell to her knees. She donned one of her shapeless frocks over that and added a heavily embroidered tunic cinched at her waist with a wide jeweled belt. The ensemble was part of Brishen's bridal gift to her—apparel far more sumptuous than anything she'd brought with her from Gaur and uniquely Kai in its cut and style.

The best part was she didn't need Sinhue's help to put it on. She looked as shattered as Ildiko felt when her mistress sent her away to rest.

Ildiko sat on the chest to lace up her boots and paused, closing her eyes. The image of Brishen's expression when Serovek stabbed him would haunt her nightmares until she died, along with the memory of his body, still and bloody in the snow and his blue-eyed eidolon staring down at it with a dispassionate gaze.

"*I leave my heart and my kingdom in your capable hands, wife.*" They were his last words to her before she fled the tor ahead of the dead's summoning.

She raised her hands to stare at the trembling and curled them into fists before hiding them in her lap. Brishen had made her regent, putting all his faith in her ability to hold his kingdom together while he tried to stop the *galla* from tearing it apart. Ildiko had never been more terrified in her life—for her husband, for the Kai, for herself.

She took several shallow breaths and finished lacing her boots. Giving into her fear of failing him or losing him was a luxury she didn't have. If he returned—*when he returned*—she'd fall apart and cry herself sick. For now, she had a *sejm* to meet with and a country to rule. A young human queen over non-human Kai. What could possibly go wrong?

The *sejm* already crowded the council chamber when Ildiko arrived. While Anhuset had refused an appointed place on the *sejm*, she was present, a grim sentinel eyeing the rest of the chamber's occupants from a spot where she could watch the door.

Ildiko's first order of business was an abbreviated accounting of the events at Saruna Tor, and she fielded several requests for more detail.

"What spell did the king use to raise the dead?"

That one she could answer honestly. "I don't know. It was in a language I don't speak. Neither bast-Kai nor any human tongue I've been taught." She glanced at Anhuset. "Did you understand it?" The Kai woman shook her head.

"Stragglers leaving Escariel last say they saw a great mass of shadows cross the Absu and attack the *galla*. The were led by strange riders on horses with white eyes and seemed impervious to injury from the *galla*." The councilor recounting the eyewitness accounts was skeptical. "Surely, that can't be the king and the humans?"

Ildiko shrugged, surprised by how fast Brishen and his army of revenants traveled. "The dead and their generals aren't bound by time and distance as we are. Who knows how fast they can travel. Did the witnesses say if the *galla* were overwhelmed?" A blessing from the gods if they were, but if the scout reports held true, the greatest horde was yet to be encountered.

Mertok answered her. "I've stationed watchers near Escariel. I received a report shortly before you arrived. No *galla* have been seen on the river banks, but you can still hear them in the distance. Likely the main body of the horde following the Kai who left Haradis."

"We can't stop anyone returning to Escariel if they wish," she said. "But warn them just because it looks like His Majesty's army has pushed the *galla* back, it doesn't mean there aren't more still lurking on the shore or in the township."

Another councilor broached a subject that made Ildiko stiffen with dread. "We've had widespread complaints, mostly from the older population. A sickness. Every Kai of adult age has complained of it, though it doesn't seem to affect the young. Some fear it's the beginnings of a plague."

Ildiko willed herself not to glance at Anhuset. "Are any of you experiencing these symptoms?" She knew the answer but adopted a puzzled expression when each councilor nodded or replied in the affirmative. "Have they grown worse?" When they all said no, she tapped her chin and pretended to consider. "If it's plague, we'll know soon enough. Make sure the wells are kept clean and free of debris. We have a lot of people gathered in one spot. It will be too easy to poison the water supply from simple carelessness and neglect."

No amount of clean water would chase away the strange sickness the Kai suffered, but she'd use the assumption to her advantage to make sure they took necessary precautions to prevent a real outbreak of disease. Even without physical symptoms of illness manifesting, they'd learn their magic was gone the moment they couldn't reap a mortem light from a dead loved one. She'd have to lie through her teeth, pretend ignorance of its cause, blame it on the *galla* and pray the Kai's fear and hatred of the horde would convince them her suggestion held merit.

Until then, she had more than enough immediate concerns to keep her sleepless. Their dwindling stores of food alarmed her most. With as many refugees as Saggara housed now, and more to come, it wouldn't be long before they were decimated, even with strict rationing. Transport animals would become food, with the oxen teams slaughtered first, followed by the horses.

"Place additional guards at each storeroom and barn and watches on the horse herds," she instructed Mertok.

The meeting lasted for hours, and Ildiko was more exhausted when it was over than she was from the journey to and from Saruna Tor. Mertok lingered after she dismissed the other *sejm* members.

"Your Majesty," he said. "You should know there's already talk among some of the vicegerents and others that it's wrong to have a regent who isn't Kai ruling Saggara in the king's stead."

Anhuset's eyes turned a paler gold and narrowed. "Who are they? I'll be happy to disavow them of the notion."

Ildiko smiled. Thank the gods she had such a fierce supporter. "I don't think we need your particular method of persuasion just yet, sha-Anhuset."

She wasn't surprised by Mertok's revelation. Discontent and disapproval among the newly elevated Kai nobility had been a given the moment Brishen revealed his plan to appoint her regent.

"They'll have to swallow their gall for now. Brishen has named me regent, and I'll do what I must to hold the throne until his return." She'd likely be well and truly hated by the time her regency ended, but her husband would still have his throne. "Increase the presence of your troops in the great hall during supper," she added. "It's best to get a clear message across now instead of waiting until someone challenges me."

She didn't have to wait long for the challenge.

Supper, as usual, was a crowded affair, even more so as those who normally didn't eat in the great hall attended to hear Ildiko's summary of the Wraith Kings' plan to banish the *galla*. She answered numerous questions, careful not to elaborate on the ritual's effect on the five men and verified that yes, Gaur had sent a general of its own to help Brishen. She didn't mention they'd sent an expendable exile or that he'd come unaccompanied by troops.

She described how the magic used to make Brishen and the others Wraith Kings, rendered them mostly impervious to any harm inflicted by the *galla* and allowed them to control the dead who followed them. The *Elsod* attended the supper and confirmed everything Ildiko said.

One question rose above the din of voices. "How long will it be before the king is victorious and returns to Saggara?" The hall filled with an expectant hush.

Of the many questions she'd been prepared to answer, this was the one she'd rehearsed the most in her mind. "I wish I could tell you he is on his way back now, but there are many miles to ride and many *galla* to fight. If all goes as we hope, then it may be as early as a fortnight. If not, then longer." She refused to say he wouldn't return if he failed. Her mind shied away from such an awful and altogether possible outcome.

A cheer rose at the prospect of Brishen riding back to Saggara in two weeks, victorious. Some of the nobility exchanged speculative looks, and Ildiko made note of those. She'd given a time frame, one that gave the Kai a choice: wait patiently and let her do the job Brishen had appointed her to do or frantically conspire and plan a way to remove her from the throne or maneuver her out of a place of power. She hoped they chose the first. She braced for the second.

Supper commenced as it had for the past several days with a repast much reduced and not at all grand—a bowl of soup and bread for each diner. Brishen had instituted rationing immediately and Ildiko and the *sejm* upheld the edict.

A hard bang on one of the tables near the high table made Ildiko jump. Plates clattered and wine spilled from overturned goblets. The culprit responsible threw down his napkin and glared at the contents of his bowl.

"I refuse to eat another bite of this swill," he declared. Ildiko recognized him as a mayor from one of the villages closest to the Absu and in the most danger of being attacked by the *galla*. He had arrived at Saggara with great fanfare and proceeded to make himself a fawning toady of Vesetshen Senemset. That sly matriarch watched his antics from her seat across the hall with a measuring gaze before turning to stare at Ildiko.

The mayor waved his hand over his bowl. "Humans with their weak blood might call this food, but we're Kai nobility." He puffed out his narrow chest and sneered. "We deserve better than this. A Kai regent would see to it."

Ildiko wiped her sweating palms on her skirt before reaching for her goblet to sip. The silence in the hall was absolute as the mayor glared at her. Too focused on how Ildiko might react, he didn't notice Anhuset appear behind him. Ildiko nodded to her.

Shocked gasps and cries went up when Anhuset gripped the man by the back of the head and slammed him face first into his soup bowl. She held him there, easily subduing his struggles as he drowned in the supper he thought too pedestrian to eat.

Several Kai stood, then abruptly sat when Ildiko signaled a second time. Saggaran troops emerged from the corners and shadows of the great hall, all armed, some with swords unsheathed, others with arrows nocked onto drawn bow strings.

Anhuset yanked her victim up long enough for him to choke and inhale a saving breath before shoving his face into the bowl once more. He writhed in her hold, his struggles growing weaker.

Sickened, but equally determined to quash any future attempts at subversion of her authority, Ildiko stood and swept the horrified audience with a hard gaze. She gestured to Anhuset who released the hapless mayor. He slid off the bench on which he sat to disappear under the table. Retching sounds filled the quiet.

"Most of Bast-Haradis is camped outside those doors, with little shelter, few possessions and even less hope," Ildiko said. "I assumed it obvious to all, but apparently not. We must ration until this is over. Eat soup, eat gruel, and be grateful we have something to eat at all." Some of the Kai bowed their heads while others looked away, shame-faced or fiddled with their spoons.

Ildiko continued. "Lest we forget, the king and the men who ride with him fight an enemy who would devour us to the last man, woman and child. Kai or human, it doesn't matter to *galla*." Several of the Kai went ashen. Good, Ildiko thought. "Brishen Khaskem has appointed me regent in his absence to secure a kingdom undivided and a throne intact when he returns. I will see it done no matter what it takes." She stared at several of the nobles she considered a risk. None returned her stare. "Sedition," she declared, "will not be tolerated and will be punished swiftly and without mercy. Am I clear?"

Except for a few mumbles, no one replied. Ildiko didn't expect them to. She had made her point. Now she could only pray they took it to heart. A quick gesture from Mertok and the soldiers lining the great hall's perimeters stood down, lowering bows and resheathing blades.

One woman stood, cup in hand. Ildiko held back her smile for Ineni, Cephren's discerning daughter. The girl boldly raised her goblet in a toast. "To the king," she said. "And the queen regent. Long live the house of Khaskem. Long may it reign."

Others rose to join her, and soon everyone in the hall, with the exception of the mayor Anhuset almost drowned, was on their feet making loud toasts in Brishen's and Ildiko's honor. Ildiko wagered such enthusiastic support would last three days at most.

The meal concluded without mishap, and Ildiko later met with both Anhuset and Mertok in the royal bedchamber. She poured three small glasses half full with Dragon's Fire and passed two of them to her visitors. The glass was warm in her hand, the libation scorching on her tongue.

"And how is our poor mayor recovering?" she asked.

Anhuset downed her drink in one swallow. "I have no idea," she said between gasps. "Nor do I care."

"I didn't expect you to drown him."

"I almost drowned him. There's a difference." Anhuset lifted one shoulder in a half shrug. "Besides, it was good soup."

Mertok choked on his mirth and a mouthful of Dragon's Fire, slowly turning a dark shade of slate before Anhuset thumped him between the shoulder blades. He handed his empty glass back to Ildiko. After a few wheezy breaths, he spoke. "We should double your guard, Your Majesty. After what happened in the great hall, someone will be planning your death."

Ildiko disagreed. "I don't think so. All that applauding and toasting is temporary, but they'll step carefully now. That Kai was testing the waters with his little display. First to see if I'd back down and second, to learn how loyal Brishen's troops are to him when he isn't here."

"Then that was a foolish waste of effort and almost got him killed," Anhuset said. "Mertok and I have faithfully served Brishen for years. Our loyalty is absolute, and I can say the same for the rest of his garrison. I can't believe some in the hall thought otherwise."

"They certainly don't now." Ildiko was still shocked herself at Anhuset's ruthless assault.

"And he's my cousin," Anhuset added.

Ildiko gave a humorless chuckle. "Familial connections can be the easiest vulnerability to exploit. Traitors and assassins are often relatives with dreams of power. Surely, a Kai court ruled by Djedor and Secmis taught you that."

Anhuset's tone was especially acerbic. "I avoided court as often as possible. I don't make it a habit of lounging in a scarpatine pit."

"If you won't allow more personal guards, consider more in the manor itself. A continued show of strength," Mertok suggested.

Ildiko liked the idea. "Agreed. Just don't thin your troops too much on the redoubt's grounds. With more people arriving every day, we need them to keep the peace. We also need fresh scouts ready to reconnoiter the territory daily. I doubt Brishen has managed to capture every *galla* in such a short a time, and even one can do horrific damage and incite chaos if it somehow makes it across the water."

Mertok nodded and bowed before quitting the room, leaving Anhuset behind.

"You should take the extra guard," she said.

Ildiko sat on the chest at the end of the bed and unlaced her boots, giving a pleasured sigh when her stocking feet were free, and she could wiggle her toes. She wondered idly if Sinhue still rested. The servant was usually at her side even when Ildiko didn't summon her. "I will as soon as I see the need. Whichever nobles were out there conspiring together to kill me, they'll realize it isn't in their best interest to do away with me just yet. A monarch avenging his wife's death won't be in the mood to grant favors or listen to sly persuasion."

"True. Brishen isn't easily led on a good day, much less if he were grieving."

A knock at the door interrupted their conversation, and Sinhue called out to her mistress. She peeked around the door's edge at Ildiko's bid to enter, easing it wider and bowing before glancing over her shoulder at something in the hallway.

The servant behaved oddly. "What's wrong, Sinhue?" Beside her, Anhuset stiffened and dropped her hand to her sword pommel.

Sinhue bowed again. "My lady, do you remember the maid who served with me when you arrived in Haradis?"

"Kirgipa?" Ildiko smiled at the memory of the young girl who acted as one of her lady's maid during her stay in the Kai royal palace. Brishen had carried her brother Talumey's mortem light to their mother and sister. She'd chosen to stay behind with her family when Ildiko left with Brishen for Saggara. "She's here? She made it out of Haradis?" At Sinhue's nod, she clapped her hands, delighted. "Send her in!" The news was a bright spot in a succession of dark days.

The brightness dimmed when Sinhue told her she hadn't arrived with her sister or mother. "She's here with two palace guards, my lady. They refuse to leave her side. They're in the hallway."

Ildiko met Anhuset's yellow eyes. This was strange. "Send them all in," she said. The servant darted out of the room.

"Are you sure that's wise?" Anhuset's grip on the sword tightened.

"Somehow, I doubt Kirgipa wishes me harm."

"But the palace guards might. These are elite soldiers. I was one in the past."

"Then I'll rely on you for the protection you and Mertok insist I need."

Sinhue returned, followed by a bedraggled looking Kai woman wearing a stern expression. Kirgipa, equally tattered, entered behind her, a bundle of rags in her arms. A Kai male practically tread her heels. His features softened in recognition when he spotted Anhuset.

"Sha-Anhuset," he greeted her with a quick fist thump to his chest, the salute of one soldier to another of superior rank.

Anhuset tilted her head. "Necos?" Her stance didn't relax, nor did her hold on her sword. "It's been some time since we shared a flask."

Intent on Kirgipa, Ildiko only half listened to the conversation. "Kirgipa, I'm glad to see you." She approached the maid, hands outstretched in welcome and was instantly blocked by the Kai woman who entered the bedchamber first. She held her ground even as Anhuset drew her sword.

"Stand down, Dendarah," Necos said softly. "We're among friends."

Kirgipa's eyes had rounded to gold coins as she stared at the bristling Anhuset. "Truly, Dendarah, we're safe here," she said, adding her own assurances to Necos's.

Dendarah reluctantly eased back. "Forgive me, *Hercegesé*. We have good reason for our caution."

"Her Majesty," Anhuset growled.

"No. *Hercegesé*," Dendarah insisted. She pointed to the bundle Kirgipa held close to her chest. "*That* is Her Majesty." Her words fell like anchor weights into the room's quiet. Ildiko gaped, as did Anhuset.

Kirgipa eased back part of the rags to reveal a tiny head covered in a cap of white hair. The small face was relaxed in sleep, bubbles blowing gently out of her pursed mouth. "We've come a long way for your help and protection, *Hercegesé*. I hold the only surviving child of His Highness Harkuf and his wife, Tiye. This is the Queen Regnant of Bast-Haradis."

CHAPTER EIGHTEEN

Haradis, capital of Bast-Haradis, sprawled on either side of the Absu river, a diseased ruin emptied of the Kai and overrun by the *galla*. Somewhere in the shattered heap that had once been the royal palace, a wound in the world bled out abominations in an endless, frothing spume.

Brishen stared at what was left of his childhood home and hummed a dirge low in his throat. He had built good and bad memories here, had hated court and loved the city itself with its lively docks and teeming market places. All gone now, snuffed by the malevolent darkness spilling out of a breach created by his twisted mother.

They had traveled along the riverbank, battling and trapping *galla* the entire way. It didn't matter that the *vuhana* they rode traveled faster than any living horse. The journey to the city had been a hard, bitter slog of droving and fighting. Even now, each king cut through an attacking demon, sending the thing back to the breach where it would immediately emerge once more. It had become a thing so constant, Brishen likened it to swatting swarms of flies. Gaeres galloped past him, the consummate drover as he whistled and barked sharp commands to the dead who snatched fleeing *galla* and walled them into the now colossal pen packed tightly with demons.

269

"How do you intend to trap them inside the city?" Serovek bellowed to be heard above the continuous shrieking din behind them. *Galla* and their captor revenants screeched at each other.

The kings had used the double envelopment tactic multiple times in their chaotic drive to the destroyed capital, maneuvering *galla* against the river as they outflanked them, encircled them and herded them into the straining net created by the dead. It wasn't an optimal solution, but it was the only one they had until they could push the horde back to Haradis and seal off the city.

Brishen gestured for Megiddo. When the monk drew closer, he asked him "How big can you make your rune circle?"

"How big do you want it?"

He pointed out several spots that encompassed the broken palace. "A small one around the palace only, where the breach originates. We can use it to contain the emerging *galla* until I close the breach. A bigger circle around that one. Big enough for the dead to herd the rest in so we can cut the *galla* down and banish them back to their spawning ground."

"Do you realize how many of those bastards we'll have to slice up?" Andras, who was near enough to overhear, stood in his stirrups to behold the massive horde behind him.

Brishen shrugged. "You heard the *Elsod*. We don't tire. We don't sleep." And hacking these vile things to dust might finally ease his thirst for vengeance against them. Unlikely, but he relished the chance.

"I can draw down the wards, but they'll drain your power," Megiddo warned. "And they'll be as temporary as the one I drew at my brother's house." He leaned down, impaling a lunging *galla* on his sword. The thing slid down the blade and sank its teeth into his vambrace before disintegrating.

Brishen scowled as he hacked another one in half. "We don't need them to be permanent," he said. Megiddo was right. Warding circles that large would sap him of most of the power he possessed, and he feared he might not have enough left to return all the kings back to their bodies. He pushed aside the concern. He had no other option. He needed the containment the circles provided, no matter how risky or temporary.

The *galla* herd fought against their prison as the dead forced them into the city, while the kings battled their way toward the palace, scattering piles of Kai bones they rode past. Those not yet caught attacked in waves, spilling across the devastated city to leap at and crawl over the kings like roaches on a carcass. Swords slashed a swath toward the castle gates.

Brishen dismounted, cleaving a *galla* in two as he did. He called to Megiddo above the noise. "Can you cast the smaller circle around the palace itself?" At Megiddo's nod, the two men set to work.

The monk dismounted. Brishen, Serovek, and Andras joined him, providing shield and sword to protect him so he might build the ward uninterrupted. He was mesmerizing to watch, and Brishen regretted that he was too busy battling *galla* to simply stand and admire.

Megiddo stretched out his hand, spoke a word in a tongue unknown and sketched a symbol in the air with graceful fingers. The symbol lit, not with the blue magic of necromancy, but with amber radiance, as if he drew forth the memory of warm summer and wrote with the ink of sunlight. A *galla* grazed the glowing rune as it sped past and recoiled with a shriek before rushing back for a closer inspection. Brishen imagined he heard the thing sniff.

"My sorcery alone won't hold them. Not this many." Megiddo said. "You'll need to follow with me as I draw and repeat the words I recite to infuse the runes with death magic."

"Cut down as many of these vermin as you can as fast as you can," Brishen instructed Serovek and Andras. The more they sent back to the breach, the more they could trap within the palace.

He shadowed the monk, carefully repeating each word Megiddo recited and touching the floating amber symbols as he did. They pulsed under his fingertips, their heat bleeding away into the winter air as their color changed to a sullen green and finally to frigid blue before fading away. The ground below them caught fire but didn't burn. Cerulean flames gave off light but no warmth as they etched a circle's perimeter into the earth. Brishen knew none of the words Megiddo spoke and he repeated, but their power coursed across his tongue and down his arm to flow through his fingertips. The warding sapped his strength, and they still had another circle to draw after this one.

Andras and Serovek fought ceaselessly as the *galla* swarmed around them. Many hurled themselves at Brishen and Megiddo, only to be thrown back by the closing circle. It was slow work, and Brishen staggered from the onslaught of the spell's drain, but soon the palace's facade glowed from the light cast by the warding circle.

"It is done," Megiddo pronounced and watched with a faint smile as demons within the ward threw themselves against an invisible wall as strong and unyielding as the one made by the river. He casually stepped outside the ward to a chorus of furious screams. Brishen followed, and for one sweet breath of a moment, nothing attacked them.

"Gaeres, can you control the herd alone long enough for the rest of us to reach and close the breach?" Brishen needed three kings with him for support, and the Quereci chieftain's son, with his expertise at herding, was the best choice to remain behind and keep the trapped herd under his control.

"I'll do what I can." Gaeres swatted a *galla* trying to climb the back of his *vuhana*. "But make it quick."

Brishen raced into the palace with the Serovek, Andras, and Megiddo. He halted in the throne room long enough to flinch at the sight before him.

The great statues of Kai kings and queens that once lined the walls lay toppled, littering the floor with rubble. Tattered remains of banners and royal crests that had always hung from the high ceiling, clung to the twisted metal brackets of burnt-out torches. Blood, dried to brown stains, spattered the walls in a grisly mural. There were no bodies, only bones half hidden by bits of clothing.

This had once been both pleasure hall and battlefield, in which the great noble houses engaged in political machinations and pursued life's earthly delights under the gazes of successive Kai kings and queens. It was a charnel house now.

He turned his fury at the devastation on the *galla* scuttling down the walls towards them. The kings battled their way to the lower floors where demons filled every space with a wet, oily presence. The floors made for treacherous crossing, coated in a slippery film Brishen chose not to ponder. The air hung damp and rancid in the stairwells and corridors. Despite his eidolon's immunity to the residual foulness of demon-kin, he still tasted their presence on his tongue.

Twice, he was lifted and thrown against a wall by an upsurge of *galla* as the breach vomited them forth like sickness from a plague sufferer's mouth. Serovek's curses rang harsh and loud in the cloying darkness.

"I'm going to soak in a horse trough full of boiling water and lye when this is over," he vowed. "Thank the gods we're harnessed."

"Where's the damn breach?" Andras shouted as he body-slammed a cluster of *galla* against a wall before slicing through the entire lot with one clean stroke.

Brishen scanned the wide corridor that led off one of the many staircases and split into four more hallways. All of them were obscured by the oily bloom of *galla* bubbling up from the depths, but one pulsed darker than the others. It led to the palace's buttery and storerooms where perishables were once housed. He pointed to the spot. "There."

They cut through the ever thickening mob of *galla* in their fight to reach the rupture. Sharp nails and teeth scraped across Brishen's mail and brigandine, and numerous fingers spidered up and down his legs, jabbing and scratching. Once, Andras lost his footing, sending both him and Brishen tumbled down a short flight of stairs before crashing into the splintered remains of a door.

"Good work, lads," Serovek crowed and jerked both men to their feet. "You've found the breach."

The wound between worlds, and cause of so much misery and death, pulsed in a chamber tucked away in the palace's lowest level. The walls literally breathed with the cacophony of endless screaming hurtling from the black. Secmis, in her obsessive search for ever greater power and dominance, had split open the barrier between this world and a void that imprisoned every horror imagined by humans and Kai alike. Brishen likened it to a disembowelment more than a birthing. The breach spewed out *galla* the same way a gutted warrior spilled his blood and intestines into the dirt.

Demons poured from the wound and immediately launched into an attack, punching, scratching, biting. Brishen echoed Serovek's gratitude that they wore armor. No matter the *Elsod*'s assurances that Wraith Kings were impervious to damage inflicted by the *galla*, he was glad his armor shielded him from their vile touch.

Megiddo, Andras, and Serovek formed a half circle around him as he faced the breach. The ancient spell of a long-dead Kai sorcerer spilled from his lips. Power coiled in his belly, burned away the sludge of demon touch and surged through his limbs in sizzling bolts. Light filled the room, searing away darkness. Had he the vision of a Kai instead of a spirit, he'd be blinded. *Galla* screamed, and the howl of a sucking wind accompanied their cries.

The breach buckled under the spell's onslaught, warping as if crushed by an invisible fist. The *galla* emerging from its depths tried to escape, skeletal hands clawing the air, the floors and walls. Anything to anchor themselves in place as the rupture narrowed.

A chorus of shouts and cries that weren't *galla* almost made Brishen stumble with the incantation. The sight that greeted him when he turned his head would have frozen his blood had it flowed in his transformed veins. *Galla* arms, skeletal and insectile, stretched out of the breach to snatch at Megiddo's legs.

They yanked him off his feet. He scrabbled for purchase on the slick floor, still clutching his sword.

Andras clasped his forearm and held on, sliding as the *galla* dragged their captive toward the breach's maw. Serovek joined the struggle, wrapping an arm around Andras's torso and lowering his elbow below the knee to lock himself in place. *Galla* swarmed around him, leveling blows on his head and shoulders.

Megiddo cut away at the clawing *galla* with his sword to free himself, but for every arm and skeletal hand cut, four more took its place.

Brishen shook with the urge to help, but he dare not interrupt the invocation. Ancient and unpredictable, it would either collapse and burn out if halted or create a nightmare scenario of backlash and split the breach even wider. He watched helplessly as Andras and Serovek struggled to save the monk as the breach collapsed further inward. Multi-jointed fingers rode higher up Megiddo's legs until they dug into his hips and torso before reaching for Andras.

In a moment frozen in time, Megiddo halted his struggle and stared at Brishen. Seconds became centuries. Those blue eidolon eyes, still oddly human, blazed until they were almost white. Horror filled the monk's face before a hardened resolve replaced it. "*Farewell*," he mouthed.

Brishen's "No!" thundered inside his head, while the incantation poured from his mouth unabated.

Megiddo twisted, raised his sword arm higher and brought it down hard. A shock of blue light flashed as the blade severed *galla* limbs and Andras's hand where he clutched Megiddo's forearm. The injured Wraith King's cry ricocheted off the walls.

He fell backwards, knocking Serovek down. Wisps of blue smoke spilled from the stump where his hand had been as if bleeding ethereal blood. Serovek shoved him off and leapt to his feet.

The *galla* claimed their victim in a swarm of claws and teeth, along with the trophy of Andras's hand. Before the maw of the breach swallowed him whole, Megiddo flung the sword across the floor where Serovek caught it and beheaded a demon. Brishen swayed on his feet as power poured out of him like water through a sieve.

"Get him out of there!" Andras roared, even as he fought off *galla* one-handed.

Too late. Too late. The breach had thinned to nothing more than a sliver of black ribbon, the shrieking echo of banished *galla* the only thing emerging from it. That closed, disappearing altogether with a convulsive ripple of air.

Brishen crashed to his knees, dizzy and sick. For all that he was spirit made solid and unaffected by the weaknesses of the flesh, his eidolon still suffered the aftereffects of the spell.

Serovek's hand on his shoulder made him look up. "It's done," he said.

Brishen shook head. "Not yet." The image of Megiddo's face in those last moments filled his vision, and he couldn't hold back the choking gasp of grief. His mother, twisted, warped bitch that she was, had thrown her people—the entire world even—to a pack of ravenous, ethereal wolves. As a Kai and her son, he'd accepted the burden of righting the wrongs she committed, correcting an apocalyptic mistake. He'd closed the breach, but it had been a human—a courageous, quiet monk—who'd given the ultimate sacrifice and saved a nation of people not his own.

"We could have saved him," Andras snarled. He glared at Brishen, his eyes blazing above his face shield. Hostile, haunted, disgusted—every emotion Brishen experienced himself.

"No, we couldn't. They would have pulled you in too, along with Serovek, before I could close the breach. Megiddo knew it. Otherwise you'd still have your hand."

Andras held up his arm. Revenant smoke curled around his wrist. "We've consigned him to a horror beyond even unclean death. Cowards all," he said. "We are all cowards." He sliced through a *galla* that hurtled in from the stairwell.

He didn't utter a sound when Serovek shoved him hard enough against the wall to knock him off his feet. "You might want to rethink that notion, exile." The two swords Serovek held pulsed with light, one his, the other Megiddo's. He used both to cut away at *galla* still filling the chamber. "Our purpose was, and is, to close the breach and send those accursed demons back to where they spawned. The monk sacrificed himself for all of us. Honor that brave deed by going home and recounting it to the daughter you fight for."

He sheathed his sword for a moment and offered Andras a hand up. The Gauri lord stared at him for a long moment before accepting, and Serovek hauled him to his feet.

Brishen leaned heavily against one of the walls, making half-hearted swings at the *galla* snapping at him. "I know it's no consolation," he told the Gauri lord, "but I will carry his loss the remainder of my life." He didn't lie. Megiddo's expression was etched in his mind as deep and fiery as the wards he'd burned into the ground.

Andras's eyes flared for a moment before dimming. "You're right," he said. "That's no consolation whatsoever." He turned away and strode out of the room, his steps on the stairs hardly a whisper of sound. A procession of *galla* dogged his heels.

"Those who survive the battle often suffer guilt," Serovek said. "He'll come to terms with Megiddo's fate over time, as we all will."

"It won't matter if he does. His rancor doesn't change the fact I had to close the breach no matter the cost." Brishen gazed at the human who once saved his life and called him friend. "You understand I wouldn't have altered anything had that been you instead of Megiddo?"

Serovek chuckled and batted away a demon with the back of his hand. 'I'd hope not. I didn't much relish the idea of being skewered, resurrected and thrown on a sham horse so I can chase demons all over the place. You ruining the entire plan because you had a fit of the vapors about sacrificing me wouldn't endear you to me."

The weight of Megiddo's horrific end didn't lessen inside him, but Brishen cracked a smile at Serovek's jesting. His amusement faded as fast as it appeared. "If I thought it might free him, I'd kill his body." The three were connected—eidolon, sword and body. But if the body perished before the eidolon, the spirit was doomed to wander, and in Megiddo's case, remain trapped in an eternity of unimaginable suffering.

"Andras or I should have taken his head instead of holding him," Serovek groused. "He'd be free then. Dead but free."

They followed Andras out of the palace, Brishen pausing for a final view of the throne room thick with confused, screeching *galla*. The thrones were still in place, undamaged. A vision of Secmis seated in hers, a ghastly spider in the center of her web, made him shudder. He turned his back and walked away.

The kings gathered in front of the dead, Andras looking at no one, Gaeres's features drawn with shock at the news of Megiddo. Thinned of power, Brishen sensed the dead's restlessness, the return of their anger at being yoked to the commands of a Wraith King. Time grew short along with his power. Soon, they'd shrug off his control, and if the *galla* were not banished, set the horde free once more to join their brethren who currently plagued them like fleas on a dog.

"How will we create the outer circle without the monk?" Gaeres asked.

"I remember the spell he had me repeat, and the runes to be drawn. I'll be the one to give its power, just like the smaller circle," Brishen said. A power that was now a lantern's light inside him instead of the bonfire he first carried into this battle.

He swung onto the back of his *vuhana* and called to the dead. "Herd them toward the palace and hold them." The dead screeched and whooped, and as one body, shoved and pulled the captive *galla* farther into the city. Brishen sought out Andras who finally stared back with a withering expression. "Slash and cut until there are none left standing. They'll return to their spawning ground. With no breach to escape, they'll stay there." he said. He raised his sword in salute. "We fight for the fallen."

"We fight for Megiddo," Andras said.

Brishen gave a brief bow. "We fight for Megiddo."

CHAPTER NINETEEN

Sunlight gilded the edges of the closed shutters, painting gold threads across Ildiko's hands where they rested in her lap. It was mid afternoon, a time when humans went about their daily work, and the Kai slept. She had adopted the Kai's nocturnal schedule when she married Brishen, but sometimes she stayed awake long enough to sit on the balcony off her room and welcome the sun's rise. By this time, she was usually sound asleep, spooned against Brishen's warm body.

Not today. Nor, indeed, for many days. Sleep had eluded her for hours in her lonely bed, and she finally gave up the battle. The floor lay icy under her feet as she slipped on a robe and wrapped in a heavy blanket for extra warmth. She was tempted to stoke the nearly dead coals in the hearth but changed her mind. An infant and her nursemaid slept in the room with her, and Ildiko didn't want to disturb either with her rustlings. Instead, she padded to her favorite chair by the shuttered window and listened to the stirrings of the day patrols that watched over Saggara while everyone else slept.

The redoubt was still overcrowded and strained beyond its limits in providing sanctuary to the displaced and the homeless, but the crowd slowly thinned. Scouts had ridden out daily to reconnoiter the surrounding territories and the Absu in both directions. None had seen or heard the *galla*, and all scouts returned accounted for. The Kai were relaxing, some of the more adventurous ones packing their possessions to return to their holts and villages, believing the newly crowned king had succeeded in banishing the *hul galla* from their land and world.

Ildiko wanted with all her soul to believe it as well. Seventeen days earlier Brishen had wielded an ancient necromancer's magic to become like the dead and lead an army of revenants into battle. Except for reports from the traumatized Kai who finally arrived at Saggara, she'd heard nothing more.

The reports themselves were both epic and incredulous, a battle between demons and the dead witnessed from the banks of the Absu by more than a thousand Kai fleeing Escariel. They had recognized Brishen as a Kai by his armor and described how five generals in various harness had plunged into the sea of *galla*, with the screaming dead encircling them. Cold sweat trickled down Ildiko's back whenever she listened to the eyewitness accounts. Even when each person she spoke with assured her the Wraith Kings had succeeded in containing the horde, she still quaked inside. The hardest task remained: driving the horde back to Haradis and closing the breach. There would be no reports or witnesses emerging from the ravaged city, nothing to assuage her terror and worry that, despite the power and protection of his transformation, Brishen might not survive. The thought tormented her relentlessly, and today wasn't the first time she'd abandoned her bed thanks to her tortured thoughts.

The intermittent sounds of snuffling and smacking made her smile. The infant Queen Regnant slept in a hastily constructed baby bed, unaware of the dangers she had survived and the ones that still faced her now. A nursemaid Sinhue had brought to relieve Kirgipa's tireless care slept on a mattress next to the bed.

Ildiko had insisted on them staying in her chamber with her. Outside her door, a pair of soldiers stood guard. The baby's arrival meant a shift in Brishen's and her circumstances, one that affected every level of government and power base in Saggara. New alliances would form, allegiances broken between one set of parties and reforged between others. For the child's safety, Ildiko had ordered those who knew her identity not to reveal it. She wholeheartedly agreed with Necos's belief that there were those residing in Saggara who'd benefit from an infanticide.

Kirgipa protested vehemently when Ildiko relieved her of her duty. "Please, my lady. I've been a devoted nursemaid. Why am I being punished?" Her young features twisted in anguish.

Ildiko captured her hand, fingers sliding along the smooth curve of Kirgipa's claws. "I'm not punishing you, Kirgipa. And when this is settled, you and your loyal guards will be generously rewarded for what you've done and your role reinstated if you wish, but to have you remain as the queen's nursemaid for now will raise inconvenient questions. The Kai will think it the oddity of a human woman to suddenly adopt an 'orphan' Kai baby as her own." Especially a human queen considered barren by her Kai subjects. "But they'll simply shrug, toss me pitying looks and prattle amongst themselves how Brishen Khaskem managed to shackle himself to such a wife." She smiled when she uttered the last, imagining the tut-tutting that would take place beyond her hearing.

"But I was a royal nursemaid," Kirgipa argued. "Won't they think it reasonable that I continue the role for your orphan?"

Sinhue, who stood beside her, scowled and thumped her on the arm. "Kirgipa! Remember your place and accept Her Highness's decision."

The young woman went ashen and stuttered an apology.

Ildiko waved it away. "No, she has a point." She waited until Kirgipa lifted her bowed head to meet her gaze. "Your argument is sound, but new nursemaids with no ties to the Khaskem family won't elicit any interest. I'd rather have no questions than a dangerous few. If you wish, you and Sinhue may choose the candidates for me to review." A new thought occurred to her, one she was sure would trounce any more protests Kirgipa had. "I know you wish to hunt for your sister. Atalan is probably out there somewhere in the redoubt. Necos has said he'd find her for you. Why not accompany him?"

Kirgipa had embraced both ideas with fervor. Ildiko heard days later they had located Atalan among the survivors. She met with Mesumenes to arrange a position for both women in the manor itself. She'd do much more when Brishen returned. This family had suffered great hardship and loss in its service to the Khaskem dynasty, including insuring the line would continue. Brishen owed them much. Ildiko believed she owed them everything. Kirgipa had saved her marriage with the safe transport of Harkuf's only surviving heir to Saggara.

She rose from her seat and tiptoed to the baby's bed. Even with her eyes more adjusted to darkness, she still couldn't make out the details of the baby's features. It didn't matter. The light of a candle didn't reveal any more than the darkness did. A Kai girl child, distinguished in her gender by the obvious genitalia and the cap of silvery-white hair. Beyond that, Ildiko couldn't say if the infant resembled any member of the Khaskem family in a defining way. She had only her trust in Kirgipa's honesty and the zealous protection exhibited by Necos and Dendarah to rely on. She had no way of proving this child was the heir to the Kai throne. That task lay with Brishen, and she wondered how he might validate the claim when he returned. If he returned.

The baby cooed in her sleep when Ildiko lightly traced the soft curve of her cheek. She had accepted the fact she'd bear no children while she was Brishen's wife, and since her greatest wish was to remain his wife until she died, there would be no children for her ever. Fate, in its strange and twisted humors had proclaimed otherwise. This child, still nameless until her first year, was now not only a queen, but an orphaned one. Brishen, as her uncle, might no longer be king, but he would become regent, with all the responsibilities of a monarch until the baby came of age to independently rule. He would be her advisor, her mentor and ultimately her father. And Ildiko, her mother.

The reality of impending parenthood knocked the breath out of Ildiko's lungs, and she pulled away to stifle a gasp behind her hand. The role of regent had frightened her, but she embraced it with dogged determination. Ruling a kingdom was one thing; raising a child something else. Something far more terrifying. The baby slept on, oblivious to her observer's churning emotions.

Ildiko tiptoed back to her chair, feeling faintly ill. She could never replace Tiye as the baby's mother, but she could be a second mother and love her in the way Ildiko's mother had loved Ildiko— with all her heart. A burgeoning excitement soon chased away the sickness.

She froze in front of the chair when the chamber door creaked open. Every instinct she possessed screamed a silent warning, one verified when a dark shape slid stealthily through the narrow opening and crept inside on soundless feet. A pair of yellow eyes glanced at the bed where Ildiko usually slept, taking in the bunched covers that looked as if she slumbered there now. The intruder's gaze moved to the sleeping nursemaid and settled on the baby bed.

Whoever this was hadn't seen Ildiko by the window, and she used that fact to her advantage. She slammed the shutters open with both hands. Bright sunlight flooded the room, revealing a Kai man dressed in nondescript clothes and holding a bloodied knife.

He reeled from the blinding light and raised both hands to shield his eyes. Ildiko inhaled a deep breath and screamed at the top of her lungs. The earsplitting shriek startled the groggy nursemaid wide awake and sent the baby into a chorus of equally deafening howls.

"Guards! Guards!" Ildiko shouted until she was hoarse, but no one burst into the room. The would-be assassin squinted at her and snarled before returning his attention to the baby bed. The nursemaid added her own shrieks as she snatched the wailing child out of the bed and backed herself right into the far corner of the room.

The attacker's feral grin curved triumphant as he crept toward them, knife blade gleaming in the sun's light. Desperate, Ildiko searched for something, anything to stop him. Her gaze landed on the shutter pole leaned against the wall behind her. Used to unlatch and open the shutters too high for arm's reach, it was the same length as the long *silabat* stick she used to train with Anhuset.

Concentrated on his prey and unconcerned about the weak human woman hiding in the opposite corner, the assassin didn't anticipate Ildiko's attack. She grasped the shutter pole like a spear and rammed the weighted brass hook end into the back of his knee with all her strength.

He crashed to the ground with a scream of his own, the knife flying out of his hand to spin across the floor. Ildiko didn't pause. She pivoted on one foot, swung to the side and smashed the pole down on his head, striking his temple. A sickening crack followed. Ildiko struck him a second time. Sounds erupted from her throat, animalistic grunts and snarls as terrified rage cast a red haze over her vision. She raised the pole for a third blow only to stumble when it was seized from behind. She spun, hands still clutching the crimson-stained stick to stare wide-eyed and gasping at Anhuset. She screeched and tried to wrestle the pole free until the Kai woman roared directly in her face.

"Ildiko, stop!"

She froze, startled back to awareness of her surroundings. She looked frantically for the nursemaid and found her still huddled in the corner, clutching the howling baby to her. "Are you alright, Imi?" she croaked. The nursemaid nodded, her eyes huge in her face.

"Let go, *Hercegesé*."

Ildiko returned her attention to Anhuset and discovered they both still gripped the shutter pole. Behind her, a crowd of onlookers filled the room, mostly troops with swords drawn.

Anhuset could have easily yanked the makeshift weapon out of her hand. She didn't. She waited, stern features calm and watchful, until Ildiko loosened her grip and tucked her trembling hands under her arms in a self embrace.

"Is he dead?" she whispered.

Anhuset skirted around her, still holding the shutter pole. A short silence reigned before she spoke. "You shattered his knee and caved in his skull. I think it's safe to say he's dead."

Ildiko slowly pivoted and wished she hadn't. The Kai sprawled on the floor, leg bent at an odd angle. Bits of bone and brain dotted his cheek. Blood pooled under his ear and trickled out of his mouth. Ildiko raced to the wash basin and promptly emptied the remnants of her supper into it.

"He tried to kill the Queen Regnant," she said after rinsing her mouth with a cup of water someone handed her. She groaned at the slip. For all her warnings to everyone else not to reveal the baby's identity, she just virtually shouted it from the rooftops.

Anhuset's dry response didn't make her feel any better. "No use fretting," she said. "If he came to kill her, then your secret is already out." Her tone changed, became sharper. "Someone close those shutters before I go completely blind," she snapped. "And haul that sack of horse dung out of here so we don't have to look at it. Find out who knows him and bring them to me."

Ildiko pitied whoever might suffer an interrogation from sha-Anhuset. She ordered Ildiko to sit in one of the chairs by the hearth and sent a shaken Sinhue down to the kitchens to fetch wine for both her mistress and the nursemaid who looked on the verge of fainting.

"Do you want to retire to another chamber while this gets cleaned up?" Anhuset jerked a thumb to the spot where the dead Kai had sprawled.

Ildiko avoided looking in that direction a second time and shook her head. Her nails carved half-moons into her palms before she relaxed her hands, marched to one of the chairs near the fire and turned it so it faced away from the scene. She sat down, holding on to the threads of her dignity even as shock shredded it like wet flax. "No," she said in flat voice. "This is my room. I will not be driven out by some baby-murdering bastard Kai. Or his ghost. Just make sure the stain is good and gone."

Her gaze sought out Imi and the baby hovering nearby. She dimly registered that the little queen's wails had subsided to into soft hiccups and snuffles as Imi made shushing noises. Ildiko gestured for the nurse to bring the baby to her. "You're free to leave, if you wish Imi. Just send Kirgipa to me."

"I'd like to stay, if you please, my lady," Imi said in a soft voice and passed her charge to Ildiko who settled her on her lap.

Infant Kai and human woman stared at each other for a long moment, and Ildiko wondered what the baby saw when she looked into a face different from her kin. She stroked the tiny head, feeling the soft hair tickle the spaces between her fingers. The little queen cooed and blew a spit bubble between her pursed lips. Her small fists waved in the air, one opening to grasp the finger Ildiko held out to her.

"I suspect all of Saggara will be on fire with chatter about you, little one," Ildiko said. She glanced at Anhuset who watched them both from the chair she claimed. "You'll have to assign a guard to Kirgipa, at least until the fervor about one of Harkuf's children being alive dies down. Otherwise, she'll be inundated with questions and driven to madness by them."

"I'll assign Necos. He and Kirgipa are friends, and as a former palace guard, he'll handle any overly persistent curiosity monger with the right amount of...persuasion."

Ildiko concentrated on running her fingers lightly over the baby's plump body, a far more pleasant pastime than remembering the sight of the dead Kai on her bedchamber floor. "The assassin killed the guards, didn't he? I screamed for them but none came."

"Yes," Anhuset said. "Both their throats cut. They were good soldiers. All I can think is someone found out they were on guard duty today. The right amount of dream flower powder in a goblet of wine won't give you visions, but it will make you slow. Dim your senses. Easy to sneak up on and overpower."

Ildiko lifted the baby and kissed her forehead before returning her to her nurse. "I couldn't sleep. No word from Brishen or about him in more than a fortnight. I was too worried, so I got up and sat by the window. I saw the door open and the Kai sneaking inside." She shivered and stared at Anhuset. "What if I had been asleep?"

Anhuset shrugged. "Then the queen would be dead," she said flatly. "And likely the nurse and you." Her mouth turned up at one corner. "You were paying closer attention to those *gatke* lessons than I thought you were."

Ildiko raised a hand to show the other woman how badly it trembled. "I've never killed anyone before," she said. "I had to. I know this, but it doesn't make it easier to accept." She returned Anhuset's slight smile with a bleak one of her own. "I am not a warrior."

"You were when you needed to be."

Straightforward words without lavish, empty praise and yet Ildiko fancied she'd been given both absolution and the highest of compliments. Anhuset, whom she'd respected and admired since she first met her, approved of her actions.

When Sinhue returned with the wine, Ildiko and Anhuset toasted each other and Imi, emptied their cups and refilled from the pitcher. Ildiko glanced at the nursemaid who, with Sinhue's help, prepared an early breakfast for the baby. The chamber had slowly darkened, and Sinhue lit the candles in a candelabra for Ildiko's benefit.

Anhuset finished her second goblet of wine and set it aside. "Always a good way to break your fast," she proclaimed. Again, her mouth turned up briefly at Ildiko's chuckle. "I think now you'll sleep," she said. "You've been dealt a shock or two. Your mind needs the rest as much as your body."

At her words, Ildiko surrendered to a huge yawn. She shook it off. "I don't have time to sleep. The *sejm* will want to meet to discuss the Queen Regnant, and we need to find who sent an assassin to kill her."

"The *sejm* can wait, and I don't need your help to hunt down criminals." Anhuset gave a short bow. "No disrespect intended, *Hercegesé.*"

Ildiko was thrilled with her old title. Lower in status and so much lighter on her shoulders. She still occupied the role of regent, but she was no longer queen consort. Thank the gods for that. Another yawn stopped her from replying, and Anhuset left the room before she could stop her.

Brishen's cousin was right. A sudden fatigue plagued her, as if she had rowed a merchant ship single-handedly into Pricid's harbor. Memories of the earlier violence weighted her soul , and her mind shied away from the grisly image of the Kai assassin, dead by her hand. She sought her bed and crawled under the covers, eyes already half closed. Sleep claimed her even as Sinhue tugged the covers over her shoulders.

The servant's voice was only a vague murmur in her ears. "Well done, Your Highness. Well done."

She awoke to a room made gloomy by shadows and the low firelight cast by the lit hearth. The lack of sunlight edging the window shutters told her it was still nighttime. Had she only slept a few hours? There was no one to ask. She was alone, and her heart slammed against her ribs at the sight of the empty baby bed nearby and no nursemaid in sight.

Blankets tangled around her legs, and she frantically kicked them aside. The baby. Where was the baby?

Sinhue's serene voice stopped her from catapulting out of the bed. "You're awake, my lady."

Ildiko spotted her in the room's deeper shadows where the firelight didn't reach. She must have kept watch while Ildiko slept. "Where's Imi and the queen?"

"Imi is attending personal business. The queen is with Kirgipa and half the garrison keeping watch over them."

The amusement in the servant's voice and confirmation of the baby's whereabouts sent a surge of relief through Ildiko. She rubbed at itchy eyes. "How long did I sleep? Surely more than a few hours."

Sinhue opened one of the chests that held Ildiko's clothing and laid underskirt and tunic on the bed. "Since yester eve. The day has come and gone."

Ildiko's eyes rounded. "That long? Why didn't you wake me? I can't waste my time sleeping." Her rest hadn't even been restful. Dark dreams plagued her, visions of the Kai she killed interspersed with those of Brishen and the low, stunned sound he made when Serovek ran him through with the sword.

"Sha-Anhuset said not to disturb you unless the *herceges* himself strode through the redoubt's gates." She handed Ildiko a new shift and stockings, a smile curving her mouth. "Only the foolish and the reckless ignore an edict from sha-Anhuset."

"I'm supposed to meet with the *sejm*." She shrugged on a soft woolen shirt and stepped into the underskirts Sinhue handed her. "The gods only knows what rumors are swirling about regarding the queen." She suspected half the council accepted Ildiko's inadvertent admission that a child of the heir apparent had survived the *galla* attack in Haradis while the other half soundly rejected it. This would be a contentious meeting.

Sinhue laced the underskirt until it fit snug against Ildiko's waist and held the long tunic while she slipped her arms through the arm holes. "The *sejm* has been told to gather whenever you're ready. Shall I bring you something to eat or do you wish to eat in the hall?"

"Here, I think." She'd savor the solitude before facing the *sejm* to answer a slew of questions and probably as many accusations about keeping the Queen Regnant's identity a secret for her own nefarious purposes.

She was slipping on her shoes when a frantic beating at the door made her and Sinhue exchange wary glances. *"Hercegesé, come quick!"*

"Oh my gods," Ildiko whispered. "The baby." She bolted toward the door and jerked it open. A Kai soldier stood on the other side, her eyes shining like twin lamps in the dark corridor. "Where's the queen?" Ildiko snapped.

The soldier backed up, a confused frown lining her brow. "With her nurse and guards, Your Highness." She gestured with a tilt of her head toward the stairwell. "Sha-Anhuset sent me to find you. Riders approaching the redoubt with an army behind them. Scouts say it's the *herceges* and his Wraith Kings."

She almost didn't move out of the way in time before Ildiko was running down the corridor toward the stairs with Sinhue calling after her. "Your Highness, your shoes!"

Ildiko ignored her. Shoes be damned. She'd destroy hers within seconds of entering the muddy bailey, but she refused to take precious time changing into her boots.

For the first time since Ildiko had come to live at Saggara, the bailey was empty except for carts and a pig loose from its pen. Everyone had gathered on the surrounding plain outside the gates. The soldier Anhuset dispatched to fetch her touched her elbow, guiding her through the throng of Kai. Many bowed as she passed, some whispering her name, Ildiko *Hercegesé*, in admiring tones. Word of her fight with the Kai assassin had spread.

She found Anhuset with Mertok at the front of the crowd. Kirgipa stood nearby, the Queen Regnant in her arms and a contingent of guards encircling her. Ildiko calmed at the sight. The baby was safe.

Anhuset pointed to a line edging the horizon, darker than the descending twilight. "Brishen and the dead," she said.

Ildiko peered in the direction the other woman pointed but couldn't make out anything other than the darker line of demarcation. She listened for the sound of distant hoof beats or marching steps but heard only the rumbling conversation of the gathered crowd who watched with her.

The dark line widened across the plain, spreading like a nebulous high tide as it drew ever closer to Saggara. Soon the entire plain, once dusted in starlight, turned black. Some of the Kai uttered prayers to their gods while others wondered if any of their deceased loved ones rode with the *herceges*.

Vaporous shapes roiled within the cloudy depths, vague outlines of people with ever-shifting faces and will-o-the-wisp eyes. Chills spread down Ildiko's back and arms. The dead, Kai and human, covered the dormant carpet of dropseed grass in a purling shroud. Silent. Watching the living Kai watch them.

They halted, as if waiting for a command, and soon horsemen emerged from the revenant line's flanks, two on either side. They rode to the front, where three reigned in simulacra horses and a fourth advanced toward the Kai. Ildiko gave a dry sob at the sight of her husband in beaten, gouged armor.

She left Anhuset's side and stood in the open space between the living and the dead. Brishen dismounted and strode toward her. He stopped an arm's distance away and pulled off his helmet. Gasps filled the frigid night air as the Kai faced a Wraith King for the first time.

Even Ildiko, who had witnessed Brishen's transformation at Saruna Tor, consciously planted her feet so as not to skitter away from him. He wore the same face, carried himself with the same grace and power, but the eye that gazed at her and the people he had battled *galla* for wasn't Kai yellow, but ethereal blue threaded with lightning. It stared through them instead of at them. The sword he carried glowed with the same otherworldly luminescence as his eye. Shadow clung to him, as if he not only wore darkness but spawned it as well. It hollowed his features, casting the fine bones of his face into a spectral gauntness.

Ildiko blinked, and he was Brishen once more, leader, loving husband and friend. She crushed the hem of her tunic in her hands to stop herself from trying to touch him. Neither living nor dead, he shimmered in front of her, a lodestone to which she would always be drawn.

She had no idea why he returned to Saggara with the dead still bound to him, but she thanked any god listening that he was here. "Prince of night," she said, and reached out to caress the air in front of him. "Welcome back."

His rigid stance eased a fraction, and he leaned toward her, yearning rippling in every slope and bend of muscle covered by leather and mail. A smile played across his mouth. "Woman of day," he said, and the endearment held the worship of a supplicant before a beloved deity. "I've missed you."

He was so close, a breath away from her fingertips, and lethal to any living touch. Still, Ildiko's hands tingled with the temptation to grasp him, assure herself he was real and unharmed, even in this unholy incarnation. Instead, she asked the question she knew hovered on the tongue of every Kai behind her. "Are the *galla* gone?"

Once more his phantasmal gaze swept the crowd. "They're gone," he said.

The crowd erupted into thunderous cheers and applause. Ildiko didn't join in. Instead, she looked beyond Brishen to the three Kings who waited in the distance with the dead. There should have been four. Her heartbeat sped up. "Where is the fourth King?"

Brishen's shoulders drooped as if the question carried the weight of a thousand sorrows. "Taken by the *galla*." The echo of ghosts whispered in his answer.

The crowd continued to cheer behind them, but their voices seemed far away. "Who?" She dreaded his answer. Not Serovek, she pleaded silently, picturing the Beladine's laughing eyes and the way his teasing drove Anhuset to distraction.

"Megiddo."

Ildiko closed her eyes, recalling the monk's quiet dignity and unhesitating bravery in volunteering to help Brishen. To suffer such a fate… "I'm sorry," she said.

"So am I," he replied, the chime of mourning in his voice.

Brishen turned his attention to the crowd, and their cheers quieted. He raised his voice, its tone no longer mournful but sure and strong. "I come to you now so you may know it's safe to return to your homes, your farms, your holts and villages. And soon I will return to Saggara."

More cheers followed his declaration along with shouts from the crowd. "The Queen is safe! The Queen is here!"

Brishen tilted his head, puzzled, and looked to Ildiko, the obvious question in his expression. She grinned, relieved to offer good news to blunt the horror of Megiddo's fate. "There's someone you should meet," she said and motioned for Kirgipa to come forward.

The nursemaid handed the baby to Ildiko and bowed before stepping back. Ildiko tucked back swaddling and turned the infant to face Brishen.

He only looked more puzzled. "Who is this?"

"Harkuf's youngest child. The daughter born a few months ago."

Brishen inhaled sharply, gaze darting back and forth between Ildiko and the baby. He opened his mouth to say something else but was interrupted by a frantic screech. A single, swirling cloud of black erupted from the revenant army and hurtled across the stretch of grass toward Brishen before taking form.

Ildiko cried out, startling the baby. Screams and sharp cries rose from the crowd as almost all of Saggara dropped automatically into genuflection. Anhuset leapt forward, blade drawn, and shoved Ildiko behind her. Guards flanked either side, enclosing regent and regnant within a cage of armor, weaponry, and grim-faced Kai with no inclination to join the others in subservient posturing.

Secmis. As terrifying and malevolent in death as she had been in life, her form smoked and roiled before Brishen who showed no surprised at finding her there.

"I wondered when you'd show yourself," he said in a bored voice.

Secmis flung a skeletal arm at Ildiko who huddled even closer behind Anhuset. The baby squawked at her tightening grip. "Give the baby to me! She is blood of my blood."

Another cry rose from the ghostly throng, and Ildiko swore she recognized the voice of Tiye, the baby's dead mother. "No! Brishen, I beg you! Don't!"

Brishen's attention never wavered from his mother. Secmis's demands gave way to cajoling. "You have proven yourself far beyond my expectations, excelled beyond your father and spineless brother. A worthy ruler of Bast-Haradis." She pulsed with dark light, a creature born of maledictions and the suffering of others. "Give me the child, so I may live once more," she whined. A sour hint of bile surged into Ildiko's throat at the hungry desperation in the plea. "I will rise as queen again, rule by your side and raise you above the throne of Bast-Haradis, over all kingdoms of the world until there is one king and one queen. Our children will be spoken of in legends."

If Ildiko's stomach wasn't already empty, she'd have retched right there. The Kai, on their knees, recoiled, many abandoning their subordinate posture to rise and gape in disgust at the scene before them.

Brishen's upper lip curled as if he smelled something rank. "What manner of legends, dearest mother mine? Abominations? Monsters worse than the *galla*? You would possess an innocent child, crush her soul and turn her body into your vessel." The loathing of decades painted his words, thick and curdled. "Is there nothing you won't defile or debase in your quest for power?"

"I will make you a god," she boasted.

More dark light spilled out of her at his contemptuous laugh. "You would devour me." His eye blazed bright. "I saw you murder my sister," he snarled. "I released her spirit and took her mortem light before you could use either for whatever foul purpose you had in store."

Secmis shrieked and lunged at him, ghostly hands curved as if she'd rend him apart with her claws. He opened his arms wide and caught her in an embrace.

It was the hold of a lover—if that lover were vengeful, murderous and eaten with hate. Brishen's hands pressed into Secmis's back, crushing her against him until she arched like a bow. Stars died in her shadow as she writhed in his unrelenting grip and wailed her fury.

Cracks split Brishen's armor, small fissures opening in his chain mail and brigandine. Ethereal blue light burned hot through the breaks. They spread, splitting the skin of his hands and face until he resembled parched earth gasping under drought, his form held together only by the bondage of an internal sun. The cold light snaked out of him to pierce Secmis whose screams pitched and dipped, furious at first and then agonized and drawn out as Brishen first broke her soul on an invisible wrack and then tore it apart. His splintered face remained implacable.

Ildiko had often wondered how her thoughtful, infinitely loving husband could be the child of parents like Djedor and Secmis. At the sight of his expression, merciless and indifferent to his captive's agony, she wondered no longer. In those moments, when he shredded Secmis's soul as easily as *galla* shredded flesh, Brishen Khaskem was truly his mother's son.

Searing light pulsed around his body, and Ildiko flinched away from the brightness. When she could see once more, he stood before her, solitary and no longer fissured. His eye, a cerulean blue, burned almost white now. His gaze swept the shocked and silent crowd before returning to her. "Good riddance at last," he said softly.

No one spoke; no one breathed. They had just witnessed an execution the like of which they had never seen before and would probably never see again. Ildiko suspected she stared at Brishen with the same expression every Kai around her wore: stunned amazement, horror, and no little fear. What power did this transformed king possess that he could destroy a soul at will? She knew, and that secret would die with her.

"It's about damn time," Anhuset said in a loud voice. "I never could abide that jackal in fancy dress. At least now I won't be ashamed to say I'm related to you, cousin."

Her irreverent remark broke the gravid quiet. Ildiko chortled, a mixture of true humor and shattered nerves. Brishen joined her, and soon laughter echoed through the crowd. It wasn't the twisted amusement of watching vengeance so finally delivered, but the joy of relief, of hope.

The living shield wall around Ildiko opened so she could return to Brishen. His face softened as he stared at the baby in her arms. He drew closer, blue eye no longer as incandescent as he took in the sight of his niece. He then dropped to one knee and raised the ensorcelled sword he carried in offering instead of threat. His declaration, earnest and resolved, carried across the plain. "The queen is dead. Long live the queen."

CHAPTER TWENTY

S erovek studied his body with a critical eye. "At least my beard didn't get any thicker while we were gone."

They were once again at the peak of Saruna Tor, with the dead swirling restlessly around them. The physical bodies of the kings lay undisturbed, features peaceful as if they slumbered without worry or care. Brishen's gaze settled on Megiddo. Deathless sleep. Dreamless, soulless, trapped in a state of waiting for a spirit that would never return.

They all appeared unchanged until something caught his eye. Andras's body, supine beside Megiddo's, was not as they had left it. He lay with his arms crossed over his chest in the pose of a supplicant, fingertips resting against the opposite shoulders. At least the fingers of his right hand were. The left hand was deformed, shriveled into a twisted claw encased in necrotic skin.

Megiddo's severing of Andras's eidolon hand had left its mark. Andras might not have bled blood or suffered pain when it happened, but his physical body displayed the effects. The hand wasn't missing, but it was as useless to the Gauri lord as if it were.

"Do you get used to it?" Andras stared at Brishen with bright, bitter eyes.

Brishen didn't need to ask what he meant. Many had leveled the same question on him after he healed from his injuries, half

303

blind with the loss of his eye. He shrugged. "What other choice is there?"

He turned away from the bodies and faced the vast army spilling down the tor. He was done. Done with the feel and taste of death, of unlife that coursed through his eidolon's spectral veins. They were poisoned with the lingering essence of Secmis's venom.

She'd thrown herself at him, and he seized the chance, the moment, to do what he swore he'd accomplish all those years ago when he freed his murdered sister from her diabolical clutches. The *galla* had consumed Secmis's body; Brishen obliterated her soul. The power that gave him dominion over the dead also gave him the ability to destroy them and left a stain on his spirit. Profane. Unclean.

"General Hasarath," he said.

A revenant separated from the ghostly crowd and shaped itself into the memory of the old Kai general who sacrificed himself for so many at the Absu. "Sire," he replied and bowed.

"None will forget what you and the others did at Haradis. Every generation of Kai born from now forward will know the honor and bravery of Hasarath, of Meseneith, of Satsik..." He named each of those who stood before that first wave of *galla* and made themselves willing prey so that others might reach the safety of the river. He'd build monuments to their names, temples in their honor, and have scribes write of their heroism. Just like humans did.

The Kai could no longer rely on the reaping and storing of mortem lights with their precious memories. Those Kai too young to have their magic manifest yet had escaped the thievery of

Brishen's spell. But who knew if the power they inherited would be strong enough to reap the memories of their elders. The magic of the Kai, if not completely dead, flickered weakly in its final days.

His voice softened when he spoke Tarawin's name. She floated toward him, her shadowy features still kind, still gentle. "My family is indebted to yours for all time, Tarawin. Your son fought under my command, and now so have you. Your daughter Kirgipa rescued my niece. That act alone saved a dynasty and a marriage. I will raise her up, ennoble her and the children she will bear. Your house will be exalted and your daughters the matriarchs of princes."

Tarawin drew closer until the smoky mist of her essence drifted over his arms and shoulders in the lightest caress. "Live long, *Herceges*. Live happy." She withdrew into the miasma, becoming nameless and faceless once more.

Brishen bowed before the dead. The other Wraith Kings did the same. "We release you from service with our eternal gratitude," he said. "May your journey continue beyond the reach of this world, and may you find peace."

A rippled flowed through the gathering, accompanied by a drawn sigh, and the dead faded away. No epic whirlwinds or howling faces in spinning vortices. Only a quiet vanishing as if they had never been there at all.

Brishen listened, savoring the whip and swirl of the natural breeze spinning between the encircling menhirs and lifting strands of his hair from his shoulders. No frightful screaming from ravenous *galla* rent the quiet. Instead, he heard the muted thud of hooves and the encouraging commands of riders as they coaxed their horses up the tor's pitch toward the peak. Gaeres's men. They had kept sentinel at the tor's base while their leader rode with Brishen into battle, retreating only far enough away to avoid the returning dead. That danger was gone now, and they climbed the tor to reach Gaeres.

"What happens now?" Gaeres asked.

"We become whole again." He hoped so. He prayed so. Brishen bowed a second time, this time to Megiddo's still body. "At least four of us."

"And what of the monk?" Andras's belligerence hadn't lessened. Tiny forks of lightning arced around his handless wrist, and he glared at Brishen.

"I'll bring his body back to High Salure," Serovek said. "His brother's family are my guests there for now. Either they will take him or return him to his monastery."

"So he'll just stay like that for eternity? Dead but not, and a captive of the *galla*? This is wrong!"

"Then give me an alternative," Brishen snapped back. "If we destroy his body, his spirit has no place to return. I will not—*will not*—reopen the breach for any reason. I couldn't if I wanted to. What power I have left, and it isn't much, will be used up reuniting our spirits with our bodies. All we can do for Megiddo now is protect his body until someone finds a way to retrieve his eidolon."

He braced for another volley of arguments, but Andras stayed silent, mouth thinned to a tight line. Gaeres clapped a hand on Serovek's shoulder. "My men and I will help you bring Megiddo to his family before we return home."

Serovek thanked him and turned to Brishen. "Let's finish this. We've spent long enough chasing demons."

Brishen couldn't agree more. "Unless anyone objects, I'll reunite you first." He removed the ward surrounding Serovek's body and called up the words to reverse the incantation that separated each man into body, sword, and eidolon.

The strength of the spell rode hard on him. It didn't require the blood and violence of its counterpart, but the force of its draw made Brishen see double. He touched the sword Serovek held. "The king is the sword; the sword is the king," he incanted in a language long dead and long forgotten. The blade's light pulsed as lightning crackled up and down its length. Two radiant flashes, and the light shot up the hamon line, through the guard and grip to sizzle along Serovek's arm.

The margrave's eidolon convulsed in one great shudder before collapsing in on itself until it was nothing more than a shining sphere. The sword fell to the ground, once more a weapon made only of steel and the labor of a swordsmith's arm. The sphere hurtled into Serovek's body, sinking into his chest through harness, clothing, and flesh. He gasped, arching his back, and his lids twitched open.

Brishen bent over Serovek and peered into his eyes, no longer an encompassing spectral blue, but cold-water dark, with pupils and irises and the strange white sclera the Kai found so repulsive in humans. "Welcome back, my friend." He backed away before Serovek could touch him. Gaeres signaled, and the Quereci who had made it to the tor's peak rushed forward to help Serovek stand and retrieve his fallen sword.

Andras chose to go last, and Brishen repeated the incantation over Gaeres and finally the Gauri exile. By then, his power was almost extinguished. What faint threads might remain once he recombined belonged to Megiddo. A chance to rescue the monk and return his spirit to his body, while improbable, wasn't impossible. Brishen would guard those last drops of sorcery inside him until he found a way.

Performing the incantation on himself proved strange. The sword in his hand bore a life of its own, that portion of his will and awareness that had hacked through *galla* and bore their taint. Since the start of this macabre journey, he'd felt hollow, incomplete. He was. When the part of his spirit occupying his sword sank into his eidolon, he almost shouted his astonishment to the heavens. When the muscles of his body screamed in agony, and his eyelid slammed shut against the harsh sunlight, he laughed out loud.

"I'm not mad," he assured a concerned Serovek and Gaeres as they helped him to his feet. "I'm whole again."

"Well said," Serovek replied with a grin.

Their celebratory hugs weren't shared by all. Andras stood to one side, his withered hand tucked away from sight. He already held the reins of his living mount, watched over by the Quereci while he was gone. The simulacra they rode faded as the dead had once Brishen was whole and the incantation complete.

"My daughter awaits me," Andras said and swung into the saddle. "Do you need me for anything else?"

Brishen shook his head. "No, though you have the thanks of a kingdom for your help. You saved a world, Andras."

The Gauri lord looked at Megiddo, still within the protective ward, and back to Brishen. "Don't garland yourselves yet," he said with a sour scowl. "There are no heroes here." He nodded to Gaeres and his Quereci and tapped his heels into his mount's sides. Horse and rider trotted out of the menhir circle to descend the slope.

"There goes a man eaten alive by guilt," Serovek said, his gaze fastened on the spot where Andras had disappeared.

"I couldn't halt the incantation. I wouldn't, nor would I alter my decision if I had to do it again." Brishen was as gut-strung by Megiddo's fate as Andras. They all were, but he didn't lie to himself or the others. Closing the breach trumped everything. Megiddo's self-sacrifice had proved he understood that.

"We know," Serovek replied. "So does the Gauri. He just needs time to accept it and to understand that no matter if he had double or triple the strength, he wasn't going to pull Megiddo free. By the time they got that first claw around him, it was already too late."

"He may not wish it, but I'll confirm with Sangur the Lame that Andras Frantisek was instrumental in banishing the *galla* and deserves to have his lands reinstated to him. He may not accept my accolades, but I hope he will."

"He will. You heard him when we first met. He has a daughter to dower, and if he was willing to face *galla* for the chance to do it, he'll accept your accolades and the lands resulting from them."

They lingered at the tor only long enough to build a simple sled and carefully transfer Megiddo onto it. His ensorcelled sword glowed brightly in the sun before Serovek wrapped it in layers of fur and leather before tying it to his saddle. He, Gaeres and the Quereci would start the trek home as soon as everyone was mounted and Megiddo secured to the sled.

"Are you sure you don't want us to ride with you to Saggara? It isn't that much of a detour." Serovek, looking not at all troubled by his tenure as a Wraith King, wiggled his eyebrows suggestively. "I'll take any excuse to see the fair Anhuset again."

Brishen chuckled. "You just saw her a day ago."

"That doesn't count. I was playing nanny to the dead and was too far away to work my charm on her."

"Your charm will get you killed." Brishen shook his head. "I want to travel alone, see if I can enter Saggara without much notice or fanfare. That would be hard to do with an entourage of eight humans and a Wraith King in tow. Besides, you need to get Megiddo to High Salure for his safety and to tell his family."

Serovek lost his jocular demeanor. "The worst of all tasks."

Brishen parted company with the others under a cold winter sky. As he did with Andras, he bowed to Gaeres, professed his gratitude and promised any and all aid in the future if it were needed. He and Serovek clasped forearms. "Fair journey to you, friend. It seems I will be in your debt forever."

The other man released his arm to punch him in the bicep. Brishen's arm went numb for a moment, even through the double layers of chain mail and padded gambeson. "No debt," Serovek said. "But I want an invitation to your next *Kaherka* festival, and I'll claim a dance with the beautiful Ildiko."

"I'll make sure the kitchens prepare your own scarpatine pie."

Serovek grinned. "You've always been an exceptional host, Brishen Khaskem."

Brishen watched them ride away before turning his horse to Saggara. Unlike the *vuhana*, his earthly horse's gait didn't cover leagues in minutes, and he didn't arrive outside Saggara's gate until mid morning of the following day.

The grasslands that stretched from Saggara's patch of young woodland was empty of tents and the vast multitude of Kai who had descended on them over the course of weeks. A few yurts hugged the tree line, and small knots of horses grazed on the short, brittle grass peeking through shallow snow drifts. While the Kai may have returned to their homes, they'd left behind a trampled swale littered with the remains of campfires and scattered animal bones. Brishen guessed two summers would pass before the grasslands reclaimed this patch of earth and wiped away any hint that half a kingdom had once huddled here.

His breath hung in the frigid air, a misty cloud, but he paid no mind to the cold. Saggara loomed ahead, with its walls and fortifications and its legions of soldiers who helped him guard territories. Once it had been the summer palace of an ancestor. It would be so again. Not nearly as grand as the royal seat in Haradis had once been, and not as haunted.

Ildiko waited behind those walls, and a niece to whom he would now surrender his crown. He grinned and nudged his horse into a faster gait.

Brishen hadn't truly believed he might sneak into the fortress unnoticed, but the hue and cry raised the moment he was sighted made him flinch. He rode into the bailey, swung out of the saddle and tossed the reins to an open-mouthed stablehand. People bowed as he strode to the manor, some reaching out to touch his arm as he passed. He didn't stop, didn't linger to talk or greet those who called to him or begged him to wait.

His steward tripped and stumbled to his knees when he saw him. Brishen paused long enough to lift the man back up by his tunic and asked the most important question any man had ever asked of another. "Where's my wife?"

Mesumenes had barely uttered the word "wild" before Brishen bolted down the hall, through the chaotic kitchens and out a back door that led to the wild orange groves. He slowed, though his breathing sped up to harsh pants.

Ildiko sat on a bench alone, pale face turned up to the sun, eyes closed. She hadn't heard him approach. The bench had been one he ordered put in this particular spot. It hugged a stone wall near the secret alcove where he'd hidden his sister Anaknet's mortem light from his mother years earlier.

He planned to one day send it to Emlek once Secmis was dead. Now that she was, he found himself reluctant to part with the light. Anaknet's mortem light didn't have any useful knowledge for future generations. Its importance lay strictly in the personal value Brishen placed on a connection to his sibling. It would remain here. While he might no longer have the ability call up that gentle spark and see her brief, indistinct memory, he held the image of her tiny face in his mind, as clear now as it was when he was eleven years old. How fitting that he find the person he treasured above all others sitting next to the treasure he'd defied a malevolent queen to save.

As eidolon, he'd been a fractured creature. Powerful, yes, but incomplete. United once more in both body and soul, he still hadn't felt whole—until now, in the presence of his human wife, who sat wrapped in quiet dignity with her pale face tilted up to the sun.

Something alerted Ildiko she was no longer alone, maybe the sensation of being watched, or the hitch in his breath as he admired the proud lines of her profile limned in morning light. She opened her eyes but didn't move except to slide her gaze askance. He didn't even flinch. "Are you real?" she asked in a hesitant voice. "Or am I wishing too hard?"

A tree branch dragged across his pauldron as Brishen navigated the narrow path cut between the orange trees to reach her. He held out his hand, noting how it shook. Ildiko didn't hesitate and clasped his fingers. She opened her mouth to say something else, but he stopped her with a finger pressed to his lips. He coaxed her off the bench, and immediately swept her into his arms.

She was light as thistledown and even softer. He carried her back to the house, through the kitchens and past the servants who gaped at them, up the stairwell and into the corridor where their bedchamber waited. Neither spoke, and Brishen tightened his hold when she buried her face against his neck.

He met Ildiko's personal servant halfway down the hall. Sinhue's eyes grew huge and her jaw dropped before she fled in the opposite direction, back to his bedchamber from which she emerged. By the time Brishen turned the corner, a small crowd had gathered outside his door and were striding toward him, Sinhue in the lead. This time she bowed as she passed him and grinned. Two soldiers followed her, and behind them a groggy young woman he didn't recognize cuddling a baby he did. His niece. Two more soldiers flanked her and all bowed to Brishen as they trekked toward the stairs without comment.

Brishen broke the silence he had imposed on himself and Ildiko. "My gods, wife, how many people are sleeping in our room now?"

Her body shook with quiet laughter. "Just the nurse and the queen, and that's for my benefit more than anything." She kissed his neck, a soft flutter that made him increase his pace. He kicked the door shut behind him and set her gently on her feet.

The world shrank to the candlelit room and the two of them. They had lapsed mute once more, and Brishen was glad for it. He didn't want to waste time or effort on words. He wanted nothing more than to relearn his wife, to assure himself that she wasn't merely an apparition created from dreams dreamed in his bleakest hours.

She stood still under his gaze, and except for the occasional shiver, still under his touch. And Brishen touched her everywhere. Her slender neck and shoulders, the twin knolls of her collarbones and the hollow of her throat. She closed her eyes as his fingers glided over the curve of her breasts, pausing to cup them before moving onto the expanse of her belly and the curves of her waist.

Candlelight burnished her hair in a way the sun didn't, softening the fiery red color so that it shimmered, instead of blazed. She wore it partially up, locks braided into a crown. Brishen released their ties, and the braids fell down her back. He took his time, unweaving each one until long waves flowed over her shoulders and chest. He reached to pull her against him and stopped.

His armor was a wall between them. He expertly shucked everything until he stood naked and scooped Ildiko into a tight embrace. Her fingers dug into his arms before flattening and her palms slid over the hard muscles of his shoulders and back. He buried his face in her hair and inhaled the scent of wild orange flower and mint.

She was life and hope and strength, and he drew on all three as he bent his head to kiss her deeply. Her simple gown soon lay abandoned at the foot of their bed. Brishen mapped the terrain of her body with his mouth and hands, rediscovering those places he had laid claim to many times since their marriage. It was never enough and never would be.

When Ildiko uttered his name in a breathy sigh and clamped her thighs against his hips, he forgot everything—kingdoms and fragile queens, lost monks and fallen cities—and found both solace and ecstasy in her loving embrace.

Afterwards, they lay curled around each other in the gathering gloom. Brishen remained quiet, doing nothing more than stroking Ildiko's long hair as the first hot tears trickled down his neck and soon became a river. She sobbed softly, soaking his hair and pillow where she hid her face. Her arms and legs wrapped tightly around him, and she chanted his name over and over until the sobs faded, and she relaxed in his hold.

"I think I drowned you," she said and hiccupped into his ear.

He leaned back to better see her face. She was a mess. Splotchy skin and eyes nearly swollen shut from her crying fit. She snatched up a corner of the blanket to wipe her nose. Brishen found her watery smile lovely and envied her the ability to weep. When he had a moment, he intended to escape into the orange grove where the trees grew wildest and thorniest and there keen his own grief in a dry-eyed, solitary requiem.

"I take it you missed me then," he teased gently.

She hiccupped again and smacked him on the arm. "Only a little, and don't let that puff up your pride."

A comfortable silence grew between them until Ildiko cupped his cheek in her hand and stared at him for several moments. "What horrors you carry behind here," she said and slid her thumb across his forehead. "I can see them in your face, in the changing shades of your eye. Will you not let me ease your burden, Brishen?"

He caught her hand and brought it to his mouth for a kiss. "You already are, wife. You're my sanctuary, my refuge." And when he could speak of it to her, he'd recount his time as a being of great power and unnatural existence, of his sense-fractured emptiness and the deep sorrow of losing an honorable man to a merciless fate. For now though, he'd simply savor the feel of his wife against him, in the bed they shared, in the fortress he ruled, in a kingdom not yet perished.

EPILOGUE

"**W**ell?" Ildiko asked Sinhue. "Will I do?" She spun on her heel, the many folds of her layered skirts billowing out around her. The sleeveless coat she wore over her silk shirt weighted her shoulders with its opulent embroidery of gold thread and tiny jewels sewn into the design. It was a most important day for several reasons, and she'd chosen the finest, most formal outfit she owned, another gift from her generous husband.

Sinhue stepped back to eye her handiwork. She and Ildiko had closeted themselves in the chamber the *Elsod* had finally surrendered to her once she returned to Emlek with her *masods* and set to work preparing for the coronation. "You look very...regal, *Hercegesé*."

Ildiko laughed aloud at her servant's pause and diplomatic reply. She turned to the full length mirror, admiring the emerald skirts and tunic with its intricate lacings and knotwork designs that decorated the hems of coat, skirts and shirt cuffs. The shirt itself was a shade of pearl that caught the light and reflected back soft shades of pink, blue and peach.

The ensemble highlighted Ildiko's red hair and bleached her fair skin an even paler shade. "A very respectable mollusk, even if I do say so myself," she said and announced herself ready to receive visitors.

317

Brishen was the first to arrive, and he took her breath away. Unlike her own vibrant colors, he was garbed in black with accents of indigo at the collar and cuffs and silver in the clasps that closed his tunic. Except for the saffron-yellow eye that narrowed when he smiled at her, he was a study in lush darkness. "Hello, pretty hag," he said.

"Wolf," she teased. "You look good enough to eat."

One of his eyebrows rose. "Why is it when I tell you that, you look ready to bolt for the door?"

She braced her hands on her hips. "I do not," she said, indignant. "At least not anymore."

He surveyed the room, noting the empty baby bed. When the *Elsod* left, they had turned Ildiko's former bedroom into a nursery and occasional changing room. Brishen hadn't protested the proximity, especially after Anhuset recounted the assassination attempt and her continued search to find who put him to the task. Guards still lined the corridors outside the royal bedchambers, and the door between the chambers stayed open when he wasn't making love to Ildiko in their bed. They had both quickly learned the absolute and indisputable importance of *not* waking the baby.

"Where's my niece?" he asked.

"I'll fetch the nurse," Sinhue volunteered and left the room after receiving assurances from Ildiko she was no longer needed.

Ildiko sashayed to her husband and raised her face for his kiss. Brishen tried to pull her close, but she danced out his reach. "You'll muss my hair, and Sinhue will string you up by your guts if you ruin all her hard work. I'm terrified of even sneezing in case I do something to it and suffer the same death."

Brishen scowled, his expression both exasperated and puzzled. "Just wear a hat."

She refused to dignify the ridiculous suggestion with a reply. Men. Instead, she asked him the same one she'd been asking for the past week. "Have you decided on your niece's name yet? Her coronation is less than an hour away, Brishen. You can't just call her 'Queen Little Girl.'"

"Why not? I rather like it."

Again, she graced him with the same expression she'd worn when he suggested she wear a hat. The Kai tradition of not formally naming a child until they had reached the end of their first year was all well and good unless that child happened to be the Queen Regnant. "Tell me you've thought of something." He had waved off her numerous suggestions, all good Kai names taken from the family trees recorded in the scrolls stored in Saggara's library. Brishen would have none of it, nor did he reveal what he might have in mind. Until now.

"Tarawin," he said, and his features sobered. "Her name will be Tarawin."

Ildiko blinked hard, forcing back the tears that filled her lower lids and threatened to spill over. She didn't need to look any more like a shellfish than she already did. Crying only made it worse.

He'd chosen a commoner's name, specifically the name of a common woman with more nobility in a drop of her blood than entire royal dynasties. She'd lost her son during his service to Brishen and sacrificed herself to the *galla* on the banks of the Absu, along with other brave Kai men and women, so that many more Kai might survive.

Her eldest daughter Kirgipa had braved a hard journey and left behind a beloved sister to make certain she delivered the only surviving child of Harkuf Khaskem to his brother. Today, before Brishen formally abdicated the throne to his niece, he planned to ennoble the faithful nursemaid and her sister, bequeathing both land and title to them and their descendents.

"A small thing," he'd told Ildiko earlier, "of far less value than the life she saved and the one she gave back to you and me. I'd give her a country, if I had an extra to spare."

He hadn't forgotten the palace guards either. Both had looked horrified at his suggestion of ennoblement, though equally happy when he offered the alternative of generous coffers and a place among the highest echelons of court guardianship, second only to Anhuset and Mertok.

"What do you think?" Brishen said when Ildiko continued to stare at him without replying.

She gave him a watery smile. "It's a good name. A name more than suitable for a Kai queen. Kirgipa and Atalan will be overjoyed." She toyed idly with a lock of his hair. "You're a fine man, Brishen Khaskem."

"It's hard work remaining worthy of you, Ildiko Khaskem."

"You've a velvet tongue."

"That's what you said yesterday when I had my head between your—"

She shushed him with a shocked laugh. "Stop that." She turned for a final check in her mirror.

Brishen came to stand behind her. He stroked her shoulder with a clawed hand and met her gaze in their reflections. "I'll do this poor child no favors by turning the throne over to her. We celebrate today with heavy hearts. The Kai rejoice at the galla's banishment and grieve for the loss of their magic because of the demons."

His gaze never wavered as he recited the lie both he and Ildiko had told the panicking Kai when news spread through the kingdom of their inability to conjure the simplest spell or worst of all, reap a mortem light.

She stroked his hand resting just under her breasts. "She won't rule alone, Brishen. You'll still be regent until Tarawin is an adult."

"That role I'm happy to take on. With you by my side, I'll relish it." He bent to kiss the sensitive spot under her ear.

A pleasurable shiver rode down Ildiko's back and arm. "I much prefer Princess Consort over Queen Consort anyway." And far, far more than Queen Regent. She truly understood now why Brishen hadn't welcomed his elevated status as monarch.

He straightened but continued stroking her shoulder. "I only have one regret," he said.

A faint frown line stitched her brow. "What's that?"

"I'll never be able to call you Queen Ildiko. It has a nice ring to it."

Ildiko resisted the urge to turn and instead gripped his hand in hers. She stared at his beloved, scarred face, the black eye patch and yellow eye, the toothy smile behind the lovely mouth that drove her to distraction. "No. Nothing so grand. I'm content to live my life as just Ildiko," she said softly, repeating words similar to those he once whispered in her hair when he thought her asleep. "Who is loved by Brishen."

ABOUT THE AUTHOR

Grace Draven is a fan of fantasy worlds, romance, and the anti-hero. Storytelling has been a long-standing passion of hers and a perfect excuse for not doing the laundry. She lives in Texas with her husband, three kids and big, doofus dog. You can check out her latest projects at www.gracedraven.com.

Made in the USA
Columbia, SC
22 March 2021